JACK OF
HEARTS

JACK OF HEARTS

Aces & Eights – Book One

SANDRA OWENS

Montlake
Romance

Text copyright © 2017 Sandra Owens

Published by Montlake Romance, Seattle

www.apub.com

Amazon, the Amazon logo, and Montlake Romance are trademarks of Amazon.com, Inc., or its affiliates.

ISBN-13: 9781503941380
ISBN-10: 1503941388

Cover design by Eileen Carey

Printed in the United States of America

*To the readers of the world who know there is
nothing better than getting lost in a good book.
Without you, authors wouldn't exist.*

PROLOGUE

As an investigative reporter with a deep belief in the laws of our country, I've used my pen to fight injustice wherever I found it. Over the years, I've exposed politicians and those in power who've hurt and/or stolen from the very people they are supposed to protect. I've never hesitated to unmask these villains living among us . . . until now.

As you sit at your kitchen table drinking coffee, or in your recliner, or wherever you are while reading this, I will be praying that my family understands why I had to write this article. If I'm aware of criminal activity, no matter how close to home it hits, and don't expose those responsible, then my life's work means nothing.

Michael Parker again read the last two paragraphs of the front-page story that would run next week. Although he thought he might be sleeping on the couch afterward, he planned to give his wife and daughter the article to read tonight.

"You gonna let me read that yet?" Jack, his editor, asked, poking his head around the doorframe.

"Tomorrow." His family would read it first, then Jack could have it. Michael had never been this secretive with his editor before, so the man was biting at the bit to know what his award-winning journalist was working on.

"Coffee in my office in the morning then. I'll buy."

Michael rolled his eyes. "No you won't. I still refuse to drink that shit from the vending machine, you cheap mofo. I'll pick up coffees on my way in tomorrow." Which Jack had known Michael would do. It was a game they played, one Jack enjoyed more than he did since Michael was always the one buying.

As soon as his editor left, Michael shut down his computer. He pulled out the thumb drive, putting it in his briefcase. Unlike any of his other stories, this one wasn't saved on his computer. It existed on this thumb drive only, staying with him at all times.

It was going on ten o'clock, time to go home and face the music. He'd called earlier to say he was finishing up a story and would be late. Most nights, he looked forward to going home to his wife and daughter. Not tonight, though. He swiveled his chair around, his gaze falling on the bookshelf behind him. The photo of him with his family at his daughter's high school graduation caught his eye, and he sat for a good five minutes staring at the two most beautiful women in the world.

He'd never been prouder than when he'd listened to his daughter give the valedictorian speech. That girl had stolen his heart the moment she was born and he'd laid eyes on her. When he'd held her in his arms for the first time, he'd made a promise to his baby girl that he would do his part in making the world a better place for her. Over the years, he'd done his best to keep that promise, to be a father she would be proud of.

Briefcase in hand, he rode the elevator to the ground floor, waving to the night security man as he walked out of the building. This late, he was the only one on the sidewalk, which suited him. He wasn't in the mood to talk to any of his coworkers. His car was parked in the garage across the street, and as he waited for the light to change, he stared ahead, seeing nothing.

This story had Pulitzer Prize written all over it, but the thought didn't excite him as it should. He just wanted to get it published, deal with the repercussions, and put it all behind him.

The revving of an engine penetrated his brain, and he blinked, focusing on the car headed straight for him. The hell? He tried to get out of the way, but he'd waited too long. The impact sent his body flying through the air and crashing into the building behind him.

Funny, shouldn't he feel pain? His vision grayed, but before fading out altogether, he thought he saw a man grab his briefcase, then take off running. "My story . . ." he tried to say, but his mouth refused to work.

As the world turned to black, tears leaked from his eyes. *I'm sorry, my beautiful girls. So damn sorry.*

CHAPTER ONE

The fight was as good as over before it started. Alex Gentry walked to the bar, grabbed a pitcher of beer meant for the dudes playing pool in the back room, then returned to the biker lying facedown on the floor. He stood over the heavily tattooed man and poured the contents over the guy's head.

"Get up, Spider," he said when the man's eyes blinked open and he sputtered. Spider laughed, turned onto his back, and opened his mouth, catching the beer. The dude was fucking crazy.

"Good stuff," Spider said when the pitcher ran dry.

"I sure hope you're not giving away free beer again, bro."

Alex managed not to show any surprise at hearing the voice of his oldest brother. He glanced over his shoulder and glared at Nate. "Stop sneaking up on me like that."

Nate smirked. "But it's so much fun. Why's Spider drinking his beer while lying on the floor?"

"He bet me I couldn't knock him out with one hit." They both stared down at the man who seemed as comfortable on a floor sticky from spilled beer and crushed cigarette butts as he would be on a barstool. Spider grinned back at them.

"How much did he lose this time?" Nate asked.

"A hundred." So far Spider had lost around five hundred bucks making ridiculous bets with Alex. Not that Alex was complaining. Most of the bills were counterfeit and were passed on to Denzil Rothmire, the head of Miami's FBI office—their boss. The one or two real hundreds, Alex put in the tip jar for their two employees to split.

Alex held out his hand. "Pay up."

Still sprawled on the floor and grinning like an idiot, Spider dug into the pocket of his dirty jeans and pulled out a wad of money, peeled off one bill, and handed it to Alex. "You're fun losing money to, Heart Man."

Alex snorted. "And you're crazy, dude."

"I know," Spider answered, pushing up to a sitting position.

"What was the bet this time?" the third Gentry brother asked, walking up to them.

Alex eyed Court. "He didn't believe I could put him on his ass with one punch."

"Dude, back in high school Heart Man was state champion in boxing." Court slapped an arm around Alex's shoulder. "Our baby brother forget to tell you that?"

"Slipped my mind," Alex said.

For some reason Spider found that hilarious, and they left him wallowing on the floor.

"Keep an eye on things for a few minutes," Nate said to Riker, their bartender, as they walked by.

"You bet, Boss Man." Riker went back to wiping down the bar.

Alex paused. "Pour another pitcher of beer and take it to the dudes in the pool room."

Riker gave him a two-finger salute. "You bet, Boss Man."

"That one real?" Nate asked after he'd closed the door to the office. The room had been soundproofed, and every morning Court swept it for bugs.

Alex stuck the bill under the ultraviolet light. "Nope."

"Spider's stupid for passing out counterfeit Benjies instead of tens and twenties. Nobody pays attention to the small bills," Court said.

Alex nodded. "I also think he's too stupid to be making them, so we need to find out where he's getting them. You gotta like the dude, though. He's the happiest biker I've ever met."

"That's 'cause he's a pothead." Nate threw himself down on the leather sofa, stretching out his long legs.

"Well, I give him credit for not touching anything else. Other than his beer and his joints, he's clean."

Court gave him a look of disbelief. "Christ, Alex, I can't believe you just said that. Other than his beer and joints, he's clean? That's like saying other than Dad guzzling his Johnnie Walker, he didn't drink. And you left out the part about Spider passing out counterfeit bills around town."

"Yeah, well, Spider amuses me, so sue me." Alex pushed Nate's feet off the couch, taking the space on the opposite end. A strand of hair fell across Alex's forehead, and he brushed it back.

Although two years apart in birth order, the three brothers looked so much alike that by unspoken agreement they each wore their hair differently. Nate kept his long black hair tied back into a low ponytail with a leather strip, while Court liked his cut military-style. Alex preferred his to curl around his collar, but not an inch longer than that. He'd often thought that, unconsciously, they had matched their hair to their personalities.

"Anyone besides me getting worried about Ramon being MIA for a week now?" Court said.

"The word on the street is that his father sent him to Mexico." Alex leaned over and adjusted the gun in his boot where it was rubbing on his ankle. "I'm guessing he's meeting with their suppliers."

Nate frowned. "Where'd you hear that?"

"Here and there. You outta get out more, bro." Although here and there wasn't exactly the truth. The information had come from a source close to the Alonzo drug cartel family, one he was keeping to himself.

"What the hell is he doing back?" Nate narrowed his eyes as he stared at the large monitor mounted on the wall. "I kicked him out earlier. Told him he was banned for a week."

Alex glanced at the screen to see Dirty Dan walking up to the bar. "Guess he didn't believe you. What'd he do this time?"

"Caught him behind the bar stealing beer again." Nate stood and headed for the door. "Idiot," he muttered.

"I'll come with you." As Alex pushed up from the sofa, his phone pinged with an incoming text, and he pulled it out of his pocket.

Need to see you!

The exclamation point was code for ASAP. "Sorry I'll miss all the fun, but my snitch needs to see me." Dirty Dan coming back so soon after he'd been evicted meant he was looking for a fight. Like his brothers, Alex loved a good brawl.

"Spooky Man the one who told you where Ramon was?" Court asked.

"Yep." To keep the other two FBI agents in the room from trying to arrange a meeting with his snitch, Alex had told them his source spooked at the drop of a pin. That if either of them came anywhere near him, he would disappear, never to be heard from again. They'd dubbed the informant Spooky Man, which amused him.

"Go ahead and take off. I'll back up Nate." Court followed Nate out.

As soon as Alex was alone, he sent a text.

On the way

Before leaving, he grabbed a plain black T-shirt from the closet where he and his brothers kept spare clothes. He pulled off the personalized one he was wearing, not wanting to show up at Spooky Man's stinking of cigarettes and biker groupies' cheap perfume. Each brother's work shirt had inspired their customers to give them nicknames. Alex's had a jack of hearts playing card above the Aces & Eights logo of a deck of fanned cards, earning him the nickname Heart Man.

Court's had a king of clubs, so he was simply King. Top dog Nate had the ace of spades card on his shirt, making him Ace. The bar was the queen of diamonds, and a demanding queen she was as far as Alex was concerned. She ate up all their time, masquerading as a front for their undercover work.

Grabbing his helmet and jacket, Alex went to the garage they'd added at the rear of Aces & Eights, pressed the door opener, then mounted his Harley. Fifteen minutes later, he parked his bike under a streetlight a block from his destination. Clicking on the alarm, he walked the rest of the way to High Tea and Black Cat Books. Going to the back of the building, he climbed the fire escape, careful not to make any noise.

When he reached the window two stories up, he tested it to see if it was locked. It was. Good, she had listened to him. His first visit, it had been open, and he knew better than most that there were night monsters looking for easy access to a woman's bedroom.

He tapped a prearranged code on the glass, and the window immediately slid up. After stepping inside, he closed the window, locking it. It was undeniably odd to be sneaking into a woman's room for reasons other than joining her in her bed.

They'd tried to think of a neutral place to meet, but Ramon had spies all over South Miami. Madison Parker, cousin to Ramon Alonzo, was running scared, and ever since stepping between her and Ramon when the jackass had tried to kiss her, Alex had accidently fallen into the role of champion. Since that worked to his advantage, he'd encouraged her to contact him if Ramon ever messed with her again.

Why he was keeping her a secret from his brothers was a question he refused to examine too closely. She was a prime source for information on the Alonzo family. There was no one in the world he trusted more than Nate and Court, but he was feeling weirdly possessive where Madison was concerned. A damn red flag there. He didn't do possessive.

The reason he'd lied to his brothers sat crossed-legged on the end of her bed, leaving the only chair in the room for him. The bedside lamp was dimmed, and in the low artificial light her fiery red hair reminded him of the flames of a campfire, changing colors whenever she moved. Her eyes almost appeared black, but in the daylight they were a captivating green. *Cat eyes,* he'd thought the first time they met.

It had been on a Saturday morning three weeks earlier when he had first laid eyes on Madison Parker. He'd been at Ramon's house, playing a game of pool with the man, doing his best to lose a hundred bucks. Not an easy thing when his opponent kept missing the pocket. Alex had already learned that Ramon didn't like losing, no matter what the game was.

He quietly sighed when Ramon missed again. Alex bent over the table and lined up his cue. He was going to have to put this one in the pocket, or it would become obvious he was missing on purpose. If Alex could manage to lose to Ramon, the man would be happy and might even brag a little about his drug business.

Just as Alex pulled his arm back to take the shot, a woman walked into the room, and he hit the ball so hard that it flew over the rim of the table and hit the wall. Jesus, she was gorgeous. Red hair curling halfway down her back, green eyes, and a splash of freckles across her nose, she took his breath away. A first for him.

He liked women, maybe a little too much if you listened to his brothers, but never had he wanted to lay claim to one at first sight—until now. Who was she? She glanced from him to the dent in the wall then back at him, and full lips that wore nothing more than clear gloss lifted in a grin.

"Nice shot, Ace."

He straightened, dropped the cue stick, and walked around the table, his hand out in front of him. "Hi, I'm Alex, and you are?" She put her hand in his, and he had the unsettling thought that he was never going to let it go.

Her gaze fell to their joined hands. "I'm—"

"My cousin," Ramon said, stepping next to her and putting his arm possessively around her shoulders.

"You don't look anything alike." It was a stupid thing to say, but he had the urge to call Ramon a liar. If she was a member of the Alonzo family, she was off-limits, and that was a heartbreaker.

She tugged on her hand, and he reluctantly let go, then she slipped out from under Ramon's arm. "I'm Madison Parker, and you're very observant, Alex."

There was mischief in those cat eyes, but it faded when Ramon wrapped his hand around her hair and pulled her roughly back to him. She didn't seem to like her cousin, if they were in fact cousins. Alex wasn't sure he believed it, but he also hoped she wasn't Ramon's girlfriend.

"Ramon's father and my mom are twins."

So it was true; they were cousins. He wondered where the red hair and green eyes came from, but he reminded himself that as a family member of the man he was investigating, she was untouchable, no ifs, ands, or buts. Where that gorgeous hair and those beautiful green eyes came from was not his concern.

When she tried to pull her hair out of Ramon's fist, Ramon's eyes flashed with annoyance. Alex gritted his teeth and forced himself not to give Ramon a bloody nose.

She slapped at her cousin's arm. "Ouch. That hurts, Ramon."

As fast as a striking snake, Ramon backed her up to the wall, pressed his body against hers, and crashed his mouth down on hers. She whimpered as she tried to push him away.

Alex saw red, dark blood red. He grabbed the man's earlobe and twisted it hard until Ramon let go of her.

"What the hell's wrong with you?" Ramon said, rubbing his ear after Alex let go.

"She's your damn cousin, man. The better question is, what's wrong with you?"

Ramon looked at her and sneered. "Does she look like my cousin? I think my aunt brought the wrong baby home from the hospital."

"I'm proud to say I got my looks from my dad," Madison said to Alex. She swiped the back of her hand across her mouth. "The next time you touch me like that, *cousin*, you're gonna want to guard your balls, because those are what my knee will aim for." She walked out of the room with her head held high.

"Damn, she's hot," Ramon said, his gaze on her ass as she left.

Alex visualized how Ramon would look without teeth.

Sitting in her room with her now, he was still disturbed by the incident. And although he had reminded himself a thousand times since then that *Spooky Man* was off-limits, his protective instincts were off the chart.

"Thanks for coming so quickly," she said quietly.

Remembering that she had a roommate, he kept his voice low. "Well, there was an exclamation point at the end of your text."

She smiled, her even white teeth gleaming in the semidarkness. "Maybe you shouldn't have told me to use one in an emergency. I like exclamation points and tend to overuse them."

"So there's not an emergency?" His eyes were drawn to the bottom lip she chewed on, and his reaction was instantaneous. *Down, boy.* His dick apparently didn't comprehend the meaning of off-limits no matter how many times it was reminded, and Alex subtly shifted in the chair.

Was it an emergency? Madison had thought so when she'd messaged him because the text from her cousin had panicked her. With a little time to calm down, however, she doubted Ramon's demand qualified as urgent. She should have just texted Alex and asked him to get in touch with her when he got a free moment.

Where Ramon was concerned, though, panic was lately her first reaction. The boy she'd once played hide-and-seek with had grown into a perverted man. Not that it was a total surprise, considering his creep of a father.

She really needed to learn how to put on her big girl panties and deal with her cousin on her own. But Alex was here now—and wasn't it just the pits to have a man in her bedroom whose bones she wanted to jump, but who'd figuratively put up a "No Touching" sign?

A little embarrassed that she'd overreacted, she shrugged. "It felt like an emergency at the time, but now, I don't know. I shouldn't have bothered you." She had always wondered, when she'd read that someone gave a strangled laugh, just what that sounded like, but now she knew because Alex gave one.

"Bothered?" Another laugh that sounded as if something amused him. "My problem, not yours." He shifted as if the chair was uncomfortable.

Were they even speaking the same language? "So, um, Ramon texted me." As if she'd waved a red cape in front of a bull, Alex turned such an intense focus on her that she had the urge to run. Not for the first time, she wondered just exactly who he was. When she had met him at her cousin's house, she had immediately classified him as an a-hole since he was obviously a friend of Ramon's. A very sexy a-hole, but one nevertheless. She might have misjudged him.

"He'll be home tomorrow and wants me to meet him for drinks."

"No. Just tell him no." He stood and paced around her room, observing everything as if cataloging all that she owned.

"I did text him back and said no, but you know Ramon. He doesn't understand the word."

He stopped, putting his hands on his hips. "Then just do a no-show."

"He covered his bases on that one. Called my mom, told her he expected to see me at the Flamingo Bar at exactly five."

"You're an adult, Madison. She can't make you do anything you don't want."

He didn't understand, and she wasn't ready to spill the dynamics of her family. "That's true, but I'll never hear the end of it if I don't go." That was as close as she was willing to get to the truth.

Alex began to pace again. He raked his fingers through his hair, then stopped and stared off into space. After some seconds, he nodded as if coming to a decision. As she watched him, she was struck by how magnificent he was. From his black collar-length hair, dark-as-midnight eyes, high cheekbones, and olive skin, she guessed he had some American Indian ancestry. Whatever his makeup, God had been good to him, very good indeed.

"Okay, here's the plan. Meet him . . . be on time so he doesn't get riled, and I'll happen to show up about fifteen minutes later."

"You don't have to. I mean, that's not why I told you. I . . . what I was going to ask is, would you show me how to defend myself from an assault?" Because she knew the day would come when Ramon would go too far. After witnessing the way he had handled Ramon when her cousin had kissed her, she didn't doubt Alex could teach her how to fend off an attack.

Alex's eyes turned hard and cold, and his body seemed to expand into all rippling muscles with dangerous vibes radiating from him. "If he ever touches you like that, I'll kill him."

Holy cannoli! The man had morphed right in front of her into one scary dude. But strangely, instead of frightening her, this new side of him made her feel safe, not to mention all that alphaness he had going on was downright hot.

"Well, I don't want to have to visit you in prison." Something that seemed like amusement flashed on his face, and that didn't make sense.

He already had one strike against him as far as the law was concerned just by owning a biker bar, and who knew what went on there.

"Don't worry about me, Madison." He sat on the edge of the bed. "I'll bring a date with me so Ramon won't get suspicious. You invite us to hang out with you."

He was so close to her that she could feel his body heat, could see the flexing of the muscles in his arms, and she wondered if their decision to meet in her bedroom had been a good idea.

Alex's words sank in. At the thought of seeing him with a date, something that felt a lot like jealously unfurled, and she swallowed hard. This was her first time experiencing such a thing, and she didn't at all like it.

"Sounds like a good plan," she lied. "You never answered my question. Will you teach me how to defend myself?"

There was a slight hesitation. "Yes, but some other time. I need to get back to Aces and Eights. I'll see you tomorrow night. Lock the window behind me."

Like a thief in the night, he slipped away, and she dutifully turned the lever, locking herself in. Without him, the room suddenly felt empty, and she stood for a moment in the quiet. What did she know of him other than he was Ramon's friend, he owned a biker bar with his brothers, and he qualified on all counts as a bad boy?

Bad boys were Lauren's thing. Her roommate was the one with a weakness for the creatures, not Madison. Well, not until this one, anyway. But what truly bad boy climbed a drainpipe to retrieve a child's ball? The same day he'd hauled Ramon off her, she witnessed Alex pulling over his motorcycle, alongside a little boy who was crying. She'd left her uncle's house right after Alex, and upon seeing him stopped, she had nosed her car into a parking spot where he wouldn't notice her.

He had squatted next to the sobbing boy who she guessed to be around four, and after a brief conversation, Alex had peered up. She'd followed his gaze, but hadn't seen anything. Then he'd patted the child on the shoulder before standing and shimmying up the drainpipe like a freaking monkey. At the roofline, he'd reached up, fumbling around in the gutter, and then, viola, a baseball had appeared in the hand he held out for the boy.

The child broke into a wide smile as he clapped his little hands. It was what Alex did next, though, that had ruined his bad boy image as far as Madison was concerned. He'd slid down the pipe, picked up the boy, walked up to the door of the house, and rang the bell. When a man answered, from where she sat, it appeared Alex had given the guy a stern talking-to. Madison wanted to applaud Alex for stepping in where others wouldn't have, because who left such a young child alone on the street these days?

That was the day she'd moved him from bad boy status to hero status. So when he'd told her to call him if she ever needed him, she'd suggested her room as a meeting place.

Along with having a roommate who would come running if she screamed, she kept a knife under her pillow, should her cousin decide to make a surprise appearance, which she wouldn't put past him. She felt pretty well protected.

Alex had balked at first, telling her that she didn't know him well enough to be making such an invitation, and that had only served as further reason to trust him. South Miami Beach was a small community where, except for the tourists, everyone knew everyone, she'd argued. If they met anywhere else, sooner or later Ramon would hear about it. Since Alex couldn't deny that, he'd finally given in.

Problem was, what had started as a kind of business relationship between them was evolving into her having naughty thoughts about him. Too bad he didn't think of her the same way.

CHAPTER TWO

Alex rode back to Aces & Eights sans helmet, something he'd never done before. But he needed the cool night wind on his face and whipping through his hair after being so close to Madison. There had to be somewhere else they could meet, a place that didn't have both her and a bed in it.

His brain had gone on vacation when he'd agreed to teach her self-defense. That would mean touching her. Just being close to her tonight, he'd felt her heat, inhaled her lemony scent, and wanted nothing more than to put that bed of hers to good use. If he followed through on the promise of showing Madison how to protect herself, he'd definitely have to find a place without a bed anywhere near the premises. Of course, that would still leave the floor, up against the wall, atop a desk if there was one . . .

He took the corner hard, scraping the bottom of the foot peg across the asphalt, the grinding noise echoing in the night. Throttling up, he tried to outrun thoughts of a woman with cat-green eyes.

It worked for a few minutes as he raced down the empty street, but then she crept back into his mind. He couldn't tell her he was FBI for fear that she would slip and say something around Ramon. Nor was he entirely certain that she was clueless about the family business and what Ramon and his father were involved in.

Worse, he was the lead on an operation to take down part of her family. When that came about and she realized he had helped make it happen, she would hate him. That trust in him shining so brightly in her eyes would vanish when her cousin and uncle were hauled away in handcuffs.

Better not to know what he might be missing, so no kissing her. Ever. No doing any of the things he'd fantasized about since he'd first met her. She was a source for information and nothing more. When he returned to the bar, he would tell his brothers about her. Once she wasn't his personal secret, his fascination with her would diminish. Satisfied he had his priorities straight, Alex eased back on the throttle and turned the bike toward Aces & Eights.

"When you gonna tell us who your informant is?" Nate asked.

Court brought three ice-cold bottles of beer to the table, sliding into the booth next to Alex. "Yeah, you've never been so secretive before. What gives, bro?"

Good question. Alex enjoyed the end of the day when, after locking up, he and his brothers would have a beer together before heading home. Sometimes they'd have some laughs over something Spider or some other dude had done, but usually they'd go over their progress on building a case against the Alonzo family. With Ramon MIA, things had stalled a bit.

Although he'd decided to level with them about Madison Parker, a.k.a. Spooky Man, Alex hesitated, that damn need to protect her surfacing again. If his brothers knew about her, they'd push him to use her to the fullest extent. Although he would do that, he wanted to do it his way. Hell if he knew exactly what that way was. There was a black hole in his mind, one he wanted to fill in before he gave his brothers Madison's name. He also hoped to ascertain her innocence first, if she was innocent.

Being FBI agents, they were naturally suspicious of anyone with connections to the bad guys. Once he knew which side of the line Madison was on, and if it was the right one, he could better argue her case. If it turned out he was wrong about her, then she'd go down with her uncle and cousin. Yeah, he needed to know more about Madison Parker before he turned over her name.

"Ramon will be back tomorrow. He'll be at the Flamingo Bar around five, and I plan to just happen to go there with a date."

He'd never been able to pull one over on Nate, who narrowed his eyes. "Spooky Man tell you this?"

It was close, but Alex managed not to squirm as if he were still ten years old and in trouble with his older brother. "Yep. I need a date."

Court snorted. "Just pick one of the many outta that contact list of yours."

"And put an innocent woman in Ramon's sights?" There were a good number of female names stored in his phone, and he tried to think of one who could hold her own against Ramon. There were a few biker groupies in there, and any one of them probably could, but he was still uneasy about bringing any of them into contact with the Alonzo family.

"Taylor Collins."

Alex gave Nate an appreciative nod. "Good thinking." Taylor was a fellow FBI agent, and he should have thought of her.

"I'll call Rothmire first thing in the morning and set it up." Nate slid out of the booth. "I'm heading for home."

"Me, too," Court said.

Alex collected their bottles. He hoped their bureau chief agreed to loan them Taylor. Once she showed up on his arm, the man was going to want her. That was Ramon, wanting whatever anyone else had, especially a beautiful woman.

At least Taylor was trained to protect herself. He had taken a *Krav Maga* class with her and had been duly impressed with both her determination and skills. He'd never been at the gun range with her but heard that she put it through the bull's-eye every single time. So, yeah, he was good with introducing her to Ramon.

After dropping the beer bottles in the recycling bin, Alex followed his brothers to the garage. As their three Harleys roared onto the street, he fell into his usual position, with Nate in the lead, Court in the middle, and him in the tail gunner position.

Alex liked riding behind his brothers where he could keep an eye on them. It felt like he was protecting Nate and Court, something he owed them both for taking care of a confused, angry boy.

Even though Nate had mostly raised him, growing up, Court had also kept an eye on him. Court was the one Alex had gone to when he needed to confess a sin before Nate heard about it. Together, the two of them would devise a story that would put Alex in a better light than he deserved. Because he'd often found himself in trouble, he had a special place in his heart for Court. That didn't mean Court hadn't given him hell, but Court's hell was easier to take than Nate's. Disappointing Nate had always made him feel like a brainless slug.

As he followed his brothers home, for some damn reason he thought of his mother and wondered if she'd be proud of how they'd turned out. It had been twenty-two years since he'd last seen her, and because she'd made no attempt to contact them, he guessed he'd never know. They didn't even know if she was still alive.

At the security arm blocking their way to the lower-level parking garage, he pulled up next to Court while waiting for Nate to punch in the code.

"You going to head back out?" he asked Court. Alex was feeling restless and wasn't sure he was ready to pack it in.

"Nah. I'm worn out." Court grinned like a mischievous boy. "Might ruin my reputation if I tried to make a lady happy tonight."

"And here I thought nothing could keep you from getting it up." He leaned his bike toward Court's, reached over, and punched his brother's arm. "You're no longer my hero."

"Liar. I'll always be your hero."

The security arm lifted, and Court followed Nate into the garage before Alex could retort. If he'd had the chance, he would have said, "Both you and Nate are my heroes." And he would have meant it. Without them, Alex Gentry would have been crushed under his father's heavy hand.

There were ten floors in their condo complex, and Alex lived on the eighth. Court had his place on the ninth, and Nate's condo was on the tenth.

When the elevator came to a stop at the eighth floor, he waved a hand at his brothers. "Let me know if Taylor's a go."

"I'll call you after I talk to the boss," Nate said as the door closed.

Alex walked down the hallway, passing two condo units before he came to his own. After letting himself in, he took out his phone to check for messages. Nothing from Madison, so that should mean she was tucked snugly in her bed, safe and sound.

And there he went again, thinking of her in bed.

Madison had dreamed of Alex. In a way, that was surprising because she had never dreamed about a man she actually knew. Sure, in high school she'd had some about various teen heartthrobs, but never about one of her boyfriends. In her dream, Alex had given her a toe-curling kiss.

"Why are you sighing?"

Startled, Madison spilled coffee over the side of her cup. "What?" She'd totally spaced out, forgetting her roommate was in the kitchen with her.

Lauren grabbed a paper towel and handed it to her. "You've been sitting there, staring into space and sighing. You're crushing again, aren't you?"

Madison groaned, wishing Lauren didn't know her so well. "Can we talk about something else? Like how much we still have to do today if we're going to open tomorrow?"

Madison and Lauren had met in college when they'd joined the same book club and had hit it off immediately. When they'd discovered each dreamed of opening a bookstore, they had teamed up, pooling their resources. High Tea and Black Cat Books was scheduled to open tomorrow. They'd agreed on a soft opening, planning a grand splash for a month later. Madison loved that when she'd suggested adding tea, coffee, and baked goods, along with selling books, her friend had jumped on board with the idea.

Lauren had come up with the name, and they'd scouted the no-kill shelters for the perfect black cat. Hemingway, the one they'd come home with, was—unlike every other cat in the world—not a morning person. At the moment, he was sound asleep flat on his back, legs splayed, in the middle of the kitchen floor. They didn't try to be quiet around him because nothing woke him until he was ready to be woken.

On a rainy afternoon they had found the shop, the last place on their list for that day. Discouraged by what they had seen so far, they had almost blown it off. Every place they'd looked at either had needed so much work that it would take a fortune to make it a bookstore, or was so expensive that it was out of their league.

Then they had walked through the door of a former coffee-slash-souvenir shop, and had said at the same time, "This is it." The place had been perfect. The previous owners had set it up to sell coffee, with tables spread around for those wanting to hang while they had their morning fix. In the other half of the space, they had sold souvenirs. Cheap Miami Beach ones, based on the left-behinds Madison discovered when she'd found a box of rubber dolphins and mermaid lamps tucked away in the crawl space under the stairs.

The best part, though, was a two-bedroom, two-bath apartment above the shop where they could live. Next best, it was a little under their max budget. They had spent the previous five weeks painting, retrieving boxes of books from storage, and setting up their upstairs living space.

Lauren went to the sink and rinsed her coffee cup. "Yeah, I guess we better get to it. I peeked downstairs when I got up, and the book fairies didn't get a thing done while we were sleeping." She leaned back against the counter. "You do know, one way or another, I'm going to find out who you're sighing over."

Madison didn't doubt she'd try. When Lauren Montgomery made up her mind, get out of her way. But Alex was Madison's secret, one she had no intention of sharing. Hemingway chose that moment to blink open his silvery-blue eyes. He stuck one front paw in the air in a halfhearted stretch as he yawned.

"I'll feed him," she said. "Go get started, and I'll be down in a minute." It would give her a little time to get her wayward mind back on track, purge it of a black-haired, black-eyed best dream kisser in the world.

Lauren gave Hemingway the stink eye. "I told you at the shelter that there was something wonky about that cat. But *nooo*, you just had to pick this one."

Alone with Hemingway, Madison mixed some tuna into the dried cat food. "Here you go," she said, setting the bowl on the floor. "Just the way you like it."

Hemingway was such a silly cat, and she couldn't help but smile. She never tired of watching him eat. He dropped his belly to the floor, spread out all four legs, and buried his face in the food, making a weird humming noise as he ate.

"You're the laziest cat in the world," she told him. As always, he fell asleep halfway through eating, his neck arched over the bowl, his chin resting atop his meal. He would awaken after twenty or thirty minutes, finish eating, then saunter downstairs. His favorite napping place was in the front window, where they had set up a little bed for him, one that was surrounded by a charming display of books, which Lauren had arranged.

"She loves you, you know," Madison told the cat. She just refused to admit it.

Hemingway snored on, not caring who liked him or didn't. Madison smiled, giving him a loving stroke down his back before heading downstairs to join her bookstore partner. Satisfied that she'd banished the Dream Kisser, she worked alongside Lauren, getting High Tea and Black Cat Books ready to open. Her nerves hummed with excitement. They'd done it. They had made their dream come true. Who cared if a man with smoldering black eyes never kissed her?

Later that afternoon, Madison stood next to Lauren, their arms linked, as they surveyed their shop. The tall ceiling and the crown moldings, original to the old building, were just plain awesome. The cashier's counter—the front painted by an artist friend of Lauren's to look like shelves of old books—was the coolest thing Madison had ever seen. She especially loved the display of art deco books they'd set up near the cash register, and she was certain they would sell well to tourists wanting to take home a souvenir that would remind them of South Beach.

The real wood bookshelves they'd splurged on, the groupings of comfortable seating spread around, the rich aroma of coffee filling the air . . . Madison loved all of it. South Beach was famous for its art deco buildings, and the front of theirs was painted in the pastels popular in the 1930s when their store was originally built as a hotel. It had since been divided into four shops, and she'd pinched herself many times to make sure she wasn't dreaming.

Elation buzzed through her veins, and she couldn't wait until they opened the doors for the first time so she could watch the expressions on their customers' faces as they got their first look inside High Tea and Black Cat Books.

Although she would love to sit and admire what they had accomplished, she had just enough time to shower and dress before meeting her cousin. Ramon hadn't always been a creep, but the boy she'd once liked before he'd grabbed her breasts at her fifteenth birthday party had grown into a man she could barely tolerate. If not for her mother, she would have cut all ties with her uncle's family.

Then there was Uncle Jose's loan, which Madison regretted taking the first time Ramon had hinted that she now owed him a favor. What that favor was, she didn't know, but having it hanging over her head made her physically ill whenever she thought about it, so she tried not to. If she hadn't already invested the money in the bookstore, she would have given it back. She should have found another way to come up with her share instead of accepting anything that would tie her to her uncle and cousin.

Already, Ramon was using the threat of closing down the bookstore whenever she balked at being at his beck and call. If it weren't for Lauren, she would say the hell with it and let him. Probably. The thought of losing what she and Lauren had created made her want to find a paper bag and breathe into it. Why did Ramon have to be such a jerk?

It was tempting to put on a pair of sweatpants and an oversized T-shirt since she knew that would annoy her cousin, but Alex would be there, and she couldn't bring herself to show up looking like a slob. As she flipped through the clothes in her closet, she spied a white dress with splashes of color, as if a mad artist had taken a paintbrush and gone wild. She'd seen the dress in a store window a few weeks before and had to have it.

Madison loved color, something she recognized as a bit of rebellion against her mother trying to dress her in bland colors as a child because of her red hair. As an adult, Madison refused to own anything beige, black, or white. After a shower, she slipped on the dress, loving how the full skirt swirled around her knees. The bodice wasn't low-cut, which was a plus because Ramon wouldn't be staring at her boobs all night. For shoes, she chose a pair of strappy red sandals with low heels.

After one last check in the mirror, she decided she'd do, and hoped Alex's date didn't make her wish she'd opted for something sexier.

CHAPTER THREE

Alex opened the door of the taxi, and when Taylor Collins stepped out, he gave a low whistle, while patting his chest. "Be still my heart." The black dress clung to her in all the right places, and the do-me black heels drew his eyes right to her long legs.

The tall blonde leaned back and eyed him from head to toe. "You clean up nice yourself, Alex. I'm trying to remember if I've seen you in anything but black leathers." She tapped a finger against red-glossed lips. "There was that one time at Rand's bachelor party. If memory serves right, you ended the night wearing a grass skirt and nothing else."

"Now, now, Taylor. You promised never to mention that." The only female in their field office, she had somehow managed to get them to think of her as just one of the guys. She had certainly been the only woman at the party and had been as rowdy as the rest of them. On the job, though, she was all business and sharp as a tack. If he had to pick someone to back him up in a dangerous situation, other than his brothers, she would be high on his list.

She laughed. "I lied."

"Of course you did. Nate said he briefed you about tonight. Any questions?"

"Only one. Do you want me to pay more attention to you or to our bad guy?"

It was a good question, and one he hadn't considered. "We'll play it by ear. Ramon will be with his cousin, and he has an unnatural attraction to her." He held open the door, following her into the Flamingo Bar. "We're headed up to the rooftop," he told the hostess.

"Does she return these unnatural tendencies?" Taylor asked when they entered the elevator.

"No. I don't know the family's dynamics other than her mother and Ramon's father are twins. From what I've gathered, Madison's mother puts pressure on Madison to spend time with her cousin. I think there's more to it, but what that is, I don't know." Yet. But he was sure going to find out.

"So if he gets too familiar with her . . . that's disgusting by the way, maybe I should try to divert his attention?"

"I think she would appreciate that." The assessing look Taylor gave him made him uncomfortable, but he kept his face blank.

When they reached the rooftop, he scanned the area and, locating Ramon and Madison, he said, "There's our target, along the rail, third table from the left."

"Good-looking man."

"And he knows it. If he makes you feel at all uncomfortable, kick me under the table, and I'll knock out one or two of his teeth. Won't be so good-looking then." Ever since he'd pulled Ramon off Madison, he'd been itching to rearrange the man's face.

She slipped her hand around his arm as they approached the table. "Tell me this isn't personal for you, Alex," she said quietly.

He'd said too much. "No, just can't abide a man going where he's not welcome, that's all. Let's walk by them first, see if he'll call us over.

Make him think it's his idea we join them." He turned his attention on her as they passed. "Laugh at something I said."

She laughed as she leaned her head toward him, her cheek brushing his shoulder. "You're such a funny man, Alex. You know what they say, a hot guy who can make a girl laugh is a deadly combination."

Her words were spoken softly so that only he could hear, and to an observer, it would appear as if they couldn't take their eyes off each other. That there was no sexual chemistry between them, he found interesting. Actually, he'd not picked up on any of his fellow FBI cohorts thinking of her as anything but one of the team.

She was a woman who turned the heads of every male she walked by, though, and he didn't miss the envious looks directed his way. If she had a steady man in her life, no one knew, although being the gossipy men they were, they'd often speculated about her private life.

Just when he thought they were going to have to pretend to notice Ramon and Madison, he heard his name called. "Showtime," he whispered. He put an arm around Taylor and led her to the table. "Ramon, dude, didn't know you were back in town."

Ramon stood, his eyes on Taylor's chest. "Just got back today. Have a seat and catch me up on what I've been missing."

The bastard pulled out the seat next to him, clearly wanting Taylor close to him. Alex let go of her and sat next to Madison. Her lemony scent was the first thing to hit him. It reminded him of the hot summer days when his mother would bring him an ice-cold glass of lemonade to make the chores his father had assigned him tolerable. He hadn't thought of those times until recently, when he was close enough to Madison to catch her scent.

Shaking off the direction his thoughts had veered, he said, "Ramon, you devil, you try to steal my date, we're gonna have words." As expected, Ramon's eyes lit with pleasure that he'd been challenged. The fool. If anyone could best Ramon at his own game, it was Taylor.

"Introduce us," Ramon said, his head bent, giving him a better view of the cleavage showing above the low cut of Taylor's dress.

Alex would have killed him then and there if he'd leered at Madison like that. *You gotta stop thinking of Madison as yours, dude.*

"Ramon, this is Taylor. Taylor, my friend Ramon Alonzo." He nodded at Madison. "This is Madison Parker, Ramon's cousin." He'd intentionally left off Taylor's last name. If asked, they would tell Ramon it was Crawford, an alias already set up if anyone was curious enough to check.

Ramon, being the ass that he was, slipped his hand under Taylor's and brought her fingers to his lips. While Ramon's attention was on Alex's partner, Alex slanted his head and gave Madison an eye roll. She smiled back, but it didn't reach her eyes. Had Ramon already acted inappropriately with her?

Their waiter arrived to take their drink orders. "I always forget what I like," Taylor said, giggling. "It's pink and fuzzy, and it tickles my nose."

Madison muttered something under her breath, and Alex leaned toward her. "Pardon?"

She gave a little shake of her head. "I'll have a glass of Merlot, whatever your house brand is," she said to the waiter, as Ramon attempted to help Taylor figure out what kind of drink she wanted.

"My date," Alex nodded toward Taylor, "wants a Magic Fuzzy Pink."

"That's it!" Taylor exclaimed, giving Alex a brilliant smile as if he were a genius.

"I was just going to suggest that," Ramon said.

Alex winked at Taylor, and her smile grew brighter. The woman should be on the stage. She had Ramon thoroughly convinced that although she was gorgeous, her elevator didn't reach the top floor. His favorite kind of woman.

"I need to find the restroom," Madison said, pushing away from the table.

As Alex watched her walk away, the first thing that came to mind was how fresh and pretty she looked in her colorful dress. The second was how much he wanted to see her long red hair spread out over her pillow, and her cat-green eyes darkened with desire while he was deep inside her. *News flash, Alex. Not gonna happen.* Yeah, he had to stop forgetting that.

He didn't like the dull look in her eyes, though. Reaching his hand under the table, he slipped out his phone and made it buzz. "I gotta take this," he said. Ramon waved him off, and Alex slipped out of his seat, making his way to the women's bathroom. He leaned against the wall outside the door and waited for Madison to appear.

Madison ran a brush through her hair and then freshened her lipstick. "It tickles my nose," she muttered, mimicking Taylor's giggle. There was no denying the woman was gorgeous, but she didn't have the brains God gave a cabbage.

How disappointing that Alex would go for someone like that. In the few conversations she'd had with him, he'd seemed intelligent, like a man who enjoyed lively conversation. They had even talked about the books they liked when he'd learned of High Tea and Black Cat Books.

She supposed she couldn't hide in the bathroom the rest of the night, but she so did not want to sit at that table and watch him wink and smile at his date for the next few hours. Maybe she could plead a headache and leave the two men to battle over the bimbo's attentions, since they both seemed to be enchanted by her.

"Blah." She made a face in the mirror. Actually, Alex had done her a favor by showing her how shallow he was. As of now, she was over him. She would go back, finish her wine, and then make her excuses. After snapping her purse shut, she washed and dried her hands, holding on to the paper towel to open the door. She gave the management a nod of approval for placing a trash can at the exit.

"I was beginning to think you'd climbed out the window and gone home."

Madison came to a stop in front of the man casually leaning against the wall. The one making her heart stutter at the sight of him. Okay, so apparently she had to work on the getting-over-him part. She'd get right on that as soon as she could tear her gaze away, because *hello*, the man was serious eye candy, whether wearing black biker leathers or dressed in a pale gray silk shirt and dark gray pants. His black hair curled over his collar, and she had to mentally order her hand not to reach up and comb her fingers through it to see if it was as soft as it looked. *Get a grip, Mad. You're over him. You said so just minutes ago.*

"Madison?" He put his hand on her shoulder. "Did Ramon say or do something before I got here?"

"No. Why?" She barely refrained from leaning into his touch. And the scent of him? She wanted to rub her nose over his skin and breathe him in. When she was finally back home and alone in her room, she was going to give herself a stern talking-to about avoiding bad boys for the rest of her freaking life.

"I dunno. You don't seem yourself."

No shit, Sherlock. She might be herself sometime next week, when hopefully— please, God—she couldn't recall his scent or how it felt to have him touch her. A scolding was definitely in order. *The man likes his women dumb and beautiful, so beat that fact into your brain, Madison.*

"I'm fine," she said, then, needing to get away from him before she told him how stupid he was for not appreciating a woman with a brain in her head, headed back to their table. She'd hoped to leave him behind, but no such luck. With his long legs, he easily kept up, staying by her side.

"Madison," he said, putting his hand under her elbow and stopping her.

There he went again, touching her. He really, really needed to stop doing that. The heat from his hand was like sticking a marshmallow in a fire and watching it flame. That was how her skin felt where his fingers curled around her arm—all marshmallowy and burning hot.

"What?" she snapped.

His eyes widened. "Have I done something to annoy you?"

There was a loaded question. *Yes, Alex, you have annoyed me. You touched me. I'm afraid you implanted your scent in my memory for all time. You talked about books with me, and that made me weak in the knees. You like your women stupid and beautiful. You . . . you . . .* He'd never kissed her and she was thankful he hadn't, while at the same time she was sad about it.

"I want to go home," she said.

Sympathetic black eyes peered down at her. "Yeah, Ramon's an ass, and I don't blame you."

Uh-huh, that was the reason she was going with. "He is. I'm going to plead a headache, then leave the three of you to your fun."

"Can't say it will be fun without you, Madison."

Oh God, she wished he'd stop saying her name with that sexy emphasis he put on it. Nor did she believe him. And she didn't doubt that sometime around midnight, after he'd wrestled his dumb date away from Ramon, Alex and the I-might-be-stupid-but-I'm-every-man's-dream woman would be tangled in the sheets.

Who cared? Not her.

♥ ♥ ♥

Madison groaned as she flipped her body. She'd tried falling asleep on her left side, then on her right, and now she was flat on her stomach, no closer to sleep than an hour ago. Every time she closed her eyes, Alex was there. Seeing him in something other than his leathers, she'd literally lost her breath for a few seconds. No man had ever caused her to have those kinds of heart palpitations before, not even her last boyfriend, the one she'd thought she loved and wanted to marry.

Madison punched her pillow in frustration. "Damn you, Alex."

"And damn you, Madison. You didn't lock your window."

She shot up, a scream on her lips.

"It's me," Alex said, gently putting his hand over her mouth. "Don't yell."

Her heart was beating so fast that she pressed her hands against her chest. "You scared me. What are you doing here?" She glanced at the clock. A little before midnight. Well, if nothing else, she'd been wrong about him being in another woman's bedroom, because now he was in hers.

He turned on the lamp. "Why are you mad at me?"

"Who said I was mad?" She squinted and reached over, dimming the light.

One black brow lifted, as if he found her amusing. "You were just damning me. Must've had a reason."

Oh, let me count the ways. Although tempted, she refrained from saying it. He would want all the details. He moved to the chair and sat, as if he were visiting her in her living room during normal-people hours. As she was learning, Alex wasn't like anyone else she knew. At some point since she last saw him, he'd changed back into his leathers, which meant he'd ridden his bike to see her. She tried not to feel any pleasure in knowing that if he'd gone home to change, he'd spent even less time with his date.

"Did we discuss you coming here tonight, Alex? Because I don't think we did, so go away." If she had blinked, she would have missed how fast he moved from the chair to planting his butt—correction: totally awesome butt—on her bed, right next to her leg. If her knee inched over until it was touching his hip, it wasn't her doing. Since when was she responsible for how her knee reacted to him?

"After you left, I missed you." He picked up a strand of her hair, his knuckles brushing the top of her arm, and stared at her hair as if fascinated.

When he twined it around his fingers, she fought but lost in her effort to conceal how his touch affected her as a shiver snaked down her spine. She pushed his hand away. The man was seriously messing with her mind. Sometimes he seemed untouchable, as if he didn't want her to know the real him. Other times, like now, she thought that if she lifted the covers, he would crawl into bed with her and hold her close.

It was as if there were two of him: the daytime, all-business Alex, and the nighttime, mysterious and sensual Alex. He intrigued her and she hated that he did. She was a simple girl. There was more than her fair share of drama in her life between her mother, her cousin, and her uncle. She needed simple and easy, a guy who wouldn't complicate matters any more than they already were. Alex was not that kind of man.

He leaned his elbows onto his knees and clasped his hands, dangling them between his legs. "There are things about me you don't know and that I can't tell you," he said, staring down at his feet. "I promised myself I'd stay away from you, but here I am." He lifted his head, his eyes snaring hers. "You should tell me to go and to never come back."

There was a deeper message in his words than she could interpret; it was there in his eyes as he locked his gaze on to hers. A warning, but from what? And even though she knew with every fiber of her being that danger surrounded him, she couldn't form the words to tell him to leave.

Instead, she did what she'd wanted to do from the day she'd first met him. If nothing else, she was going to damn well know what it was like to kiss him. She crawled onto his lap, wrapped her arms around his neck, and lowered her mouth to his. He put his hands on the sides of her waist and gave what felt like a halfhearted attempt to push her away.

"I'm trying to be noble here," he said against her lips when she resisted his effort to lift her off him.

She slipped her tongue inside his mouth when he opened it to speak, and he responded with a low groan.

He wrapped her hair around his hand and tugged her head back. "You're playing with fire, Madison."

"That explains why I'm so hot," she said. He swore, then roughly pulled her mouth back to his and kissed her in a way that no man ever had. Not even trying to be gentle, he nipped stinging little bites on her bottom lip, and then soothed them with his tongue. Until Alex, she'd thought soft butterfly kisses—lips brushing against lips—were the sexiest thing ever, but his possessive demand that she let go and give as good as she got was a turn-on like no other.

When he slipped his hand under her tank top and pressed his palm flat on her lower spine, pulling her stomach to his, she pushed her bottom down on the erection straining against the confines of his leather pants, rocking herself over him.

He stilled. Breathing hard, he put his forehead to hers. "We can't do this." With little effort, he put his hands on her waist and lifted her back onto the bed.

"I'm sorry. I forgot you have a girlfriend." She tilted her head, eyeing him. "It appears for a few minutes there, you did, too." Grateful her voice didn't betray the hurt invading her heart, she pushed back against the headboard, pulling the covers up to her chest.

"That's not the rea—" He stopped. "Right, I forgot. That was wrong of me. I was just worried about you." He stood. "I should go."

He forgot he had a freaking girlfriend? Seriously? "I don't think you should come here again." *Even better, dump silly Taylor and come here every night.*

At the window, he paused. "I'll be around. If Ramon messes with you again, call me."

She doubted she would. It was too hard being near him knowing he was off-limits. "I can handle my cousin." Maybe.

"Promise me, Madison." He came to the foot of the bed and gave her a hard stare. "Promise, and then I'll go."

"Fine, I promise."

He nodded as if satisfied, then climbed out the window. "Lock this," he said, sticking his head back in. "Now." And then her very own superhero disappeared into the night.

CHAPTER FOUR

A week had passed since Madison had crawled onto his lap and kissed him. Alex could still remember the taste of her even though he'd tried every trick in the book to forget.

"Yo, Alex." Court snapped his fingers in front of Alex's face. "Where'd you go?"

"What?" He had to stop thinking of her since he obviously zoned out whenever he did. Things were heating up with Ramon, and he needed all his concentration centered on the operation.

The woman sitting next to Alex slid her hand up his thigh, and he resisted the urge to remove it. He had willingly agreed to head out with his brothers on their Sunday night off, thinking that what he needed was to find someone to take his mind off Madison. It wasn't working. Sure, Lisa—was that her name, or was it Risa?—was hot, and a month ago, he would have welcomed her attention. But she wasn't Madison, and no matter how hard he tried to enjoy the feminine hand on his leg, it just wasn't happening.

Nate and Court had scoped out the trendy bar as soon as they'd walked in, their gazes zeroing in on the three women, obviously friends, sitting at a table near the entryway. Alex had followed his brothers, letting them do the talking. Soon, they were invited to join the women, introductions were made, and everyone was having a great time. Except him. Disturbed over his lack of interest, a first for him, he'd put forth the effort to join the fun. It wasn't working, and for the last hour, he'd been ignoring the puzzled glances of his brothers.

Was Madison okay? He had checked his text messages constantly, thinking he'd be relieved there wasn't any word from her. He'd thought wrong. How soon could he get away with leaving and not getting the third degree from his brothers?

His phone pinged with a text, and he slipped it out of his pocket, discreetly reading the message. Although he was disappointed it wasn't from Madison, it gave him the perfect excuse to leave.

"Ramon," he mouthed to Nate. He stood. "My apologies, ladies, but I have an emergency."

"Will you be back?" Lisa or Risa said.

"Afraid not." He gave her a regretful smile. "I'll grab a cab," he told his brothers, leaving them the car since they'd ridden together.

"I'll walk you out," Nate said.

And here comes the third degree. "Ramon wants to meet up with me." Hopefully that would divert Nate's attention.

"I figured." Nate eyed him in the way that always made Alex want to squirm. "You're off your game, Alex. Actually, you've not been yourself for a week or so. What's going on?"

Alex came close to spilling everything, because that was the effect the Nate Look had had on him from the time he was a boy. They walked out onto the street, the steamy air from a recent rain shower hanging heavily around them. Even though it was near midnight, it was damn hot. It was time to tell his brothers about Madison, but not now, standing outside a popular nightclub. The longer Alex kept Madison a secret, the more pissed Nate would be when he learned about her. His brothers knew him too well and were already aware that something was going on with him. If he didn't explain soon, Nate would tie him to a chair and interrogate him until he blabbed all. Might as well get it over with.

"There is something on my mind." He raised a hand, waving at a taxi parked down the block. "Tell Court to meet us for lunch tomorrow, and I'll fill you both in at the same time."

"Come up to my place. I'll have sandwiches from the deli delivered."

The hand Nate had put on his shoulder was comforting, and not for the first time Alex's heart swelled with love for his brothers. Their father had been a cruel man with a quick temper and heavy hand. The day had finally come when their mother had left, and Alex couldn't blame her for that. He did, however, blame her for not taking her sons with her, leaving them with a man she'd seen knock them around at the slightest provocation. Most times the bastard didn't need a reason. If not for his older brothers, Alex wasn't sure he would have survived.

"Great. See you tomorrow." He opened the back door of the cab.

"Be careful around Ramon, brother."

"Always am."

During the ride to Ramon's, Alex tried to block the memories that had reared their ugly head, but there were times when his father refused to be banished from his mind. Like the day five-year-old Alex had dropped the heavy bucket of slop while carrying it to the pigpen. He still had scars on his back from the old man's belt buckle. For some reason, he was more of a disappointment to his father than Nate or Court. Or maybe as the smallest boy, he'd been easier to pick on. Who knew where that bastard was concerned?

It would have been worse if Nate and Court hadn't dragged him away whenever their father was in a rage, all three of them hiding in the woods until their father passed out—a nightly occurrence—and they could sneak back into the house.

Their mother had been too afraid of her husband to stick up for them, and they hadn't wanted her to. She got enough beatings on her own. Until she'd left them, there was always a meal waiting for them when they would come out of hiding.

And then there was his son-of-a-bitch father with his visions of grandeur, always bragging about how he was going to turn their five acres of dirt into a thousand-acre cattle ranch to breed prime Angus beef. Unless he'd been some kind of magician—which he wasn't, just a mean drunk—there was no way that piece-of-shit land, their three pigs, a yard full of chickens, and one ornery milk cow were going to morph into a fancy ranch.

"As soon as my useless sons get off their lily-white asses and pull their weight, we'll have us that ranch. Cain't do it all myself, boys" was the old man's favorite saying. And that was when he was in a good mood, which was seldom. Most times, they were working their lily-white asses off while ducking the old man's fists.

The only reason they hadn't flunked out of school every year was because their mother had been fierce about making them study and do their homework. Never mind that they could barely keep their eyes open sitting around the scratched-up, wobbly table each night while their father drunkenly snored away, passed out in his plaid La-Z-Boy.

"I want you boys to be more than your father, and an education is the only way that will happen" was her favorite saying.

He'd never forget the day he watched his half–Seminole Indian mother walking down the dirt road, knowing he'd never see her again. She'd gathered her sons one day when their father had gone into town, told them she loved them, but that she had to leave. When they had begged her to take them with her, she'd smiled her sad smile.

"This is the hardest day of my life, leaving you in the hands of your father. If I take you, he will find us and kill us all. This he has sworn to do if I dared such a thing. There is a reason I must go, but you are strong boys and you will grow up to be men I can be proud of." She had kissed each of them as tears streamed down her face. "Nathan, you will see that you and your brothers study hard and get good grades. Court, you will help your older brother protect Alex." She'd knelt then. "My baby. This will be the hardest for you, but be brave and strong for your brothers. Can you do that?"

Alex stared out the taxi window, remembering how he'd promised to be strong even as hot tears had flowed down his cheeks and burned his skin. He'd been seven that day, the last time he'd cried. Brave, strong boys didn't cry, and after that, no matter how heavy his father's hand was, he'd willed away his tears.

That had been the saddest day of his life. The day his father keeled over and died had been the happiest. Nate had been seventeen, and having stepped into the role of mother at age eleven—continuing their late-night study sessions, keeping them fed and clean— upon the old man's death, he had stepped into the role of father, too. He'd pushed them hard to maintain their good grades, to follow him into college, and after they'd gotten their degrees, Nate had recruited him and Court into the FBI.

No, he hadn't cried since watching his mother walk away with slumped shoulders, but his damn eyes were burning from all the remembering. Not in the best of moods to be hooking up with Ramon, he did what he knew how to do best. He crushed the video streaming through his mind belonging to that lost boy.

He paid the driver, pausing as he exited the taxi to survey the newest South Beach hot spot where Ramon had said to meet him. Purple, pink, and turquoise neon lights pulsated, screaming out the name of the club. A line of people dressed in their hottest clubbing clothes wound around the corner, hoping to get into Rage. Alex hated places like this, but work was work, so he walked up to the bouncer, knowing that because Ramon had invited him here his name would be on the list.

"Alex Gentry," he said.

The man eyed his phone, scrolling down the screen with his thumb. "Yep. You can go in."

"Can I be your date?" a pretty brunette said, slipping out of line and linking her arm around his.

He smiled at her. "Why not." Once inside, he freed his arm. "Go play," he said.

"What if I want to play with you?" She blinked long lashes at him.

"Define play," he said, lifting his mouth in a half smile that he'd learned women loved.

"I love games, if that answers your question," she said, her gaze leveled on his mouth.

Hell. He couldn't do this. There wasn't a future in the cards with Madison, but he couldn't see her again knowing his mouth had been on another woman's. And he would see her again, that was inevitable as she was Ramon's cousin.

"I'm not the man for you, gorgeous." He gave her a gentle push. "Enjoy your evening." Without waiting to hear a protest, he lost himself in the crowd. The place was suffocatingly packed, and while normally he thrived on this kind of action, all Alex wanted to do was go home.

Where the hell was Ramon? The overwhelming scents of perfumes and colognes assaulted his nostrils as he pushed his way through the crowd. About the time he'd decided to say to hell with it and walk out, a beefy hand clamped down on his shoulder.

Alex spun, caught the man's fingers in his grip, and bent one back. "Don't ever touch me like that again, man." He'd known it was one of Ramon's men, but the only way to get respect from these dudes was to be meaner than they were.

The oversized, gym-muscled man squealed. "Damn, that hurts. Let go."

"Where's Ramon?" Alex let go of the man's fingers.

"Upstairs. He's got a table."

Alex followed Ramon's bodyguard, thinking it was going to be a hell of a long night.

It had been an exciting opening week, and as Madison studied the spreadsheet detailing their expenses and income, she tried not to think of Alex. He hadn't called or texted once, obviously honoring her request not to return. Every night, she'd waited for a tap on her window that never came, and she had to stop hoping he would show up even after she'd told him not to. She could have texted him, but her pride had kept her from doing that.

She took a sip of coffee, grimacing. It had gone cold, and she eyed the clock, debating making another pot. It was after midnight, though, and she really should go to bed. Lauren was out on a first date with a guy she'd recently met, and Madison had been trying to wait up for her.

Not that she was worried about Lauren . . . well, she was a bit. Her friend was a little on the wild side when it came to men. All Lauren knew about this new guy was his name, Nelson Lopez, and that he was a drop-dead gorgeous model who liked to collect old books.

Lauren was hot in a bad girl kind of way. Madison envied Lauren's short, spiky brown hair with blonde highlights. She would love to wear her hair like that, but where on Lauren it was sexy, on her it would just look stupid.

Edgy totally worked on Lauren, though, and men were drawn to her like drone bees to their queen. There was an air about her that promised excitement and a bit of naughty fun. She was also the best friend Madison had ever had. Underneath the fun-loving, devil-may-care persona was a woman who Madison knew without doubt she could always depend on, and she hadn't hesitated to sign on as Lauren's business partner.

Hemingway dug his claws into her legs when she tried to pick him up so she could stand. "Ouch, you little monster." He blinked sleepy blue eyes at her, and she tapped his nose. "I'm not buying that innocent look." She set him on the floor, carried her coffee cup to the kitchen, and grabbed a peanut butter cookie, munching on it as she headed to her bedroom.

Their bookstore opening had been better than they'd hoped, especially considering they'd not done any advertising. The first month was all about settling into a routine, learning the business of operating a bookstore, and working out any bugs that popped up. If things went as planned, they would be able to hire a part-time person before their grand opening so that she and Lauren didn't have to be on hand six days a week, from the moment they unlocked the door until closing.

Everything was perfect in this part of her life. It was her mother who weighed the heaviest on her mind. As hard as Madison tried, it was proving impossible to pry Angelina Parker away from her twin brother's influence. As far as Madison was concerned, her uncle Jose was a control freak, and saw himself as some kind of godfather who had the right to decide what was best for his sister and her.

Ever since Madison's father had died, Angelina had leaned on her brother, allowing him to take charge of her life. As much as she could, Madison stepped between her mother and uncle, and she sensed Uncle Jose resented it. In most families, being close to a sibling was probably a good thing, but Madison couldn't help feeling that the relationship between Angelina and Jose wasn't a healthy one. It was a Cuban thing—especially with the older generation of males—this attitude that they knew what was best for the women in their life. And God forbid you should disagree with them.

Madison was still furious that Uncle Jose had taken over paying her mother's bills. Then he'd decided his sister shouldn't have to cook, so he'd arranged for La Cantina to deliver meals to her each day. Madison had seen red when she'd learned that he'd even taken to buying Angelina's clothes. Her mother needed to learn to stand on her own two feet, and Uncle Jose was doing his best to prevent that. All Madison knew to do was to continue to try and keep her mother away from him as much as possible.

An hour after going to bed, Madison gave up trying to go to sleep. Her mind was crammed too full of thoughts—worry for her mother, the bookstore, Lauren still being out, and yes, Alex—and sleep was elusive. She turned on her lamp, deciding she would read for a while. There were two books on her nightstand, one a romance, and one from her business management class. She chose the latter, figuring it would make her sleepy.

After reading a few chapters, she was nodding off when she heard a tap on her window. Alex? She waited for his special signal, and when it came, her heart screamed, *Yes! Let him in.* As she grabbed the robe she'd tossed onto a chair earlier, her brain questioned the wisdom of opening the window for him.

He had a girlfriend, and he'd made it clear that there wouldn't be more kisses, or anything else happening between them. She opened the window anyway, but when she stepped back for him to enter, he shook his head.

"I don't trust myself in a room that has both you and a bed in it," he said, leaning back on the fire escape's metal railing.

She wasn't sure how to feel about that. He'd just admitted he felt something for her but refused to do anything about it. Yet, since he had a girlfriend, she had to respect him for not being a cheater. Which only made her like him more.

Madison sat on the windowsill, noticing that he was dressed as if he'd been out for the night. It was impossible to decide whether she liked him better in his bad boy biker leathers or his trendy casual clothes. He must have been out clubbing. With Taylor? If so, why was he here instead of with her?

"How are you, Madison?"

She lifted her gaze to the sky. The earlier rain clouds had moved on, and stars twinkled against a black velvet background. Someday she'd love to go to a place where there were no artificial lights, lie on her back, and spend hours stargazing.

"I'm fine," she said, shifting her eyes to his, sucking in a breath at how intensely focused he was on her. He confused her, and she wished she could have five minutes inside his mind.

"I've been worried about you." He braced his hands on the railing behind him, causing his shirt to stretch across his chest and shoulders.

"Have you?" Her mouth dried as she imagined how he'd look without a shirt, because it was impossible to miss how muscled he was.

"I didn't want to, but . . ."—he spread out his hands—"there you have it."

"Alex, what do you want from me?"

"I don't know." He stared into the distance.

He seemed to be having some kind of internal battle. As she waited for him to say more, she asked herself what she wanted from him and was surprised to find her answer was the same as his. She didn't know, and she let out a weary sigh. The roadblock was that he had a girlfriend, and if there was one role she refused to play, it was that of the other woman. Also, his involvement with her cousin made her uneasy.

"How serious are you and Taylor?" And there went her mouth, saying things that weren't supposed to leave her mind. Eyes she couldn't read met hers. That wasn't true, though, because she realized they were troubled. About what, she didn't know, and she didn't think he was going to tell her.

"Taylor? She's a friend and we go out sometimes."

Friends with benefits? At least she'd kept that question to herself. "I see." Not really, but if they were only friends, what was stopping him from wanting to see her?

"No, you don't see. There are things about me I can't tell you, and I'm trying to stay away because I don't want to hurt you."

"And how's that working for you, Alex?" What things couldn't he tell her? That he was a drug-dealing biker outlaw? What else would be the kind of secret he couldn't talk about? And if that was the case, she needed to stay far away from him. Having one drug dealer—if she was right about her cousin—in her life was one too many.

He chuckled, but by the sound of it, he was mocking himself. "Since I'm standing on your fire escape at two in the morning, it appears it's not working so well."

"You still up, Madison?"

Madison almost fell off the windowsill at hearing Lauren's voice.

Lauren walked into the room. "Why are you sitting in the window?"

"Ah . . ." She glanced to where Alex had been standing, but he wasn't there. "Just enjoying the stars and waiting up for you." As she stood to close the window, she leaned out, seeing him at the bottom of the stairs. The man had the quiet feet of a cat. He nodded once before disappearing into the night.

Their conversation spun in her head, and although she was glad Lauren was home safe and sound, she wished she were alone so she could analyze what Alex had said. Perhaps she was a fool, but she just couldn't believe he was a drug dealer.

"How was your date?" She moved to her bed, sitting on it cross-legged. Hemingway jumped up, curling in her lap.

"I think I'm in love." Lauren dreamily sighed as she kicked off her shoes and sat on the edge of the bed.

"You said the same thing three weeks ago about what's his name . . . Brian?" She stroked the cat's sleek black fur.

"Brad, but I mean it this time."

"Of course you do. I only met him for a short time, but he seems nice." She grinned. "Definitely easy on the eyes."

"You have a gift for understatement." Lauren flopped back on the bed. "I look at him and almost start drooling. It's embarrassing."

"Try not to do that. It wouldn't be pretty." Her only concern was that this one might break Lauren's heart before all was said and done. But she shouldn't see doom where there wasn't any. There probably wasn't any reason to worry. This time next week, her friend would be in love with some other man. That was how it always went with Lauren.

"I know," Lauren said, sitting up. "We're having dinner tomorrow night. You should come. I'm sure Nelson won't mind. You can kick me under the table if you see drool dripping down my mouth."

"Thanks, but it's my mom and uncle's birthday tomorrow, and there's a family dinner planned." Which she was so not looking forward to, and she still needed to buy a present for her uncle. He collected antique swords, and although she couldn't afford to purchase anything like that, she recalled seeing a coffee table book on old swords when she and Lauren had been stocking the bookstore's shelves. Awesome! Problem solved.

After Lauren left, Madison went back to the window, opening it. Alex wouldn't like her being exposed like this, but if someone tried to get to her, she'd easily see them coming. She sat back on the sill, lifting her eyes to the sky.

"Are you there, Daddy?" she whispered. No answer from the man she missed every minute of every day. No night bird trilled an answering song, no stars shot across the sky giving a sign that he heard her.

For some reason she didn't understand, she'd never felt so alone as she did this night. Her beloved father was gone, her mother couldn't see past her own grief, and Alex would never be a part of her life no matter how much she wished otherwise.

In the distance, she heard the low rumble of a motorcycle. It wasn't Alex. He'd left long before, but her heart ached to see him walk back up the stairs, a smile just for her on his face.

Stupid tears slithered down her cheeks. She angrily swiped them away before jumping off the sill and slamming the window shut. To hell with Alex. As of this very minute, he was banished from her mind.

CHAPTER FIVE

"What's been eating you this past week, Alex?" Nate asked after they'd finished lunch.

Court punched Alex's arm. "Yeah, bro. You're worrying us."

"I'm just tired of Ramon's shit. He dangles a carrot, hinting that he's got a big score in the works, but he's cagey. I told him we were looking to expand our money-laundering operation, and that we had the means to do that through Aces and Eights, along with a few other places we owned. He's interested, but I don't think he trusts me yet."

"If he's hinting, then he's starting to trust you," Court said.

Nate nodded. "True, but maybe you need to push a little harder. Possibly imply that you have some other big dealer in mind if Ramon doesn't get off his ass and bring you in?"

"Might work." Alex drummed his fingers on the table. "I'm supposed to drop by his place later tonight. Said he wants me to meet his father, who, strangely enough, I've never seen when I've been over there."

"That's a good sign," Nate said.

"I guess so." Alex checked his watch. "About time to head over to Aces and Eights."

Nate leaned his chair back on two legs. "Not so fast, baby brother. Now tell us what's really got you moping around like a lovesick girl."

Damn. He didn't want to talk about Madison, still feeling an inexplicable need to protect her from this bad business he and his brothers were involved in. Not only was it bad, but it was going to get worse before it was over.

Two pairs of eyes identical to his pinned him to his seat. There was no getting out of telling them about her, but he didn't have to like it. "There's this girl—"

"Name?"

As soon as he heard it, Nate would connect the dots, since they knew everything there was to know about Ramon Alonzo. "Madison Parker."

Alex could almost see his older brother scroll through the list of names stored in his brain. Nate was sharp; he had to be to raise two hell-raising brothers. Not that Nate hadn't raised his own hell—but, whatever.

"First cousin to Ramon." Nate dropped his chair down on all four feet. "What the hell, bro? You've been hiding a prime link to Ramon and his father?" His gaze zeroed in on Alex's. "Questions. Does she know what her cousin and uncle are into? I'm thinking how could she not. That wasn't a question, but I have three more. Why aren't we using her for intel? Is she Spooky Man? Last one, you're not soft on her, right?" He leaned across the table and wrapped his fingers around Alex's wrist in a tight grip. "Tell me I'm right, Alex."

Alex had never been able to lie to either of his brothers. "No, I don't think she knows, and yes, she's Spooky Man, and I wish I could tell you I'm not soft on her. That answer your questions?" And that was his reason for being miserable. He glanced at Court to see sympathy in his middle brother's eyes. When Nate had you in his sights, it didn't end pretty.

"Dammit." Nate stood, kicking his chair away. He flattened his hands on the table and lowered his face until it was only inches from Alex's. "From this point on, Madison Parker is off-limits to you. I'll decide how best to use her."

Alex reared, pushing Nate away. "Like hell you will. You go near her, *brother*, and I swear, I'll . . ." He'd do what? Kill his brother? Beat the shit out of him? He walked out of Nate's kitchen before he really lost it. If he had to choose, it would be Nate who owned his loyalty, but he wasn't sure he could handle throwing Madison to the big bad wolf that was Nate. As he reached the door to leave, he was grabbed from behind.

"Does she mean that much to you?"

Alex pressed his forehead to the door. "I don't want her to, but yeah, she does."

Nate heaved a sigh. "Not good, baby brother. Not good."

Like he didn't know that.

Alex parked his car behind several others in the driveway of Ramon's house. Looked like either Ramon or his father had company. Since there were security cameras watching him, he held his phone down by his leg, out of sight. As he walked by the cars, he snapped photos of each license plate.

At the door, he rang the bell after discreetly sliding his phone back into his pocket. "Mrs. Gutierrez," he greeted the housekeeper when she answered. "Ramon's expecting me."

"*Si, señor*. Come with me."

He followed her through the house and out to the backyard. "Everyone is up there," she said, pointing to a set of stairs that led to the roof.

"Thank you." She returned inside, and Alex took a moment to look around. It was the first time in his six or so visits here that he'd seen the back, and he hadn't realized how protected the house was. There was a high stucco wall topped with a row of pointed spikes. Although they were decorative, Alex didn't doubt they were razor sharp and meant to keep out unwanted guests. He noted the security camera mounted under the eaves, figuring there were more scattered around, like in the clump of palm trees on his left, or in the sunburst mounted on the stucco wall. The place was a damn compound.

He jogged up the steps, and when he walked onto the roof, he paused. The Alonzos had created a rooftop paradise, and it appeared he was interrupting a celebration of some sort. From this vantage point, there was a great view of the Atlantic Ocean that had been hidden by the wall at ground level.

Profusely blooming red bougainvilleas wound around a pergola, under which sat a long table that could probably seat twenty people. Alex did a quick head count, pausing when he saw unmistakable fiery red hair. Madison had her back to him, and Ramon sat next to her with his arm around the back of her chair. Gritting his teeth, Alex headed toward them.

An older version of Ramon sat at the head of the table, and at the other end was an attractive woman about the same age, and both had wrapped gifts in front of them. A birthday party? If so, then the woman must be Madison's mother, Jose Alonzo's twin sister. The people facing Alex all looked over at him, causing the ones with their backs to him to glance behind them.

Madison's eyes lit with pleasure, and she smiled. Alex ignored her and, although he did it for her sake, he was sorry to be the reason her smile faded. She turned her face away, which was good because now he could concentrate on Ramon.

"Alex," Ramon said, waving him over.

"My apologies. I don't mean to interrupt."

"No, man, it's cool. Grab a seat. As soon as my father and aunt open their presents, we'll take off."

Since manners had escaped Ramon, Alex held out a hand to Jose. "Alex Gentry. Happy birthday, Mr. Alonzo."

The man eyed him, assessed him, dismissed him. Alex let his hand drop. "Perhaps I should wait for Ramon downstairs."

Jose pointed to an empty seat a few chairs down. "Sit."

Right. He would sit. His seat was directly across from Madison, unfortunately. How was he supposed to ignore her when her face was all he saw?

"I'm Trina," a sultry voice said next to his ear.

Alex glanced at the woman he hadn't noticed. "Alex Gentry." In her late thirties, he guessed, she was extremely attractive, but he wasn't interested in the invitation he saw in her eyes. Still, he smiled, playing the part Ramon would expect of him. "Pleased to meet you, Trina."

Everyone quieted as Jose opened his first present, a box of Cuban cigars. "You know I'll enjoy these." Without personally thanking whoever gave him the cigars, he grabbed the next gift. "This one's from Madison," he said, reading the card.

He tore off the paper and turned the book over to show everyone before tossing it aside and moving on to the next wrapped package.

Madison leaned forward. "You love antique swords, Uncle. I thought you'd enjoy a coffee table book about them."

"You should know I don't care about books," he said, not even pausing to look at her as he dug into the next gift.

Bastard. Alex took a moment to study the man. According to their research on Jose Alonzo, he was fifty-five, although he could pass for younger. His dark brown hair had silver streaks through it, giving him a distinguished look, as did the faint lines visible at the corners of his mouth and eyes.

The word was that the older Alonzo was grooming his son to take over. Alex wished him good luck with that. From his observation of

Ramon, the man thought entirely too highly of himself. Ramon wasn't half as smart as he believed he was.

Alex glanced at Madison, frowning at seeing her cheeks turn pink with embarrassment. Her gaze was on her half-eaten piece of birthday cake. He wanted nothing more than to scoop her up and carry her out of this place, away from these poisonous people, but he had a job to do. What he wanted didn't count. If Ramon didn't get his fingers off her shoulders, however . . . Alex tore his gaze away from the offending fingers before he did lose his cool.

Madison pushed her dessert plate aside. The evening was turning out to be pure torture. Between her uncle embarrassing her, Ramon continually touching her, and Alex ignoring her, she wished she had the nerve to get up and leave. And if Trina got any closer to Alex, she was going to end up in his lap.

If not for her mother, Madison would hightail it, but Angelina would have a meltdown if her daughter did such a thing. Angelina's problem was that she needed a man in her life, and her brother seemed more than happy to be that man. As far as Madison was concerned, there was something unsettling about their devotion to each other. She had no idea what to do about it.

Ramon twirled a strand of her hair around his fingers, and she punched his leg with her fist. "Stop it," she whispered. He chuckled and ignored her.

Pervert. He hadn't always been like this. He was her only cousin, and before she'd sprouted boobs they had been friends. One day they were playmates, and seemingly the next he'd started staring at her chest, making her squirm uncomfortably. From the moment he'd grabbed her breast at her fifteenth birthday party, squeezing so hard it had brought tears to her eyes, she'd been afraid of him. Her fear seemed to excite him, so she did her best to hide it.

She glanced at Alex and wished she hadn't. He had his head bent close to Trina's mouth as the woman whispered into his ear. Trina and

Uncle Jose were friends of the *with benefits* kind. Madison had walked in on them once and saw Trina straddled across his lap in the hot tub, both naked. She was still trying to *un*see that one. She also suspected that Trina and Ramon had the same kind of relationship. If Madison's guess was right, Trina had been with every man at the table except for Alex, and the woman was obviously working hard to correct that.

How was she supposed to sit here and watch them whisper to each other, knowing Trina would likely add another notch to her bedpost before the night was out? She couldn't. Edging her chair back, she stood and walked to the rooftop railing. Black storm clouds hung low in the eastern sky, and the ocean splashed angry waves onto the shore. She wished the sky would open and send everyone scurrying for cover so she could sneak out and go home.

"I'm sorry."

Alex. He stood so close behind her that she could feel his body heat, could smell his spicy aftershave. She schooled her face before facing him. "You're sorry for what?" Dressed in black pants and a blue Oxford shirt with the sleeves rolled up, he was beautiful to her . . . probably to every woman here. All the more reason to stop yearning for him to kiss her again.

"That you aren't enjoying yourself tonight."

He reached up as if to brush her hair back, or stroke her face or something, she didn't know, but then dropped his arm back to his side. Afraid that her hands would take off on their own and touch him, she gripped the railing and gazed out over the water. The dark clouds had covered the moon, and all she could see were the flashes of the white-caps as the waves rolled in.

"Who says I'm not enjoying myself?"

"Your eyes say. Madison, I—"

"Alex! Let's go, man."

"Coming." He gave her a sad smile. "I wish I could take you away, just go somewhere. You and me."

She wished that very same thing. "Are you going somewhere with Ramon?"

He put his hand on her arm. "Yeah, but listen. We need to talk, and I'm tired of sneaking around to see you. Meet me tomorrow for lunch."

"Not a good idea."

"I'll call you in the morning. Maybe you'll change your mind by then. Take care, Madison."

After he walked away, she pressed her palm over her arm where his hand had been, still warm from his touch. Where was he going with Ramon? It still worried her that he appeared to be involved with her cousin's business, and she needed to do some snooping, see what she could find out.

Ramon whispered something in his father's ear before grabbing Trina's hand and heading for the stairs, Alex following close behind. Why were they taking that woman with them? Madison tore her gaze away from the trio. This night sucked, and she was past ready to go home.

"Let's go," she said, walking up next to her mother.

"Not yet. Jose and I haven't had our birthday champagne yet."

Right. The champagne ritual. At the end of each birthday party, after the guests left, the twins would walk down to the beach, just the two of them, and would lift their flutes toward Cuba.

When Madison's father and Jose's wife were still alive, Madison would stand back with them, watching the twins. She'd once asked what they were saying and was told they were cursing Castro.

At the age of eleven, Jose and Angelina had arrived on the beach of Miami, along with their parents, having come over in a boat that probably should have sunk somewhere between Cuba and Florida. Somehow they'd made it, though, but their mother arrived sick and had died a week after finding freedom. For that, the twins blamed Castro, thus the annual curses.

Thunder rumbled in the distance. "It's going to rain, so you should do that soon." Since there was no way she was going to get her mother to leave before the ritual, Madison returned to her place at the railing. A few minutes later, her uncle and mother appeared below, and Madison watched as they opened the gate and walked down to the water.

At the ocean's edge, they lifted their flutes of champagne and started yelling. The curses were made in Spanish, and although she couldn't catch the words, Madison could pick up the sound of their voices. After a while, they clinked glasses, then drank the champagne. Jose put his arm around Angelina, and she leaned her head on his shoulder.

The twins had always been affectionate with each other, but it seemed to Madison that sometime after each had lost their spouses, they had grown even closer, if that was possible.

"How did the champagne tradition start?" she asked, after she'd finally convinced Angelina to leave. She wondered why she'd never asked that question before. The rain started, and she turned on the windshield wipers.

"Our father started it. Mother died on our birthday. Did you know that?"

"No, I don't think I did." She glanced over at her mother. Even at fifty-five, Angelina was still beautiful. Her shoulder-length dark brown hair was thick and glossy, and her olive skin flawless. But she was fragile, and without a man to take care of her, she was lost.

"It was a hard time for us. In Cuba, our father was important, a lawyer. Here? He was a nobody. He got a job selling shoes. But you know that already, don't you?"

"I've heard it once or twice." Or a hundred times. It was Jose's favorite story, how their father was nothing in America. Jose liked to brag that he'd been the one to take advantage of all America had to offer.

Until recently, Madison had thought he'd made his money buying and selling real estate. He did do that, but a few weeks ago she'd overheard a conversation between her uncle and Ramon about moving some merchandise that had her suspicious about just what they were involved in.

"Yes, but you asked about the tradition of drinking champagne, so I will tell you that story."

"Please do," Madison said, glancing at her mother again.

"On the first anniversary of Mama's death, on my birthday and Jose's, Father took us to the beach. We yelled at Castro and then drank champagne to honor Mama's memory. We continued to do that every year, even after Father died."

Madison pulled into the driveway of her mother's house. "You and Jose were only twelve that first time. Abuelo let you drink champagne?"

"Only a little. Goodness, it's really raining. I should have stayed at Jose's tonight."

No, she shouldn't have. As it was, Jose had hinted that his sister should move in to his house since it was so big and she was alone in hers. Aside from wanting to keep her mother out of Jose's clutches, Madison loved her childhood home. She had been happy growing up here. Memories of her father were inside those walls.

Impulsively, she leaned over the console and hugged her mother. "Happy birthday. I love you."

Angelina pressed her cheek against Madison's. "I miss your father so much."

"I know you do. Me, too." She knew her mother was lonely but wasn't sure what to do about it. "You want me to stay here tonight?"

"No, I'm tired and going straight to bed." Angelina pulled away. "Did I thank you for my present? It was the perfect gift, Madison. I'm looking forward to a day at the spa."

An idea occurred to her. "What would you think of working part-time at the bookstore in the afternoons?"

"I don't—"

"Before you say no, think about it, okay? Why don't you come by tomorrow and look around?" It would be perfect for her mother. Not only get her out of the house and interested in something, but it would mean less time to spend with Jose. "Please?"

"I would like to see your bookstore." Angelina gave her the kind of disapproving look only a mother could. "You wouldn't let me come before."

True. Madison had wanted her mother's first view of High Tea and Black Cat Books to be after they had the place finished. "I'll be there all day, so stop by whenever you want." The rain had slackened while they'd talked, and after helping her mother carry her birthday presents into the house, Madison headed home.

Lauren wasn't back from her date, and Madison took a quick shower, and then crawled into bed, moving over to make room for Hemingway. She tried not to think about Alex, tried not to wonder where he'd gone, and especially tried not to think of him being with Trina. It was a wasted effort.

CHAPTER SIX

"Wait here. We'll be back in a few," Ramon said as he and Trina exited the SUV.

"Sure thing." Alex had hoped they'd let him come with them, but no dice. Ramon opened the hatch, and when he was visible again, he carried a large duffel bag. The two disappeared into a condo.

They obviously still didn't trust him, but that was expected. If nothing else, he had a new address to check out, one he would put in as a request for surveillance. Then there was Trina. She'd not given a last name, but at the party he had taken a picture of her giving Jose a birthday kiss. It hadn't been an innocent kiss either.

During the twenty-minute drive, she had frequently leaned around the front seat headrest to talk to Alex. She had asked many personal questions, quizzing him on Aces & Eights' finances. That was to be expected since Ramon's operation would want to know how much money the bar could launder, and he'd been prepared with answers. He just hadn't expected her to be the one asking. Nor did he like the way she eyed him. She was going to be trouble, the kind he and his brothers hadn't planned for.

He was tempted to get out of the Hummer and see if there were any open windows in the condo, but the chance there were security cameras mounted somewhere stopped him. Instead, he sent Nate the condo's address, along with Trina's picture and the license plates photos, while waiting for Ramon and Trina to return. After he hit Send, he deleted everything from his phone on the outside chance Ramon somehow got his hands on it. While he was at it, he got rid of the text messages between him and Madison.

Thirty minutes passed, and Alex was getting annoyed. He got out to stretch his legs. The condo complex was upscale, and he guessed the units sold for a million or two. Considering the size of the bag Ramon had carried in, Alex figured Ramon and Trina were making a big delivery.

Ramon's specialty was heroin, and Alex wished he could make a phone call and rain down every law enforcement division available before that shit hit the streets. But they were under orders to learn the names of the dealers Ramon was selling drugs to and where he was getting his supply, which was going to take some time. Alex's greatest hope was that Madison knew nothing of her cousin's activities. If he had to put handcuffs on her, it would kill him.

Ramon and Trina finally appeared, and Alex leaned his arms on the SUV's roof, watching them. They were in a heated conversation, but, unfortunately, he couldn't hear what they were saying. Trina was the first to notice him standing outside the car. She punched Ramon, and they stopped arguing.

"I told you to stay in the car, dude," Ramon said when he neared.

"No, you said, 'Wait here,' and I did. Just stretching my legs." Alex opened the rear door and returned to the backseat, but before he could close it, Trina slid in next to him. And wasn't that just peachy? He scooted to the other side, and she came right along with him. Another inch and she'd be on his lap.

"Were you a good boy while we were gone, Alex?"

"I was a bored boy." As soon as the words were out of his mouth, he knew what was coming and wished them back.

"Poor baby." She trailed her fingers over his thigh, edging them toward his groin. "Sounds like you need some entertainment."

She had that purring, sultry voice down pat, he had to give her that. "I appreciate the offer, darling, but I have an iron-clad rule. I don't mix business and pleasure." He put his mouth close to her ear. "No matter how tempting."

"I'm pretty sure I can change your mind."

Alex grabbed her wayward hand, putting it on her lap. "If anyone could come close, it would be you, Trina. But I learned the hard way that mixing business and pleasure gets messy." He hoped she bought his off-the-cuff excuse.

"Trina, leave him alone." Ramon tossed the duffel back over the seat. "Here's your chance to prove you're not talking smack."

Alex caught the heavy bag. "How much is in here?"

"Sixty thou," Trina said.

"I believe you, but don't be offended, because I'm going to count it. Had a dude try to pull one over on us once. Best if we all agree, don't you think?" He unzipped the bag and started counting the packs of hundred-dollar bills. He counted one pack to see how many bills were banded together, then fanned through the rest to make sure the money was real.

Not only did he need to verify the amount of money in the bag but they would be suspicious if he didn't.

He zipped the bag closed, setting it at his feet. "As soon as we run this through our businesses and set up the offshore accounts, I'll give you the numbers." They were finally getting a foot in, and if the first deposit meant to test him was sixty thousand, the operation was quite possibly bigger than they thought.

"Don't try to cross us, Alex. It would be very bad for your health and that of your brothers," Trina said, her eyes cold as she stared hard at him.

"Not to worry, darling. I like my health and that of my brothers just the way it is." Offshore accounts actually would be set up, and the money made accessible to Ramon and his father. What the two wouldn't know was that the FBI would also have access. Some operations lasted as long as a year, sometimes longer, and Alex hoped this wasn't one of them. He wanted Madison separated from Ramon and his father, and the sooner the better.

After admitting to Nate and Court that he wasn't sure he could stay away from Madison, they'd had a long talk. Among the many things he loved about his brothers, they always listened, though they might not like what he had to say. And his attraction to Madison was one of those times. His feelings for Madison had surprised them because it was a first for Alex. Hell, it surprised him, too. But as much as he'd tried to resist her, he kept finding himself at her window. That couldn't continue, and his brothers had agreed.

The new plan, if he could get her to agree, was that they would openly date. His brothers liked that, believing it would get him even closer to the family. Alex wanted to find out what, if anything, she knew about her cousin and uncle's business. The obstacle to their dating would be Ramon, how he would react.

Nate believed that even if Ramon didn't like it—which Alex was sure he wouldn't—in his twisted mind, the man would think Alex had a set of big ones for going after Madison after being warned off.

"Why don't you come in with us, have some drinks, play a little pool," Ramon said when they arrived back at his house.

Trina trailed her fingers down his arm. "Who knows, I might even get you to break your no-fraternization policy."

"If anyone could, it would be you, beautiful." He squeezed her hand. "Gotta take a rain check, though. It's almost closing time, and I need to get back to the bar, help my brothers kick out the drunks." He picked up the duffel bag. "Besides, I want to get this money somewhere safe."

"When are we going to meet these brothers of yours?" Trina asked. "I don't trust anyone I don't know." Her gaze roamed over him. "Are they as hot as you?"

Alex laughed. "No, I'm the hottest of the bunch. Of course, if you asked them, they'd each claim the same. Sure, let's set up a meeting."

Ramon turned, facing the backseat. "Trina and I will come by your bar tomorrow night. Check the place out."

"Cool," Alex said. He winked at Trina. "You're in for a treat."

The woman actually licked her lips, and Alex had never in his life been so happy to get away from anyone.

"Trina's going to be trouble," Alex said. The bar was closed and he and his brothers were sitting in the office while he brought them up to speed. "One of you is going to have to step up and take her off my hands."

Court gave an adamant shake of his head. "She-wolves scare the hell out of me."

"I can handle her." Nate grinned.

Cocky bastard. Alex eyed his older brother. If anyone could tame a she-wolf, it was Nate. "She's all yours, bro. Be careful what you ask for, though."

"Hello?" Madison held her phone to her ear, her heart fluttering like hummingbird wings at seeing Alex's name on the screen.

"Hello, Madison."

The way he said her name in that sexy way of his sent a thrill through her. "Be right back," she said to her mother before walking to the stockroom.

"You there?"

She closed the door behind her. "I'm here." Refusing to make it easy on him, she waited. It still grated that he'd taken off with Ramon and Trina to God knew where. Probably clubbing, and why hadn't she been asked to come along? Not that Alex owed her any explanation, and she wasn't about to ask him for one.

"How's the store doing? Did you have a good opening?"

"Very." She didn't want to talk about the store.

"That's good. I'll have to drop by, see the place. You must be proud."

"I am." There was a long silence, and she pressed her lips together to keep from talking.

"Are you mad at me, Madison?"

Yes. "Why would I be?"

"I don't know. Have lunch with me."

"Where did you take off to with Trina and Ramon?" She was going to chop off her tongue. "Never mind. Not my business."

"Ah, I understand now. Have lunch with me and I'll tell you."

"Honestly, Alex, I don't really care." And she would keep telling herself that until she believed it.

"I don't think you mean that. At least, I hope you don't."

She opened the door and peeked out. "Listen, it's busy here and my mom stopped by. I gotta go."

"So lunch is out. What time do you close?"

"Six. Why?"

"I'll stop by tomorrow afternoon, see if I can talk you into drinks and dinner. Later, Madison."

"No—" She was talking to dead air. Damn him. How was she supposed to get him out of her mind if he kept coming around? All she had to do was be near him and she wanted him all over again. And why did he want to risk being seen together in public? Hadn't they agreed that wasn't a good idea?

She stuck the phone into the back pocket of her jeans and went to find her mother. Before she could locate Angelina, Madison spied Lauren sitting next to Nelson Lopez on one of the love seats. She had her hand on Nelson's knee and was laughing at something he'd said.

Madison detoured their way. She was feeling just grouchy enough to nose in where she probably wasn't wanted. It wasn't fair that Lauren had that kind of eye candy hanging on her every word while the man Madison had the hots for had her head spinning, and not in a good way. One minute he was saying they couldn't be together and the next he was calling to ask her to dinner. Someday, maybe she'd figure him out.

"Hi. Have you seen my mom around?" She sat on the arm of the love seat, nearest Lauren.

"She's having a ball playing barista," Lauren said, grinning. "Hope everyone loves whipped cream on their lattes because she piles it on. Said she needs to learn how to make those cute kitty designs in the foam in honor of Hemingway."

Madison glanced toward the coffee bar to see her mother laughing as she handed a woman a cup, and good God, Lauren wasn't kidding about the whipped cream. But Angelina seemed happy and that was a beautiful thing to see. It had been far too long in coming.

"I'm trying to convince her to work for us a few days a week." She shrugged. "Sorry. I should have asked you first. Would you have a problem with that?"

"That's a great idea," Lauren said. "She seems to enjoy it here, and the customers love her."

"It's not a done deal. I still have to convince her." She stood. "There's a customer at the counter with a load of books in her arms. We'll talk later."

After ringing up and bagging the customer's books, she headed for her mother. "You appear to be enjoying yourself."

Angelina paused in wiping down the counter. "It's been nice to get out of the house." She picked up a cup and held it out. "I've been experimenting with making those little designs with the cream."

Madison peered into the cup. "That's a cat face, right?" Actually, it was kind of cute.

"It's not quite right. I'm going to see if I can find an instructional video when I get home."

"Does that mean you'd like to work for us?"

Her mother shrugged. "Maybe. I had fun today, which I'll admit surprised me."

Madison impulsively hugged her. She missed the closeness they used to have before her father died. After his death, Angelina had been withdrawn, and the only person who seemed able to console her was Uncle Jose. Madison had tried not to resent that, even though it hurt not to be the one her mother had turned to in her grief. Her mother didn't seem to understand that she was grieving, too. She wanted her mother back, the one who used to laugh and shower her face with kisses if a full day passed without seeing each other.

Hope blossomed that working together might be the catalyst to finding that closeness again. Blinking against the tears for what she and her mother had lost—the love of the best father and husband ever—for the first time since his death, she thought they might find their way to acceptance and peace. That although they both would forever miss Michael Parker, the day would come when they could remember him with smiles and laughter instead of tears.

Hemingway sauntered over, sat, and looked up expectantly at Angelina. She dipped her finger in the whipped cream topping in the cup and let him lick it off.

"You're going to spoil him," Madison said.

"Cats expect to be spoiled. I'm just obeying his demands."

"Can't argue with that."

Madison spent the last hour before closing ringing up customers and straightening the shelves. Angelina tagged along, and Madison showed her how to use the register and credit card machine. Nelson had left after he and Lauren had gone to lunch together, but he'd returned, waiting to take her to dinner. The man really was drool worthy, but he didn't make her stomach twitchy the way Alex did.

Angelina left when it was time to lock up, promising to come back tomorrow. If her mother agreed to come work for them, Madison would put her on the payroll as of today.

"We're taking off," Lauren said, walking up hand in hand with Nelson.

"Have fun."

"Why don't you come to dinner with us? We can drop you back here before we hit the club." Lauren peered up at Nelson. "You wouldn't mind, would you?"

"Not at all."

The man's smile was lethal, but it didn't reach his eyes. Did he not like Lauren inviting her along with them? "Thanks, but I'm going to finish up here, then crash in front of the TV and watch *The Voice*."

"She has a crush on Adam Levine," Lauren told Nelson.

"Truth. As soon as he divorces his wife, we're getting married." She waved them away. "Go on. I have nothing better planned for tonight, so I'll wrap things up here."

"Thanks! I'll make it up to you." Lauren reached for Madison's hand and squeezed it. "In fact, you take off early tomorrow night and I'll stay."

Madison started to protest, but then remembered Alex said he would stop by. Why not take a night off? Not that she'd decided she would go to dinner with him. Even if she didn't, both she and Lauren had worked their butts off getting the shop ready to open, and she couldn't begrudge either one of them an early night off.

"It's a deal." She smiled at her friend. "I'll see you when you get in if I'm still awake."

"You're a sweetheart, Madison. I'll take good care of her," Nelson said.

"I'm counting on it." She locked up behind them and watched out the window as he escorted Lauren to a fancy black sports car. *Nice wheels, Lauren's boyfriend.* Considering the expensive clothes he wore and that car, he had to be doing well as a model. Funny that she'd never heard of him.

Did Alex own a car or just his Harley? It bothered her that she didn't know. In fact, there was a lot she didn't know where Alex was concerned, including why she couldn't get him out of her mind. Maybe he was a warlock and had bewitched her. He was certainly dangerously dark and mysterious enough to be one.

She laughed, amused at her vision of him in a black cape, fog swirling around him as he cast his spells. "Come on, Hemingway. I need to get a shower and dinner over with before it's time to watch my future husband on TV." She flipped off the light switch, picked up Hemingway, and headed for the stairs.

As she did each night before leaving, she looked back to make sure everything was as it should be. Glancing out the display window, she frowned at seeing a black Hummer parked across the street, one exactly like Ramon's. Goose bumps rose on her arms and neck. Was he watching her?

Creeped out, she hurried upstairs. Without turning on any lights, she went to the front living room window to peek out the blinds. The Hummer was still there, parked under the streetlight, and she could see that there was a man in the driver's seat, but she couldn't see his face. It didn't matter that she couldn't see him, though, because there was no doubt in her mind that it was her cousin. Considering he was parked in plain view, it was obvious that he didn't care if she spotted him.

A shiver ripped through her body. She dropped the blind back into place. Her intention had been to take a shower, put on some comfy clothes, then watch her show while plowing her way through a pint of ice cream. The thought of getting in the shower while Ramon was out there watching the building . . . nope, not happening.

Bypassing the shower, she changed into a T-shirt and a pair of harem pants, fed Hemingway, and a few minutes later peeked back out the window. The Hummer was still there. Enough was enough. She was calling the police. As if he sensed her intention, he slowly drove away.

"What kind of game are you playing, cousin?" she murmured.

CHAPTER SEVEN

"There they are," Alex said at seeing Ramon and Trina walk into Aces &
Eights at the stroke of midnight. He'd begun to think they weren't coming. The bar was open until two, but the last few hours were always the
rowdiest. Tonight they were packed, Tuesday being the Demon Riders
Club's regular day to invade Aces & Eights. It was also a big money
night, which wasn't a bad thing for the two to see.

Court eyed the monitor. "This should be interesting."

They watched as the couple stopped a few feet inside the door,
eyeing the goings-on with alarm on their faces. At the moment, Black
Jack, one of the biggest black men Alex had ever seen in his life, and
Four Leaf, an Irish man almost as big, were arm wrestling at a table
in the middle of the room. The two were best friends until it came to
competition—any competition—and then they were as likely to kill
each other as not.

The members of the biker gang surrounded them, money passing
hands as bets were made. In the middle of it all was Nate, the referee
for the match. One of the bikers, Big Dick, noticed Ramon and Trina,
and a shit-eating grin crossed his face. The two idiots had apparently

thought it a good idea to costume themselves out in shiny—obviously brand new—black leathers, and Ramon even wore a skullcap.

"Dumbasses," Alex said. If there was anyone these guys loved to mess with, it was pretend bikers. "I better go rescue them."

"You gonna bring them back here?"

"No, I don't want them to know about our office. Don't want to encourage them to come here and hang out." Another reason tonight's crowd might prove useful. Hopefully they'd get a look at the operation, realize everything Alex had told them was true, and then never want to come back again. He headed for the two, Court following close behind.

Big Dick had gotten there first, and he'd put himself behind Trina and was whispering in her ear. There was a certain rumor pertaining to his name, and Alex had no doubt the man was bragging about that to Trina. If he wasn't mistaken, the woman wasn't all that upset about what was pressed against her ass.

"Back off," Alex said, pointing his thumb toward the arm-wrestling table. "Go play with your friends."

"I'd rather play with her." Big Dick blew in Trina's ear. "Whatcha say, baby? Wanna know what it's like to ride a real man?"

Trina visibly shivered, but Ramon looked like he was about ready to take on Big Dick. Alex pulled Trina to his side before Ramon could get stupid. "You're encroaching on my property. Get lost." If there was one thing that might worry Big Dick, it was getting banned from a bar his gang liked to hang out in.

"Dude, shoulda said she was yours right up front." He backed away, his hands held up with the palms out. "You get tired of her, I got dibs."

"Back corner table," Court said quietly. "I'll go clear it out."

Alex nodded. "Sorry about that." He didn't think Trina was at all sorry, and he pegged her as an excitement junkie, especially where men were concerned. "We've got a table in the back, out of the way of these dudes."

"They all have the same insignia on the back of their vests," Ramon said.

"It's called a patch. Each club has their own. The ones here tonight are the Demon Riders. You don't want to mess with them." Spider stumbled into him. "Dammit, Spider, I thought you were going to see your old lady tonight."

"She won't open the door. I banged on it and banged on it." He grabbed Alex's hand. "Would you talk to her? Last time you did, she let me in."

Alex glanced at Ramon and rolled his eyes. "Someday the man's gonna learn how to treat a woman." He pried Spider's hand away. "Come back when you're not drunk and we'll talk."

"Thansh, Heart Man. Love ya, dude." Spider stumbled off.

Alex grinned at Spider's retreating back. "Dude's crazy but harmless." There wasn't a member of any club that frequented Aces & Eights that hadn't adopted Spider as a sort of mascot. Alex had his doubts that the man was as clueless as he let on.

"Maybe we should come back some other time," Ramon said.

"Nah. You're good. My brother cleared out a back table for us." There was a roar from the crowd surrounding the arm wrestlers, and Alex glanced over to see Four Leaf raise a victory fist. Black Jack wasn't going to like that, but Nate seemed to still have control of the gang. Nate gave him a nod, letting Alex know he'd get with them when he could.

Sometimes he wondered what they were thinking when they decided to open a biker bar as a cover for their operations. It was the perfect front, but there were days when he got damn tired of dealing with the gangs. They weren't the doctors and lawyers weekend riders, but the real thing, and there was always trouble of one kind or another. Frankly, it was getting old.

He got Ramon and Trina settled, taking a seat across from Trina, and Court pulled out a chair, turned it around, and straddled it. "This is Court, my middle brother. Big brother's busy keeping the peace right now, but he'll join us later. Court, Ramon and the lovely Trina."

Court eyed Trina. "You weren't lying, bro, when you said she was hot. Nice to meet you, Trina." The woman actually simpered, and Court winked at her. He held out his hand to Ramon. "Good to finally meet you, too." After they shook, Court said, "What's your flavor? Beer, wine, something harder?"

"I think you should guess, see how well you know me," Trina said.

Court chuckled. "I don't know you at all, but we could work on that."

Nate had walked up behind Trina, and Alex sat back to enjoy the show. Up until now, she had totally forgotten him in favor of Court, but that was about to change. All he cared about was that her attention was off him.

"I know you, beautiful," Nate said, reaching over her shoulder and setting a lemon drop martini down in front of her. "Tart and sweet, the way I like my women."

Alex swallowed a laugh as Trina lifted her face, her eyes widening at his oldest brother. Alex had overheard her ask for the drink at Jose's birthday party and had mentioned it to Nate in passing, along with Ramon's beer preference. And it was only because he knew his brothers so well that he caught the relief in Court's eyes at Nate's appearance. Court didn't want to be any closer to the woman than Alex did.

Following behind Nate, John Boy—their cook-dishwasher-waiter—placed a mug on the table in front of Ramon. "A Cubanero Fuerte for you, sir," he said in his best waiter voice.

When had they started carrying Fuerte beer? Alex raised a brow at Nate, getting a one-shoulder shrug. Sometimes Nate was full of surprises.

"Make sure his mug stays full," Alex said.

"Yes, boss." John Boy bowed as he backed away.

It was still noisy, but not as loud as earlier since the bikers had moved to the back room for a game of pool. Nate pulled a chair over, putting it next to Trina. "Nate Gentry. You must be Trina, and you're Ramon, right?"

"Interesting place you got," Ramon said. "Is every night this busy?"

Alex could see Ramon calculating just how much money the bar could launder. "No, some are busier." He shrugged. "It's a popular biker hangout."

Ramon set his mug on the table after downing half the glass. "How much you think you can pass through here?"

"How much you got in mind?" Alex countered. It was a relief to finally see the operation moving forward. If it weren't for Madison being an Alonzo family member, he would be enjoying himself, but that little fact was stealing his fun.

"Keep in mind that we have some other side businesses we can utilize," Nate said.

"Such as?" Trina stuck her finger in her martini and then sucked on it, her eyes locked on Nate's.

Nate winked at her. "None of your business, beautiful."

John Boy appeared, setting down another mug of Fuerte, then he picked up Ramon's empty one and slipped away.

"Sounds like the boys in the back are getting rowdy," Court said. "I better go keep an eye on things before they start throwing barstools. Good to meet you both. Whatever my brothers say goes for me."

Alex wished he'd thought of that excuse to leave first, but Ramon was his fish, so he was stuck with him. Trina had practically climbed onto Nate's lap and had her fingers braided through his ponytail.

"Tell me something," Nate said. "Which one of you is the boss?"

Ramon tapped his chest. "My father's turning the operation over to me. Trina's my lieutenant."

Alex darted a glance at Nate to see if he caught the glare Trina sent Ramon, and got a slight nod. That was information she hadn't wanted shared. He wondered if there was an internal battle going on for top spot. If he had to guess, Trina was the more ruthless and smarter of the two, but they were both dangerous, and he wasn't going to underestimate either one.

"That hasn't happened yet." Trina tucked in her chin, exposing her neck, and slightly parted her lips as she peered up at Nate with hooded eyes. "At the moment Ramon and I are equals."

Alex was impressed. He had a fascination with body language, and that look was a classic siren call that few women were able to master. Trina sure had.

"Beautiful, there is no one equal to you," Nate said, earning a sultry smile from the woman.

"I have something for you." Alex pulled a sticky note from his pocket. "It's the numbers for the three offshore accounts we set up to funnel the money into." He held it up. "Who gets it?"

Trina snatched the note from his hand and stuffed it into her bra. "If we've finished our business, how about a little playtime?"

Thankfully, the question was directed at Nate, and Alex stood. "No playtime for me. A few members of a rival gang just walked in, and I need to go help Court keep the peace."

He walked away, unconcerned about leaving Trina to Nate. His big brother could handle vipers just fine. All he wanted was for the night to be over so tomorrow would come, and he would be that much closer to seeing Madison.

♥ ♥ ♥

Madison had fully intended to refuse Alex's dinner invitation, which was why she was so annoyed at herself as she sat across the table from him at Havana 1957, a popular South Beach restaurant. She was supposed to be getting over him, but she obviously wasn't doing so well with that. All he'd had to do was turn those dark eyes of his on her, smile in that bone-melting way, and brush his thumb over her bottom lip as he said, "Please, Madison, have dinner with me."

The no that had been on the tip of her tongue had come out sounding an awful lot like an okay, and now here she was. Besides, he'd said he would tell her where he'd gone with Ramon and Trina. That had been bugging her ever since she'd watched him walk away with them.

"What would you like to drink?" Alex asked when the waiter appeared.

"A mango daiquiri." To keep a clear head, she should stick to water, but she couldn't resist ordering her favorite drink. "And a glass of water, please." She'd sip her daiquiri, make it last a while, then switch over to the water.

"A Michelada Cubanada for me," Alex said.

"You like those?" The cold beer with lime juice and Clamato was served over ice with a rim of salt and a lime slice on the mug.

"Love 'em. Ever tried one?"

"No. Sounds horrible." She glanced around the restaurant. Were any of Ramon's minions here tonight?

"Madison?"

"Mmm?"

"Look at me."

She'd been trying hard not to. Looking at him pleased her heart, and that had to stop.

"That's better," he said when her eyes connected with his. "You're beautiful, you know."

So was he. She could drown in those fathomless dark eyes. "The last time I asked what you wanted from me, you said you didn't know. I'm asking again, Alex, because whether I ever want to see you again depends on your answer."

The waiter arrived with their drinks, and she sat back in her chair, letting out a frustrated breath. If Alex thought he was getting a reprieve, he would be wrong.

"Are you ready to order?" the waiter asked.

"I'd like the *ropa vieja*." The shredded beef in criollo sauce was one of her favorite Cuban dishes.

Alex closed his menu. "Same for me."

"Do you actually like Cuban food, or did you just think I'd prefer it?" she asked after the waiter left. "I guess what I'm asking is if this is a"—she made air quotes—"how much can I impress Madison by playing to her heritage kind of date?" Okay, so she was feeling snarky, and maybe he didn't deserve it, but then he'd taken off with Trina, so maybe he did.

"I happen to love Cuban food. As for you, I have no idea what you like since this is the first time we've dined together. I'd very much like to change that, Madison."

She trailed her finger around the rim of the daiquiri glass as she considered how to respond. His gaze hadn't left her face, and she decided to wait him out, see if he'd finally answer her question. If he was playing some kind of game, she wanted no part of it. On the other hand, if he could convince her that he was truly interested in her, that he wasn't involved in whatever Ramon had going on, and that he wasn't playing with Trina on the side, then she might decide to explore the chemistry crackling between them. He smiled, and that sexy curve of his lips sent a tingle racing down her spine, all the way to her toes. Oh, yeah, it was crackling all right.

"Did you know that's an interrogator's trick? The keep-silent bit until the person under the white light starts sweating and squirming, and then confesses all." He lifted his glass in a salute, giving her a wink. "You'd make a damn good one, Mad. Interrogator, I mean."

Mad. She was the only person who ever shortened her name, and for Alex to do it sounded strangely intimate. As if he had the right to give her a pet name.

"So far, it doesn't seem to be working." And how did he know about interrogator tricks, anyway? And what was with the funny look on his face as soon as he'd said that?

He chuckled. "Believe me, it is. So the question is, what do I want from you?"

"And?" He had his left hand wrapped around his glass, his index finger making a trail in the condensation. As she followed his movements, she imagined how those long fingers would feel dancing over her skin. What kind of lover would he be? Tender? Demanding? She thought he would likely be both, and as she wondered if she'd ever know how it felt to be touched that intimately by him, she shivered.

"I'd give my Harley to know what you're thinking right now."

Heat burned her cheeks, and she knew she was blushing, which would only confirm that she was thinking exactly what he thought she was. When she lifted her gaze to his, she sucked in a breath. His eyes had darkened to velvety black and were shimmering with desire, intently focused on her.

"I was thinking about my grocery list. I'm out of baking soda." No way would she admit to where she wanted his fingers.

A grin flashed on his face, then he laughed. "Little liar, but I'll let it go for now. Besides"—he reached across the table and stroked his fingers, the very ones she'd been envisioning touching her, over the top of her hand—"I have a great imagination, and when it comes to you, it's working overtime."

Before she could think of a response, their food was delivered, and Alex removed his hand, sitting back in his seat. Her skin tingled where his fingers had been, and it was only because the waiter stood next to her that she didn't grab Alex's hand and beg him to touch her again . . . wherever he wanted.

"This is really good," Alex said, taking a bite of his *ropa vieja* after the waiter left.

"I can make it for you sometime." Where had that come from? He still hadn't answered her question, and she wasn't cooking anything for him until he did.

He lifted his gaze from his food to her. "I'd like that. Very much. Tell you what. Let's enjoy our dinner without any heavy talk. I'm going to answer your question, but it's a beautiful night, and I'd like to take a walk on the beach with you, then you can ask me anything you want and I'll answer."

"Anything?" Because she had a ton of questions.

"Yes."

"Deal." And surprisingly she was able to enjoy herself. Alex was interesting to talk to and seemed able to converse on any subject, but she especially liked that he shared her love of books. He'd even read a few romances and was a fan of Nora Roberts's J. D. Robb books.

"I have a secret crush on Eve," he said.

"Since she's fictional, I won't hold that against you." She groaned as she pushed her plate away. "No more for me."

"Dessert?"

"Not even, but go ahead and have something if you want. I'll have a cup of coffee if you do."

"How about we stop somewhere for coffee and dessert later? I'm ready to walk off this meal."

"That sounds good." Somehow during dinner, the turmoil that had been raging like a storm in her mind had calmed. He'd promised to answer her questions, and depending on what he said, either she would see him again or she wouldn't. It was as simple as that. Ha! Who was she kidding? Nothing to do with Alex was simple. Maybe that was why he intrigued her.

As they walked out of the restaurant, he put his hand on her lower back, and it was both a protective and possessive gesture. She liked his hand there.

It wasn't a long ride to the beach, and once they were parked, she removed her shoes, and after taking off his shoes and socks, Alex rolled up the legs of his jeans. When she got out of the car, the wind blew her dress up, and she grabbed at it.

"Beautiful view," Alex said, stepping up behind her and prying her hands from the hem. "One you shouldn't try to hide."

"Men," she grumbled.

"Yeah, we're bad boys, always wanting to see up a girl's dress." He took her hand, lacing their fingers. "I'm a happy man tonight. Want to know why?"

Madison sighed as she dug her toes into the still-warm sand. "Sure, I'll bite."

He tilted his head and peered down at her, a half grin on his face. "You can bite me anytime the urge strikes, and as hard as you want." He squeezed her hand.

She wished he wouldn't say things like that because now she was thinking of all the places on his body she could scrape her teeth over.

"I'm happy because I'm with you. I wasn't sure you'd come out with me tonight."

"I wasn't going to." He had the sleeves of his blue button-down shirt rolled up, and as they walked, her arm brushed over his. Every place he touched her prickled with awareness, and she leaned her face toward him, inhaling the starch from his shirt and the unique spiciness that was Alex.

They reached the edge of the water, and she let the waves splash around her ankles. She'd given up on holding her dress down. It was dark and there was no one else on the beach, and the warm August breeze felt nice on her legs and thighs. Sensual even, but she thought that might have something to do with the man who was still holding her hand.

"Would you like me to answer your question now, Madison?"

"Yes, please."

CHAPTER EIGHT

Alex slowed his steps but didn't stop walking. He hated lying to her about who and what he was and that he was going after her family. Although he hadn't actually lied, more like omitted important facts, but he didn't think she would see the difference. When the day came that she found out, would she forgive him? It was a risk he was willing to take because he hadn't been able to get her out of his mind no matter how hard he tried.

He had to be careful around her, though. He'd slipped when he'd told her keeping silent was an interrogator's trick. As soon as the words were out of his mouth, he'd seen the question—why did he know something like that?—in her eyes. It was hard to think straight around her, but as long as he kept on his toes so he didn't make a mistake like that again, he'd be okay.

"There's no denying that we're attracted to each other, Madison, and if we're going to see each other, I don't want to sneak around to do it. I won't sneak around like we're doing something wrong."

"I'm not sure that's a good idea."

He stepped in front of her. The wind blew her hair out behind her, and as she looked up at him, the moonlight soft on her face, he thought he'd never seen anything more beautiful.

"So we're going to allow Ramon to dictate our lives? That doesn't sit well with me. I want to spend time with you, and not just by slipping through your bedroom window in the middle of the night. You asked me what I wanted, and that's it."

"You don't understand." She focused her gaze out over the ocean.

He put a finger under her chin and turned her face back to him. "Then enlighten me."

"Can we sit?"

"Sure." He took her hand and led her up to dry sand. "Is this okay?"

"What are you doing?"

He paused with his hand on the last button of his shirt. "Taking it off for you to sit on."

"That's really sweet, but I'm not worried about my dress. It's just dry sand." She slapped her forehead. "How silly of me. By all means, take off your shirt. I'm thinking I'll enjoy the view."

"Wicked girl." He kept his shirt on, but left it unbuttoned should she decide later she wanted to explore the view. "Tell me what I don't understand," he said, once they were seated.

She brought up her knees and wrapped her arms around them. That caused the hem of her dress to slide up her legs, exposing her thighs. He told his eyes to stay on her face, but they refused to obey.

"Like what you see?"

Busted. "I'd be lying through my teeth if I said I didn't. I'm a man. Show us some skin and we turn into drooling idiots." He brushed a strand of hair away from her eyes. "Talk to me, Madison."

"Okay, it's like this. My parents loved each other and both loved me. We had a great family. A little over a year ago, my dad was killed by a hit-and-run driver when he was leaving the newspaper one night."

"Newspaper?"

"He was an investigative journalist, a damn good one. Michael Parker. Ever heard of him?"

"Hell, yeah. That was your father? He was a legend."

She nodded. "He really was. The theory is that it was someone who'd had too much to drink, but I'm not so sure. He was working on something and had seemed troubled the last few weeks before that horrible night. They never caught the person who hit him. The only person around was the night guard, and he didn't see what happened. He heard something hit the building near the entrance"—she shuddered—"and went outside to investigate. The *something* turned out to be my dad's body."

Alex wrapped his arm around her shoulder and tucked her into his side, hating the quiver in her voice. "Go on."

"Until that night, my life was perfect. So was my mother's. She loved my father and she's lost without him. She grew up in a time when it was her job to keep the men in her life happy, whether that was her father, brother, or husband. That always irritated my dad. Love him? For sure, but he hated how she always put his needs ahead of hers."

"I think I would have liked your father." And an investigative journalist killed when he was working on a story that troubled him? Alex didn't believe in coincidences, and he would pull the police report at the very least.

She smiled, her eyes lighting up. "Oh, you would have. I'm sure of it."

"What story was he working on?"

"That's the weird thing. Usually he would talk to mom and me about his stories. He trusted us not to repeat anything he told us, but this time he just kind of closed up. I guess I'll never know."

Alex's antennae twitched. "How does any of this relate to you and me having to hide that we're seeing each other?"

"My mother's lost without my father. After he died, she fell into a deep depression. Actually, and I hate even saying this, but she can't cope without a man in her life. Since my dad's death, my uncle Jose has stepped in." She made swirls in the sand with her fingers. "He's got some kind of control over her."

"I'm still not understanding."

"Ramon can be vindictive when someone displeases him. All he has to do is go to his father and complain about me. Uncle Jose will then tell my mother he isn't pleased with me, and if I don't toe the line, my uncle will get upset, which my mother can't handle." She sighed as she brushed the sand from her fingers. "She's really fragile right now."

"And what about you? You're just going to sacrifice your happiness because your cousin's a prick?" There was more to it than that. Had to be. What wasn't she telling him?

"I didn't say I liked it, and it's only until she gets stronger."

He stood, offering his hand. "I'm sorry. That was uncalled for. It sounds like she needs help, a professional to talk to."

"I've tried, but my uncle convinced her that she just needs time to get over her grief. He's a man, so his word carries more weight in my mother's mind than mine. You'd have to be a Cuban woman, especially one from her era, to understand."

"I guess I'll have to take your word for it because I agree with your father. And you're letting them do the same thing to you." She cringed, and he regretted that that had come out harsher than he'd meant it to.

"Please don't be mad, Alex."

She took his hand, and he pulled her up. "It's not you I'm angry with." More than anything, it was the situation he found himself in and the truth he had to hide from her, but her cousin and uncle were on that list, too.

But maybe her unwillingness to stand up to her family partly fueled his fire because he'd stood up to his brothers for her. And maybe that was why he slammed his mouth down on hers as she looked up at him with those big green eyes that begged him to understand. Because he didn't.

Nothing about the kiss was gentle. It was raw and hungry. He wanted to claim every part of her. When she wrapped her arms around his neck and moaned into his mouth, he pulled her against him, needing her to feel what she did to him. Her lips were soft and warm, and he slid his tongue into her mouth. Sweet, so damn sweet.

How could she deny them this? He trailed a path of kisses down to her neck, finding the soft spot behind her ear. Her hair whipped around them, and he combed his fingers into the long strands as the lemony scent of her shampoo filled his head and lungs.

Before he lost total control and took her with him down to the sand, he closed his eyes and held her close for a moment before pushing away. "Let's go get that dessert I promised you," he said roughly, taking her by the hand and heading back to his car.

"Alex?"

He knew what she was asking, and he had no answers for her. Where did they go from here? He wanted her to stand up to her family, but she was doing her best to keep everyone happy. Whether she realized it or not, she was falling into a role similar to what she'd described as her mother's. It pissed him off that she didn't see that, and he'd never been good at hiding his feelings.

The whole situation sucked, and he needed to go to the gym and kill whoever was dumb enough to get in the ring with him. Even as a child, he'd been the brother with a temper, and when he had gone into law enforcement, he'd worked hard to control the rages that would come when he got angry. The first time he could remember losing his cool, he'd been eight years old.

His father had knocked him across the room because he'd been too slow in bringing the old man a beer. It hadn't been the first time he'd been hit, but it was the first time that he'd tried to strike back. If not for Nate pulling him away, he would have gone to his grave that night or at the very least suffered some serious brain damage from his father's fists.

"Alex!" She pulled away. "You're scaring me."

Fuck. He took her hand and brought it to his lips, kissing her knuckles. "Never be afraid of me, Mad. I'll never hurt you." The lie tasted sour on his lips.

♥ ♥ ♥

Madison dipped her spoon into the hot fudge sundae with mint sprinkles that she and Alex were sharing as they sat at a pub table outside the ice cream shop. "So good. I can't remember the last time I had one of these."

"I can. Never."

She glanced at him in surprise. "Seriously?" He shrugged, and she had the feeling he hadn't meant to admit that. "Why not?"

"Too much of a luxury growing up. Then once I was a big boy . . ." He grinned. "Real men don't go around eating ice cream sundaes."

Alex could put on a pink tutu and a sparkly tiara and he'd still be all man. She giggled at the image.

"Wanna share?"

"Nope." No way she was going to share that with him.

His eyes danced with mischief as he leaned his head close to hers. "Bet I can make you."

She slapped a hand over her mouth and shook her head.

"Tell me what amused you."

When he sucked on her earlobe, she almost fell off the stool. If he kept doing that, she would tell him anything he wanted to know. She turned her face toward his, and their lips brushed. That hadn't been intentional, but his gaze locked on hers, and the mischief that had been in his eyes moments before faded. As they stared at each other, his black eyes shimmered, hot with desire.

"Alex," she whispered.

"I know."

She wasn't sure what he knew, but his mouth covered hers, and she tasted vanilla and chocolate and mint. Forgetting they were sitting on the sidewalk with people walking by, she slipped her hand around his neck, wanting more. As if she'd unleashed a tiger, he growled, shifted on the stool so that his legs were encasing hers, and pressed his thighs against hers.

Suddenly, a hand wrapped around her hair and yanked her head back. "What the hell's going on?"

Oh God, Ramon. "Let go of me!" She tried to pull her hair away, letting out a cry of pain, tears stinging her eyes when Ramon yanked harder.

Like a striking snake, Alex exploded from his chair and squeezed his fingers around Ramon's neck. "Let. Her. Go."

She'd never heard Alex sound so dangerous, and although his anger was directed toward her cousin, he scared her. It was the second time tonight she'd seen him lose his temper, and all the questions she had about him surfaced. Who was he? Because he'd just proven he wasn't afraid to take her cousin on. If he was one of Ramon's minions, would he stand up to Ramon like that? She didn't think so.

When Ramon let go of her hair, she exhaled, reached up, and massaged the back of her head. She'd been so stupid to sit out where anyone could catch sight of her and Alex and call her cousin, ratting them out. It wasn't like she didn't know Ramon had spies all over the place. So stupid.

A taxi pulled up, and a couple got out. Ignoring the two men staring daggers at each other, she grabbed her purse and slid into the backseat of the cab. She gave the driver her home address, refusing to look back as he pulled into traffic.

Tears burned her eyes, and she willed them away. A beautiful night had been ruined, and she didn't know whether to blame Alex for luring her into forgetting how vindictive her cousin could be, herself for being lured, or Ramon for being a controlling ass. One thing she did know, she would hear from Ramon.

♥ ♥ ♥

Every time the door to the bookshop opened, she was sure it would be Ramon. So far there'd been no sign of him. It was unnerving. She'd just as soon get the conversation over and done with.

What she'd told Alex was true. She was worried about her mother's well-being and the control Uncle Jose had over her. But she hadn't been able to bring herself to tell Alex about the loan from her uncle and how Ramon was holding that over her head. It was humiliating that a member of her family thought he had the right to treat her like a prized possession, and was threatening to close the bookstore if she didn't march to his tune simply because she'd borrowed money. Families were supposed to take care of each other, not make them live in fear.

After tossing and turning most of the night, Alex's questions resonating in her mind, she'd decided he was right about one thing. She needed to stop coddling her mother. It was time for some tough love.

"I did it!" Angelina clapped her hands after the customer she rang up had left.

"See. Easy." Another customer approached the counter, and Madison stepped back, letting her mother handle the transaction on her own.

"She's a natural," Lauren said quietly, coming next to Madison.

It was true. Angelina was chatting with the customer, completely at ease as she finished the sale. Since she'd come to work for them, there was a new bounce in her step, and her eyes were brighter. Maybe having a purpose to her days was bringing her out of her depression. Madison sure hoped so.

"HGA! To your three o'clock," Lauren exclaimed, grabbing Madison's arm.

HGA was their code for hot guy alert, and Madison sucked in a breath at seeing Alex heading straight for her, his eyes locked on her.

Lauren took a step toward Alex. "I got this."

"He's off-limits," Madison said, stopping Lauren in her tracks.

"You know him?"

"Oh yeah." She headed for the man who'd kept her from sleeping last night. Out of the corner of her eye, she caught Angelina's gaze darting from her to Alex and back. This was going to be interesting.

"Hello, Madison."

"Alex?" That smile of his should be bottled, a patent slapped on it, and sold to women across the country who would pay top dollar to have it bestowed on them.

"You're wondering why I'm here?" He glanced behind her—to where she knew without looking that her mother and Lauren stared at them—before taking her hand and pulling her toward the bookcases.

"That would be a good place to start." She eyed the sign above her, almost laughing at realizing they were in the romance section. That was appropriate, or maybe even better would be the mystery aisle. Still holding her hand, he faced her, and she saw uncertainty in his eyes.

"Or you could start with what happened between you and Ramon after I left." She pulled her hand away from his. "The thing is, I'm not sure we should see each other at all." Had she really said that? Today he wore jeans and a white button-down, the sleeves rolled up, which looked just as hot as his biker leathers or clubbing clothes. He was like a chameleon, one that looked beautiful no matter what color he chose.

He put his hands on the bookshelf behind her, caging her between his arms. "Is that what you think?"

No. She nodded. "I think things between us are too complicated." *Don't listen to a word I say.* Why she was giving him a hard time, she wasn't sure. Maybe she wanted to know if he thought she was worth fighting for.

"Complicated, huh?"

She nodded again. His warm breath brushed across her cheek, and she slid her eyes closed as she breathed in his scent.

"Madison," he said, putting his mouth next to her ear. "Open your eyes."

She opened them. If he knew what that low, sexy voice and wicked smile did to her, he'd use them whenever he wanted her to do something. She'd never been with a man who had the kind of commanding presence that Alex possessed. It was both exciting and scary.

"Much better." He trailed a finger down her cheek. "So beautiful. I lie in my bed at night, fantasizing about the things I'd do to you if you were there with me."

Her bones had surely turned into marshmallows. "I think about you, too."

"Do you?" At her nod—he'd turned her into a nodding fool—he gave what seemed to be a satisfied grunt. "I want to hear more about that, but over dinner. The reason I stopped by was to tell you that Ramon and I came to an understanding. He won't cause trouble, so no more sneaking around."

"How'd you manage that?" Ramon not cause her trouble? She found that impossible to believe. But oh, she wanted to. To be able to see Alex without worrying what her cousin would do? That would be a dream come true. She pushed away the guilt for not being honest with Alex, for not telling him about the hold Ramon had over her. A loan from her family was none of his business.

"I'm a persuasive man."

There was a truth. "So what's next?" Until Ramon proved Alex wrong, she was going to grab this chance to explore a side of her that no other man before him had discovered. Hell, she hadn't even suspected she had a wild side, but now that she knew it was there, she found it impossible to ignore. This thing with Alex might not last long, but before it was over, she was going to experience firsthand dirty monkey sex, not that she knew exactly what that was, but she was sure Alex did.

"Want to share why you're licking your lips, Mad?"

"For some strange reason, I was thinking of dirty monkey sex." Wow, had she said that out loud? Was this the new her? Apparently she had, because his eyes widened, followed by an ear-to-ear grin.

"Were you? Come to my place tonight, and we'll see about making that happen."

"I can't. I'm having dinner with my mom." The mom who was headed their way that very moment with Lauren at her side.

"Tomorrow then," he said. He put his mouth next to her ear. "Dirty monkey sex will be on the menu."

She exhaled a long breath. "Okay." What else was she supposed to say to that offer? No? Not possible to even contemplate. He chuckled, breathing into her hair, and she squeezed her eyes shut against the heat racing through her bloodstream that she wasn't sure what to do with.

"Okay is good." Without glancing behind him, he stepped back, putting a respectable distance between them. Did he have eyes in the back of his head?

"Madison, there you are," Angelina said, eyeing Alex with interest. "It's time to close. Do you want Lauren and me to take care of everything?"

Standing a little behind Alex and Angelina, Lauren fanned her face, and at the same time, lifted a brow. Madison got the message. She was going to be grilled as soon as Lauren could get her alone.

"Alex, this is my mother, Angelina Parker, and my best friend and partner, Lauren Montgomery. Ladies, Alex Gentry."

"I saw you at my birthday party," Angelina said. "Is that where you met my daughter?"

"Yes, ma'am. I came by to ask her to have dinner with me tomorrow night. It's a pleasure to meet you, Mrs. Parker."

He flashed that killer smile, and Madison thought both her mother and Lauren were going to hyperventilate.

"Oh, call me Angelina, please. What do you do, Alex?"

"Mother!"

Alex winked at her. "It's a fair question." He met her mother's gaze. "I own a bar with my brothers."

The frown on her mother's face didn't bode well, but at least he hadn't mentioned that it was a biker bar.

"What time should I pick you up tomorrow?" Alex asked.

"I'm still not sure—"

"She'll be done here by six," Lauren said.

Madison glared at her friend, getting a not-so-innocent shrug back.

"I'll be counting the minutes." Alex leaned toward her, mischief in his eyes. "Have a nice *night*, Madison."

Heat warmed her cheeks. She knew exactly what he meant, and yeah, she'd be fantasizing about him. Because she didn't want to be an open book, too easily read, she said, "I plan to. Dinner with my mom, followed by a hot bath, then a few chapters of the book I'm reading, and then eight hours of dreamless sleep."

Did he just snort? And she'd really like to wipe that smirk off Lauren's face. As for her mom, Angelina glanced between her and Alex, concern clearly showing.

"Mrs. Parker . . . Angelina, Lauren, it's been my pleasure to meet two such charming ladies," Alex said. He subtly moved so that he was facing only her mother. "Your daughter is a treasure, which I'm sure you already know." He stepped back. "Good night, ladies."

"Wow," Lauren said after he walked away.

"A bar owner?" Her mother frowned. "He seems nice, but I'd hoped for better for you, Madison."

"It's not like I'm sending out wedding announcements," Madison snapped. She took a deep breath, and then gave her mother a hug. "I'm sorry. He is really nice, and we're just dating, okay?"

"I'll take him if you don't want him," Lauren said.

He's mine. "Let's get closed up." The sooner she got dinner with her mother over with, the sooner she'd get to fantasizing about Alex.

CHAPTER NINE

"I told him the money-laundering deal was off if he gave me any trouble about seeing Madison," Alex said, answering Nate's question. "That shut him up real fast." It was early, and the bikers were just starting to trickle in.

They were in the office—Nate stretched out on the couch, Court sitting behind the desk, and Alex slouched in a leather recliner, one leg dangling over the arm—watching the monitor as they discussed Alex's love life. He didn't much like it. There weren't two men on the planet nosier than his brothers. They still weren't happy with him, and he tried not to let it bother him.

"You ever wonder if our mother's still alive?" Where the hell had that come from?

"Sometimes," Court said.

"Never," Nate said at the same time.

At the bitterness in Nate's voice, Alex eyed his older brother. From the time their mother had walked away, anytime he or Court mentioned her, Nate would shut down the conversation. Why was that?

Alex had never questioned it before, but something in Nate's tone made him wonder if his brother was keeping secrets.

"You know something we don't, big brother?"

Nate swung his feet to the floor. "I don't know shit, okay? She left us. End of story."

Nate had never lied to them about anything before, but Alex knew deep in his bones that he was lying now. His oldest brother's face was a slab of granite with no emotion carved into the stone. Nate knew something. That was for damn sure. Did he know why their mother had left or where she'd gone? Alex had a sinking feeling that whatever secret Nate was hiding was a big one.

He exchanged a glance with Court, who shrugged, seemingly oblivious that the rug had just been pulled from under Alex's feet. It was unsettling to learn that Nate would outright lie, but as tempted as he was to call his brother out, it wouldn't get him anywhere. Nate was a stubborn SOB and would simply dig in his heels. Might be time to do a little investigating, see if he could find out where their mother had ended up.

Back to the question of what happened to Madison's father, though, and his brothers could help look into that. "Madison's father was Michael Parker."

Both his brothers perked up. "No shit?" Nate said. "He brought down more bad guys with nothing more than an investigative article in the paper than we've ever hoped of doing."

Court nodded in agreement. "He was a legend. Remember when he wrote that exposé on those builders taking advantage of desperate homeowners after Hurricane Andrew?"

"I remember." The hurricane had decimated Miami. "According to Madison, he was killed in a hit-and-run while working on a big story that he refused to talk about. The driver was never caught. The two might not be connected, but I'm not big on coincidences."

Court sat back in his chair, eyeing Alex with interest. There was nothing that his middle brother loved more than a good puzzle. "Maybe he was afraid his story would put his family in danger."

"We might never know, but I'm definitely going to look into it."

Nate frowned at the monitor. "Sonofabitch. I'm gonna throw that asshole in a cell and lose the key."

Alex glanced at the screen, chuckling at seeing Dirty Dan leaning over the bar, filling his mug with draft beer. "Dude doesn't give up, does he?"

"It's not funny," Nate said as he headed for the door.

"Admit it. The two of you enjoy his little game." Alex shared an amused glance with Court. For some reason, Dirty Dan loved trying to pull one over on Nate, and Nate had become obsessed with catching the man.

"I admit nothing." He glanced at Alex. "Be careful tonight."

"Always am. I'll check in later if you're still up." He headed for his bike, wishing he were on the way to see Madison instead of Ramon.

"Dude's twitchy," Alex said when the man he and Ramon had gone to meet claimed he needed to go to another room to get the money. Alex didn't know how much heroin was in the duffel bag he carried, but it was heavy. He'd been surprised when Ramon agreed to bring him along, but it meant he was earning the man's trust.

Ramon picked up a paperweight that had a gold coin inside, holding it up to the light. "Javon's just nervous cause you're here." He set the paperweight back down.

Alex trusted his instincts, which had so far kept him alive. Every hair on his neck was screaming that there was more going on with the man than just having a new face show up for a drug deal. "Hold this." He handed Ramon the bag.

"What're you doing?"

"Better safe than sorry." A six-foot-tall fake plant sat near the door, and he leaned his back against the wall next to it. He palmed his gun, holding it down by his leg. At the sound of approaching footsteps, he tilted his head, listening. Ramon opened his mouth to speak, and Alex gave a hard shake of his head. Javon had worn sneakers, but by the heavy thuds against the wood floor, whoever headed their way had on boots. A bigger, heavier man than the skinny one who'd left minutes earlier.

A man wearing a black ski mask strode in, pointing a Beretta at Ramon's chest. "The hell?" Ramon said.

"Shut up," the man said. "Where's your friend?"

Alex put the barrel of his Glock against the back of the dude's neck. "Blink and you're dead. Hand your gun to Ramon, the butt toward him. Not joking when I say if you try anything, I'll pull the trigger. Two seconds is all the time you have left," Alex said when the guy hesitated.

Last thing he wanted was a dead body on their hands, so he was relieved when the man held out his gun. Once Ramon had the weapon, Alex stepped to the side, putting himself out of reach should the dude decide to try and fight his way out of his predicament.

"Face down on the floor." The man glared, but did as told. "Ramon, lock the door, then see if you can find something to tie him up with." Until he knew where Javon was, or if there were others with weapons in the house, he didn't want anyone walking in on them, catching them by surprise.

After circling the room, Ramon pulled a panel of sheer curtains from a rod, tearing it into strips. "How'd you know?" he asked as he handed the makeshift ties to Alex.

"Told you. Javon was twitchy." Alex tied the man's hands behind his back, and then bound his ankles. A quick search of his pockets produced a worn leather wallet. "Kurt Terrance," he read aloud, memorizing the address. He stuck the wallet back in the man's pocket.

Ramon picked up the duffel bag full of heroin, moved to a chair, and sat. "What're we going to do with him?"

Alex squatted in front of his prisoner. "Let me guess. Javon bragged about a big deal he had going down. You decided the drugs and the money would be easy pickings. Have I hit the nail on the head, Mr. Terrance?"

Terrance spit on Alex's shoe. "Go to hell."

Alex tsked. "Wrong answer." He stuck the barrel of his Glock against the man's ear. "Care to try again?"

"Damn, dude, you're one badass," Ramon said, admiration evident in his voice.

And, without even trying, he'd won Ramon's respect, which was everything in the world to these thugs. Go figure. "I'm waiting, Mr. Terrance."

"Yeah, man, you fucking nailed it. Happy?" Hatred shone in the man's eyes.

"Deliriously. How many men you got on Javon? One? Two?"

"One," Terrance said, giving a sigh of defeat.

"Say what?" Ramon yelled, jumping up.

Alex stood. "Keep an eye on him." He left, silently slipping down the hallway. The first door he came to was a bathroom, and after making sure it was empty, he eased up to the next open doorway. He found his man in the last room he came to.

"You can have everything. Just don't hurt them."

That was Javon's voice, and who the hell was *them*? Alex risked a peek around the doorframe, and at seeing a woman cowering on a bed, a little girl clutched in her arms, his blood threatened to boil over. Who terrorized women and children?

Alex backed up a few feet, cleared his throat, and, impersonating Terrance's voice, said, "Yo, bring that douchebag here."

"That you, Terrance?" a voice called back.

"Who the fuck else would I be?" He slipped into the room closest to where Javon was being held, and waited. Javon walked past, followed by a man also wearing a ski mask, his gun poked into Javon's back.

Alex kicked his foot up, sending the gun flying. It hit the ceiling, taking several bounces down the hallway. He twisted midair, putting the heel of his boot hard against the masked man's ear.

"Fuck," the man hollered, flattening his palm over his ear as his knees buckled under him.

Alex straddled his back, pressing his gun to the man's already-assaulted ear. "Bang, bang, you're dead." He glanced up at Javon. "Go tell Ramon I need some more ties." Instead, Javon ran back into the room where the woman and child were. Alex sighed. What a fun night this was turning out to be. He twisted the man's arm, forcing him up.

"Look what I found," he said, pushing his captive into the room. Ramon tore some more strips, and after tying up their second prisoner, Alex took out his phone.

Ramon eyed the two men lying facedown on the floor. "What're we going to do with them?"

The more Alex was around Ramon, the more he realized that the man was pretty much useless. Did Ramon even realize he'd probably be dead now if Alex hadn't ridden along tonight?

"I'm calling my brother to come get them." He punched in Nate's code.

"What's he gonna do with them?" Still clutching the Beretta, Ramon stuck it in the waistband of his jeans.

"Don't ask." He held out his hand. "Gimme that."

Ramon put his hand over the butt of the gun. "I'm keeping it."

"So if it's been used to kill someone, what's gonna happen if you get caught with it on you?"

Alex stood outside Javon's house, huddled with Nate and Rand Stevens, another FBI agent. He handed Nate the Beretta, along with the weapon he'd taken from the second man. "Idiot wanted to keep the Beretta."

"Ramon?" Nate slid the guns into a pocket of his jacket.

"Yeah. Who else? He thinks you're gonna take those two dudes to the Everglades and feed them to the gators." The two in question were hog-tied in the backseat of Nate's SUV. They'd be taken to a safe house and held under guard while the bureau chief decided what to do with them.

"So you're Ramon's hero now?" Rand said.

Alex nodded. "Appears that way." If he'd tried, he couldn't have set things up better. Whatever doubts about trusting him that Ramon might have had before tonight, they were gone.

"I better get back inside before he comes looking for me. He wanted to go with you so he could watch you feed the gators."

Nate slapped him on the back. "You did good in there, little brother."

Praise from the man who'd stepped in and raised him didn't come often, but when it did, Alex treasured the moment. Once the taillights of Nate's car disappeared, he headed back inside so he and Ramon could finish the drug deal. The sooner it was done, the sooner he could go the hell home and take a shower.

CHAPTER TEN

"So you met him at your mom's birthday party?" Lauren asked, sitting on Madison's bed.

"Yeah." That was the story Alex had given, and she was sticking to it. She held up a sundress. No, too dressy. She hung it back up. After eyeing several more outfits, she decided on a pair of white skinny jeans, a green tank top, and a pair of white flat-heeled sandals. It was a little on the sexy side, but casual.

"Work with me here, Madison. I need deets. Alex is the man you've been crushing on, right?"

She sighed. Lauren wasn't going to give up. "Don't you have a date with Nelson tonight?"

"Later. I have plenty of time to hear all about Mr. Sexy."

Hemingway jumped onto the bed and made a beeline for the white jeans. "Oh no you don't." Madison grabbed her clothes before he had a chance to shed black hair on everything.

Lauren pulled Hemingway onto her lap. "Come on. Spill. What kind of bar does he own? Have you met his brothers?"

"A biker bar, and no, I haven't met them." She riffled through her jewelry box, looking for the earrings her father had given her the Christmas before he'd been killed. The white-gold dangling bars with emeralds on the ends would be perfect. "Here you are," she murmured, picking them up.

"No kidding? A biker bar? We gotta go."

Madison glanced at her friend in disbelief. "Are you out of your mind? We're not going to a biker bar. And don't tell my mom what kind of bar Alex and his brothers own. She'll freak out."

"Get your boyfriend to take us there one night and I won't say a word." She scooted onto her knees, dislodging Hemingway. "It'll be fun."

"That's blackmail."

Lauren shrugged. "Whatever works. I want to go." She steepled her hands as if in prayer. "Please, please, please ask."

"All right already, but no promises. He'll probably say no, and that will be the end of it." Truthfully, she would like to see Alex's bar, too.

"Awesome!"

To Lauren it was a done deal, and Madison could only laugh at her friend's enthusiasm. "Go away so I can get dressed. Alex will be here in thirty minutes."

At the door, Lauren glanced back and waggled her eyebrows. "Have fun. Don't do anything I wouldn't do."

"Well, that leaves my night wide open."

"Go for it, girlfriend," Lauren said. "You're due."

Madison finished dressing, gave Hemingway a treat, and exactly on time, heard the doorbell chime. After putting her eye to the peephole to make sure it was Alex, she opened the door. Tonight he wore all black. The T-shirt hugged his chest, accentuating his broad shoulders, and the jeans rode low on his lean hips. She could stand there all night, drinking him in.

His gaze roamed over her. "Do you know what I want to do right now, Madison?"

That low, sexy voice of his washed over her, and all she could do was shake her head.

"Just this." He slipped his hand under her hair, cradling the back of her neck. His kiss was soft, a mere brushing of his lips over hers. Too soon, he pulled back, and he chuckled when she tried to follow him. "I plan to do a lot of that tonight, but if I start now, we'll get to the dirty monkey sex part of our evening right here in your foyer."

Madison giggled when he waggled his brows. He took her hand, laced his fingers around hers, and led her away. Her last boyfriend hadn't liked to hold hands, but she'd always loved the feel of a masculine hand wrapped around hers.

When they turned the corner and she saw his motorcycle, she did a little dance. "Awesome!"

He grinned down at her. "I take it you approve?"

"My dad had a BMW motorcycle for a few years, and he would take me for rides. I loved it."

"You might want to pull your hair back so it doesn't get all tangled up." He pulled an elastic band from his jacket pocket, handing it to her.

It warmed her that he'd thought of such a minor thing as her hair getting tangled. After she smoothed her ponytail in place, she took the helmet from him.

He brushed her hands away when she tried to buckle it under her chin. "Let me." He held her gaze while he adjusted the strap, and it was as if the heat shimmering in his eyes had a direct connection to her girl parts, sending a shiver through her. "There. All buckled up." Slipping off his leather jacket, he held it out. "Let's put this on you. Can't have you getting chilly."

The jacket held the woodsy scent of him and was warm from his body heat. Between that and the way he was looking at her, she wanted to climb right up him and wrap her legs around his waist. One side of his mouth quirked, as if he could read her thoughts—God forbid.

"I brought the bike tonight because I want to feel you wrapped around me like my favorite blanket. Hold on tight, okay?"

It was definitely okay. Not trusting her voice to be steady, she nodded, the full-faced helmet bouncing on her head. After he swung a leg over the bike and lifted it from the kickstand, she got on behind him, circling her arms around his waist. He put his hands on her knees and pulled her legs tight against his thighs. Her dad's bike had been a luxury cruiser, with back and arm rests for the passenger. Alex's didn't have anything for her to lean against, forcing her to wrap herself around his back. The muscles on his back rippled against her chest when he leaned forward to put his hands on the handlebar. She sighed as the pleasure of being this close to him streamed through every nerve ending on her body.

The ride through the streets of South Beach was a slow one; traffic, as usual, heavy. The sidewalks were crowded with couples and groups headed out to dinner. She caught the envious looks of other women as she and Alex passed. *Oh yeah, bitches looking at me with my arms wrapped around the hottest guy on the planet, eat your heart out.*

She pressed her face against Alex's back to hide her grin. As they rode north on A1A, she lifted her face to the wind. She could ride the night away, here on the back of Alex's bike, holding on to him, smiling back at the people eyeing them from their cars. The men probably wished they were Alex, and the women her.

"You doing okay?" he asked, glancing back when they stopped at a light.

"Are you kidding? This is great."

He grinned, gave her knee a squeeze, and took off when the light turned green. All too soon, he turned into a condo complex in Surfside, stopped at a security gate leading to an underground parking area, and punched in a code. After he parked and put their helmets in a locker in front of the space, he took her hand and led her to an elevator. A few minutes later, he unlocked his door and stepped back for her to enter.

Curious to see his home, she paused in the foyer. Before she could take anything in, Alex grabbed the waist of her jeans, spinning her around. He backed her up to the wall and stared into her eyes for a moment before covering her mouth with his. She put her hands on his waist, pulling him to her. He groaned, rocking his hips against her while pulling the band from her hair. The leather jacket slipped off her shoulders and dropped to the floor. All the while, he hadn't stopped kissing her, his tongue hot and wet as he explored her mouth. The only thing holding her up was the wall behind her and Alex's body pressed against the front of her.

Alex forced himself to pull away when all he wanted to do was lower her to the floor and cover her body with his. From the moment she'd planted thoughts of dirty monkey sex into his brain, he'd not been able to think of anything else.

But not tonight, no matter how much his dick screamed otherwise. He wanted them to spend time together, to get to know each other before they took that step. It was the first time he'd felt this way about a woman, and he didn't want to screw things up with her. He wanted to romance her, and that was a damn first.

He rested his forehead against hers. "I thought about kissing you all day." And more. Still pressed chest to chest, he could feel the rapid beat of her heart, and he called on every bit of his control to keep from scooping her up and carrying her straight to his bed.

"You didn't have to stop."

"Yeah, I did." He stepped back. Luminous green eyes peered up at him, eyes he could happily drown in. "Come on. Let me impress you with my view." He wrapped his hand around hers, liking how her tiny hand fit snugly in his. As they walked through his living room, he noted her glancing around. What did she think of his place?

Having grown up with nothing, as soon as he had enough money to buy his condo, he'd started furnishing it a piece at a time, whenever he could afford to buy something that caught his eye.

The first purchase had been a king-sized four-poster bed. His taste leaned toward contemporary in bright colors—a red leather couch, a coffee table that was a piece of art in itself, and he particularly liked the large painting an artist friend had done after seeing Alex's granite countertops. It was an abstract, slashes of varying shades of dark reds, yellows, blues, and purples that filled half the wall. A low console sat under it, housing a TV that rose at the push of a button. Sliding glass doors set in the back wall opened up to a balcony with a beautiful view of the ocean.

Alex loved the two-bedroom, two-bath condo, and he'd never thought to own such a place. He and his brothers had taken advantage of the housing market bust a few years earlier. If asked, he'd have to admit that surrounding himself with color stemmed from his childhood, when everything was a grungy gray or dirty brown.

"Oh my God, your coffee table is awesome," Madison said, letting go of his hand.

He stood back, watching as she circled the table, sliding her fingers across the wood. When he'd seen the piece in a local artist's gallery, he'd known he had to have it. It was a large piece of a door that had been salvaged from a shipwreck. One end was squared off, but the other was jagged where the top of the door had broken off.

The wood had been stained mustard yellow, and carved around the edges were different animals about two inches in size, each painted a different color. It made him feel happy whenever he looked at it.

She moved to the middle of the room and made a slow circle, and he followed her gaze, trying to see everything from her eyes. Cathedral ceilings rose to an impressive height in the large great room. Opposite the sliding glass doors to the balcony was a dining area, for which he'd yet to find the perfect table and chairs. Stainless steel appliances gleamed in the kitchen, and the granite countertops the store had called Stormy Night were the same colors as in the painting.

"Wow," she said after completing her circle. "This isn't at all what I expected your place to look like."

"No?" He got that a lot the first time someone saw his home. More than with any of the others, though, he was pleased that he'd surprised her.

"This is amazing." She moved toward him until there was only an inch separating their bodies. "I'd pegged you for all black and chrome. Dark and dangerous like you."

"You think I'm dangerous?"

"To me, yeah."

He let his gaze roam over her body, down to the swell of her breasts peeking over the green top, across her flat stomach to the white jeans covering her long legs, and when he reached her perfect little toes, he made his way back up. She wasn't model beautiful, but she took his breath away.

"Maybe you should run from me, little girl." And for reasons she couldn't begin to guess at.

A sly smile formed on her face. "Will you chase me if I do?"

"To the ends of the earth." Her eyes widened at that, and he couldn't help but smirk. "You think I won't?"

"I think you excite me and scare me at the same time. You aren't like any man I've been with before, and I'm not sure what to do with you." She lifted her hand and scraped her palm across his cheek. "Tell me, Alex, what do you want from me?"

There were so many answers to the question she kept asking. He wanted to claim her body, marking it so no other man would ever touch her. He wanted to lose himself in her goodness, hoping some of it would rub off on him. He wanted to tell her who he really was so that they weren't starting off whatever it was between them based on a bed of lies.

He put his hand over hers, leaning into her touch, and gave her the only answer he could. "I want to know Madison Parker. There's a saying in the biker world. It isn't the destination, but the journey. Take a journey with me, Mad." She pulled her hand away, and he felt the loss of her warmth.

"You have a way of never answering my questions, yet still making me want to agree to anything you ask of me." She stepped back. "Am I stupid for wanting to be with you?"

Disappointment laced her voice, and he had to grit his teeth to keep from telling her everything. "You have questions you want answered? Fine. Let's get that over with." He took her hand and pulled her out onto the balcony. He knew he was being an ass, but there had only been two women in his life that mattered, and one had left without a backward glance. The other one now stood against the railing with her back to him as she looked out over the ocean. She wasn't happy with him, and he couldn't blame her.

He rubbed his fingers over his eyelids. What the hell was wrong with him? He'd gone years without thinking of his mother, but since meeting Madison, he'd thought of her to the point where he had searched the Internet, looking for her trail. The only thing that had kept him from using his FBI resources to look for her was Nate finding out, and he would. For whatever reason, his big brother refused to even consider searching for their mother.

If he could just figure out how Madison and his mother connected in his mind, maybe he could stop being a jerk. *Your mother left because she had enough of you three snot-nosed boys. Look at the three of you. What woman would want you?*

Hearing his father's voice in his head, Alex wondered if he was losing his mind. Was that his fear? That his father was right, and he could never be a man a woman could love? To hell with that.

"Mad," he said, coming to stand next to her. "Ask me your questions."

Troubled green eyes snared his. "I think my cousin is a drug dealer. Do you know if that's true, and if it is, are you involved?"

Hell. Of course she would ask the one question he couldn't give an honest answer to. "What makes you think something like that?"

She eyed him before turning her gaze back to the ocean. "That's an evasion tactic, you know. Answering a question with a question."

It was. He put his hands on the railing, staring down at them. Because of his martial arts training, they were hands that could kill. As a boy, he had carried buckets of slop almost as heavy as his skinny body, the handle of the pail leaving indentations for hours after he'd finished his chores. His right pinky was slightly bent from the time his enraged father had broken it, leaving it to set on its own.

They were hands that longed to roam over the soft skin of the woman standing next to him, who was waiting for an answer, and if he didn't tell her something as close to the truth as possible, that would never happen.

He shifted to face her, leaning his hip against the rail. "I don't do drugs. Ever. Nor do I deal. I can't speak for your cousin."

"So why are you friends with him? That night after the birthday party, where did you go with Ramon and Trina?"

She sounded like she had something sour in her mouth when she said Trina's name. If he'd known there was a party and that Madison was there, he would have waited downstairs for Ramon. It would have saved him from having to lie to her, but as he stared into the green eyes that had captured his attention from the moment he'd seen her, he couldn't do it.

"We went to his friend's place. I only went along because he asked me to, and I didn't know Trina was tagging along until it was time to go." He put his finger under her chin and lifted her face toward his so she could see the truth in his eyes. "I have zero interest in Trina, and that's the honest truth."

"She's a man-eater." A slight smile appeared. "I know that's catty, but it's information you should know."

"I already had that figured out." He put his arm around her shoulder, leading her to the deck chairs. On a table between them was a bottle of wine and two glasses. He filled them, handing one to her.

"This is really nice. I have to tell you that I envy your view."

The view was great, but he only wanted to look at her. "Where'd you go to high school?" He truly wanted to know everything about her, but he also wanted to get her talking about anything other than her cousin.

"Miami High. You?"

"Forest High in Ocala. That's where I grew up."

As they talked, asking questions of each other, he relaxed and enjoyed having her with him. She was a bookworm, and when it came up again that he liked the J. D. Robb romance books, she made him promise to read a romance of her choosing.

"What have I gotten myself into? You're not going to make me read *Fifty Shades*, are you?" he asked, teasing her.

She laughed, surprising him when she crawled onto his lap. "Maybe instead of making you read it, I'll do a show-and-tell."

"Even better." As she lowered her face toward his, all he could do was stare into her eyes, now dilated with desire, and wonder if he had enough willpower to resist carrying her off to his bed.

CHAPTER ELEVEN

Three days had passed since Madison had last seen Alex, but he'd texted often and called her each night from his bar. She supposed that was one negative about seeing a bar owner. Their hours weren't conducive to dating like normal people.

Although she'd known him for almost two months now, kissed him in her bedroom, and had an intense make-out session with him on his balcony, she still wasn't sure what they were to each other. She didn't feel she had the right to call him her boyfriend, but she'd sure like to.

She had thought it strange that he was the one who'd put the brakes on going any further than kissing and having their hands all over each other. Wasn't it usually the guy who pushed to have sex? She had been perfectly willing, but he'd said they needed to get to know each other better first. The man was a puzzle.

The feeling that he was hiding things from her was also nagging her. Sure, he'd answered her questions, but they'd been vanilla answers, no depth to them. She was pretty sure there was more to him than he was willing to share. Even though she believed him when she said he didn't do drugs or deal them, he'd never exactly explained why he was hanging out with Ramon.

For that reason, she was determined not to fall for him. She dreamed of falling in love and getting married, but Alex wasn't husband material. So she viewed him as a man to have fun with, someone she could step out of her comfort zone and go a little wild with. When they grew bored with each other, they could walk away without any drama between them. She'd never dated a man as dangerous or edgy as Alex seemed to be, and it was exciting. All she had to do to keep from getting burned was to erect a firewall between them.

She glanced at the clock to see it was near midnight, the time Alex usually called, claiming the last thing he wanted her to hear before she closed her eyes was his voice. The man seriously melted her bones when he said things like that.

Right on time, her phone buzzed. "Hey," she said. She could hear music playing and loud voices in the background.

"Hold on a sec." She heard a door close, and the background noise faded. "There, that's better."

"Are you in the office?" That was where he usually went to call her.

"Yeah. Are you in bed?"

She squeezed her thighs together, amazed at how he could make her feel when he lowered his voice, all soft and intimate. "I am. Busy there tonight?" That reminded her of what she was supposed to ask him. Lauren had asked her a dozen times when they could go to Aces & Eights.

"Very. Missing you, though. You have any plans for Sunday?"

She was missing him, too, and the three days since she'd seen him seemed like forever. "I was going to see if my mom wanted to have lunch and go shopping."

"That's too bad. We're closed on Sundays, and I was going to ask if you wanted to spend the day with me."

"Then ask." He chuckled, and even through the phone line, the sound sent tingles of pleasure dancing through her.

"All right. Madison, would you like to spend the day with me?"

"Can I make a trade with you?"

"Uh-oh. Why do I have the feeling I won't like whatever you're going to say next?"

The man was too perceptive. "Because you probably won't. My roommate's driving me crazy. She wants to go to Aces and Eights, said if you don't take us there, we'll just show up one night."

"Okay."

Huh? Just like that? "Really?"

"Really. But it will be at a time of my choosing. There're certain nights that belong to biker gangs, and I'll give up spending time with you every Sunday of the year to keep you away from them. So yeah, as long as I can control when you come, I'll make it happen."

"Thank you. Lauren's the one pushing for this, but I won't deny that I'm curious to see your bar." She was just as curious to meet his brothers, but she left that unsaid.

"So the trade's been made. I'll pick you up at eleven on Sunday. If the weather's nice, you want us to take the bike?"

"Definitely."

"Right answer. Sweet dreams, my sweet Mad."

"Hot dreams, my dangerous man."

"When they're about you, they're always hot. Counting the minutes."

Madison stared at the phone in her hands, wishing she could crawl through the screen and land on the other side, right on top of Alex. The man had her seriously bothered, and she reached for the vibrator she'd recently named Alex.

For her Sunday date with Alex—and since it was a beautiful Florida day, meaning he would pick her up on his bike—she put on the black jeans and bright yellow T-shirt she'd bought the day before at the local Harley-Davidson store. Across the front of the shirt it read, "Wrap your legs around this." Underneath was a picture of a Harley. She'd been tempted to take a marker and X out the word *this*, writing in *Alex* instead, but that was too obvious.

She'd also bought a pair of black biker boots, since she hoped to be taking more rides with him. The helmet he'd given her to wear had been a little too big, so she'd bought her own. A small black leather purse with a chrome buckle that clipped onto her belt loops had been a must-have, perfect for holding her wallet, hairbrush, and lipstick. Her last purchase had been what the salesgirl called a do-rag—black with red roses—to wear on her head, which would hopefully help keep her hair from tangling. So what if her credit card had taken a hit. She rarely splurged, and her card wasn't even close to being maxed out.

With her hair hanging in one long braid down her back, and her boots, T-shirt, clip-on purse, and do-rag on, she went to Lauren's room. "Whatcha think?" She turned in a circle.

Sitting on her bed with a cup of coffee, Lauren eyed her up and down. "Damn, girl. You are one hot biker chick."

Madison grinned. "Cool. My old man will be here any minute, so catch ya later. May the wind always be in your face and the bugs out of your teeth."

"God help me, tell me you didn't just say all that."

They looked at each other, then burst out laughing. The doorbell rang, and Madison blew her roommate a kiss before clunking down the stairs in her biker boots. She grabbed her new helmet from the foyer table.

When she opened the door, Alex pushed his sunglasses down his nose and stared at her over the rims. "Someone's been shopping. Nice. Very nice." He grinned. "Particularly like the shirt."

"I bet you do." She walked past him, and he caught the back of her jeans, pulling her to a stop.

"We're not going anywhere before you give me a kiss."

She glanced over her shoulder. "No. You're going to have to earn your kiss." To her, he'd always had a dangerous edge, yet oddly, she was able to say things to him she would never dream of saying to another man. It was liberating.

His eyes darkened as they captured hers. "You like playing with fire, don't you?"

"I'm beginning to think I do." She walked to the back of his bike. "You just gonna stand there all day, staring at me?"

Today, instead of black leathers, he wore jeans and a plain black T-shirt. On his right wrist were three thin black leather bands. Was there a man on earth any hotter than Alex Gentry? She doubted it. Her mouth didn't know whether to go bone dry or to drool like a baby.

The man smirked. "You just gonna stand there and eat me up with your eyes?" He sauntered over and put his mouth close to her ear. "Anytime you want to eat me up, say the word and I'm all yours."

Heart. Beat. Gone. Wild. Calling on her newfound liberation, she grabbed his ass . . . jeez, the man even had muscles there. "Word."

"Madison, I warned you once about playing with fire." Before she could respond, he blatantly adjusted his jeans while holding her gaze, then slammed his helmet onto his head. "Get on," he said, swinging a leg over the seat.

Just scoop her up from where she'd melted into a puddle on a hot sidewalk in South Miami Beach. His last two words had sounded angry, but she got that the sexual tension vibrating between them was making them both testy, which only spiked her newly discovered inner devil.

"The bike?" Did he just growl? She swallowed a grin as she buckled her helmet under her chin. After she climbed on behind him, she wrapped her arms around his waist and slid the fingers of both hands under the waistband of his jeans. "Show me what this baby can do."

He squeezed the hands she had halfway down his pants. "Hold tight."

That was her intention. After a glance up and down the street, he pulled out, and as they headed down the road, she leaned against his back. Although she was curious about what he had planned for today, she hadn't asked, preferring to be surprised.

Alex hadn't forgotten Madison's request to teach her to defend herself, and his first stop of the day was at his friend's gym. After parking and locking the bike, he took her hand. "Ready to learn how to fend off a man?"

"Really?" She did a little dance step. "This is awesome. I thought you'd forgotten."

"I don't forget a word you say, Mad. Remember that." His friend Rock was in the ring with one of his students, and Alex gave him a two-finger salute as he led Madison to the private room he'd reserved for the next hour. He didn't miss the blatant admiring looks the other men—most of whom he knew—gave her. It pleased him that she was oblivious to their stares. Instead, she was all wide-eyed as she watched Rock and Blake boxing.

"I've never been in a men's gym before," she whispered.

"Glad to hear it." After they entered the private room, the floor covered with mats, he closed the door. "You'll need to take off your boots." He removed his, discretely dropping the gun he had strapped to his ankle into his boot before moving to the middle of a mat. "Come at me." When she hesitated, he said, "Pretend I'm Ramon."

Her eyes narrowed, her lips thinned, and she charged him, head down like a pissed-off little bull. He swallowed a laugh as he spun out of the way to keep her from ramming his stomach and getting whiplash. As she passed, he grabbed her from behind and pulled her against him, her back to his chest.

"Now what are you going to do?" When she tried to squirm out of his arms, he tightened his hold. "The first lesson is to stay as far away from your attacker as possible. If there's any possibility of getting away, you run. You don't look back, you just go."

She wiggled against him, still trying to get away, totally clueless what she was doing to him. He decided he was an idiot for agreeing to do this. "Be still." He was supposed to be teaching her to defend herself, not getting turned on.

"So how do I get away?" She looked up at him with those sexy green eyes.

Damn, he was in trouble. "The lesson I'm going to teach you today is how to go for the eyes, the nose, the throat, and the shin. Those are all points on a man's body where you can cause pain."

"I thought you were supposed to go for his junk first."

"If you can get a good, hard knee there, but most men are prepared for that, and they'll grab your leg, then you're in trouble. If a man is holding on to you like I am, your best weapon is the back of your head. Throw your head back as far as you can, aiming for the bridge of his nose."

"Can I try it?"

"Yes, but don't give me a bloody nose. Slow and easy, just to get the feel of it."

They spent the next hour letting her practice how to do damage when being held against her will. She was a quick study, and as the time he'd reserved the room for neared the end, her confidence grew.

"Very good," he said when she got in a good kick to his shinbone. "If you'd had shoes on, I'd be on my knees right now, and you'd be running away like your cute ass was on fire." As it was, his leg was throbbing, but he didn't want her to feel bad that she'd hurt him, so he kept that to himself.

She grinned, clearly pleased with herself. "What's next?"

Christ, he'd created a monster. "Lunch is next."

"Are you sure I can't go for his junk?"

Alex laughed. "You're a vicious little thing. Go ahead. Give it a try."

She eyed the zipper on his jeans, reminding him of a marksman sighting his target, then swung her leg up. He caught it, scissored her other leg with his, and brought them both down onto the mat, with her on top. "Gotcha."

"Wow, that was cool."

"You're something else, Grasshopper." And he was damn proud of her.

"Grasshopper?"

"You never watched *Kung Fu* reruns? No? How sad."

"Sad Grasshopper needs a kiss." She formed her lips into a pout, drawing his attention to them.

"Yeah?" As he stared up at her, it almost felt as if there were a bump in time, as if something momentous had just happened that should be marked on the calendar. His heart gave a little stutter that he wasn't sure he liked or welcomed. He blinked, cutting the connection. Crazy imagination had gone haywire there for a moment.

"Put your mouth on mine, Grasshopper." He slipped his hand behind her neck, tugging her down. One of the things he loved about her was her responsiveness, and as their tongues tangled, she framed his face with her hands while grinding her pelvis over his erection. When they did finally make love, it was going to be like having a tiger by the tail, and speaking of tails, he wrapped her braid around his fist.

He flipped them, and with mouths still fused, he settled his groin between her thighs and rocked his hips. Her low moan set his blood on fire, and he kissed a path down to her neck, nibbling and licking the soft skin under her ear.

Someone knocked on the door, and he froze. What was wrong with him? He'd been minutes from taking her on a gym mat that smelled like sweat. "Almost done here, dude," he called, knowing it was Rock telling him someone else was waiting for the room.

He rested his forehead on Madison's. "Guess we better go before we get company."

"Guess so." She smiled. "Thank you for today."

"It's not over yet." He took her hands, pulling her up with him. Unable to resist claiming one last kiss, he cupped her chin and brushed his lips over hers, while willing his heart to beat normally again.

He took her to lunch at his favorite food truck, parked near the beach and famous for their fish tacos. Another thing he was learning about her, which he really liked, was that she delighted in the simplest things. She thought getting their meal from a food truck was fun and loved the fish taco so much that she made him go get her another one.

His next stop was Vizcaya, a rambling Italian mansion on Biscayne Bay that was open to the public. As long as he'd lived in Miami, he'd never been there but had always wanted to see it. Turned out Madison had never been there either.

They strolled hand in hand through the thirty-four public rooms of the mansion, admiring the antiques, but they both agreed their favorite part was the 158-foot Venetian barge carved out of stone, sitting in the bay, serving as a breakwater piece between the mansion and the ocean.

"I wonder how many pictures have been taken of it?" Madison said, as she captured numerous photos on her phone. "It even has a teahouse, and all those statues . . . how long do you think it took to create it? Do you think they ever let anyone go on it? Wouldn't it be a cool place for a wedding?"

Alex laughed as he tried to remember the last time he'd enjoyed himself so much. "Thousands and thousands, I'd guess, and I don't know, and don't know again, and yes." She lowered her phone, looked at him, and crossed her eyes, making him laugh again. "So many questions, Grasshopper." Her enthusiasm was contagious, and he hugged her, liking the feel of her wrapped in his arms.

"I need to watch some of those *Kung Fu* episodes, see if Grasshopper is a good thing or not."

"How about we stream a few of them tonight after dinner?" When he'd picked her up, he hadn't decided how long their date would last, but as he stood in front of a mansion full of history, the ocean breeze cooling their skin, and held her against him, he didn't want the day to end.

He took his phone from his pocket, turning them so that the barge was to their back. "Smile, Grasshopper." It occurred to him that it was the first time he'd ever recorded a woman's picture to keep on his phone. What did that mean, if anything?

She handed him her phone. "I want one of us, too."

There went that funny twitch in his heart again.

Alex frowned as he watched the black Escalade in his rearview mirror. He'd first noticed it when he and Madison were on the way to Vizcaya, but then it had disappeared. Now it was back. Someone was tailing them. The traffic light turned to yellow, and he downshifted, coming to a stop.

"Madison," he said, squeezing the hands she had on his stomach. "Listen up."

She leaned her helmeted head around his shoulder. "What?"

"When the light turns green, you hold on to me real tight, okay?"

"Okay, but what's happening?"

"Not sure. Just don't let go of me." The light turned green, and he twisted the throttle to full open. The horsepower of his enhanced high-performance engine sent them off as if catapulted from a slingshot.

"Oh shit," Madison yelled, curling her fingers into a death grip around his belt.

He darted another glance in his rearview mirror. The Escalade used the middle turn lane to swerve around a pickup truck. It enraged him that anyone would chase him while he had Madison on his bike. He tried to think of who it might be but came up blank. The first order of business was to put her in a safe place.

An entrance to I-95 was just ahead, and he swerved across two lanes to make the turn, his anger growing when her helmet bumped against his and her hands pulled his belt a good two inches up his waist. He was going to kill the bastard who was scaring her.

The Escalade ran a car off the road, following them onto the interstate. Sonofabitch. By the time he came to the next exit, he'd managed to put five cars between him and the black SUV. He leaned hard right at the last minute, shooting down the exit far too fast. Luck was on his side, and the light at the bottom of the ramp was green.

Seeing a Starbucks two blocks ahead, he raced to it, scraping his foot peg on the asphalt as he turned into the parking lot, burning rubber as he braked to a stop at the entrance. "Go inside and don't come out. I'll come back to get you." When she didn't move or respond, he said, "Go, Madison."

Bless the baby Jesus, she pushed off his bike and ran inside without questioning him or looking back. As soon as the door shut behind her, he reached into his boot and grabbed his gun, sticking it into his waistband. He circled around the building, turning right onto a back street that paralleled the road he'd just come down. A few blocks later, he turned onto the street that would bring him up behind whoever was driving the Escalade that had put Madison's life in danger. He was fire-breathing furious and someone was going to pay.

He saw the moment the driver looked into his rearview mirror, seeing Alex riding his bumper. Alex didn't recognize him from what little he could see of the man's face, but he did anticipate that the bastard was going to slam on his brakes, intending to send Alex flying head over heels across the SUV's roof. He leaned hard left, missing the bumper by an inch. When he reached the driver's side window, he snatched his gun, pointing it at the face staring back at him, one he'd seen at Jose and Angelina's birthday party, one of Ramon's minions.

"Pull. Fucking. Over." Instead of being smart, the dude floored the gas pedal. Alex let him go, now that he knew who to rain down his rage on. What mattered was getting to Madison, making sure she was safe.

CHAPTER TWELVE

Madison carried the iced coffee to an empty table in the corner, set her helmet on the floor, and slouched down in a chair. What had just happened? Now that her heart wasn't still trying to beat out of her chest, she scanned the room, her gaze raking over each person. No one seemed suspicious, most intent on their laptop screens, a few others sitting with friends, enjoying a late-afternoon coffee.

When Alex had ordered her off the bike, she'd heard the urgency in his voice and knew he hadn't been kidding around, so she'd jumped to obey. Where was he and how long was she supposed to sit here and wait for him? What if something had happened and he was hurt?

Another ten minutes passed, and she fished her phone out of her little biker purse. The only person she could think to call was Lauren, but she'd give Alex a few more minutes before involving her friend. If nothing else, she'd experienced a crazy wild ride on a motorcycle, and now that her feet were safely on terra firma, she could appreciate Alex's skill in handling such a powerful machine.

The low rumble of a Harley sounded, and she breathed a sigh of relief when she glanced out the window and saw him turning into a parking space. He put down the kickstand as he quickly scanned the lot. Who was he looking for? The reservations she'd had on meeting him resurfaced. How much did she really know about him? Her heart wanted to trust him, but her mind was flashing caution signs.

Within seconds of walking in the door, he spotted her and headed her way. Almost every woman he passed noticed him, and she saw one look at her friend, mouthing, "Wow." Yeah, he was wow all right, but was he too much of a bad boy for her?

"Hey," he said, sliding into the chair across from her. "You ready to go?"

That was it? Take her on a high-speed ride through the streets of Miami, practically throw her off his bike, then take off to do God knew what, and now ask if she's ready to go as if none of it happened?

"What was that all about?"

He flicked a glance at her empty cup. "Want another coffee?"

Under his deceptively calm demeanor, she sensed he barely controlled his anger. It was there in his eyes and the firm line of his lips. "No, I don't want another coffee. I want to know what's going on."

"Just a little road rage. Dude thought I'd cut him off back on the interstate and was chasing us. I didn't want to risk you getting hurt, so I thought this would be a safe place for you to wait for me."

She didn't believe a word he said. They hadn't cut anyone off. "So you what? Chased him down and set him straight?"

"Something like that." He stood. "Let's go."

"Yeah, it's been a long day, and I'm tired." She grabbed her helmet and followed him out.

At the bike, he brushed a finger down her arm. "I'm sorry. I didn't mean to scare you. We'll go to my place, have some dinner . . . just chill a little."

Goose bumps rose under his touch, but she refused to let him see the effect he had on her. "Thanks. I had a great time today, but I really am tired, so I'm going to pass." If only he had told her the truth, but she couldn't deal with lies. If he'd tell one, he'd tell a dozen.

"Madison—"

"Ready to go?" She moved to the back of the bike as she put on her helmet. When he tried to help her buckle the strap, she brushed his hands away. "I can do it."

He pinched the bridge of his nose, then lifted his face, meeting her eyes. "We were being followed."

"How do you know? I didn't see anyone following us." If someone had been—and she still wasn't sure she believed him—she sure hadn't noticed, so why would he have? Because he was already suspicious? Was that his life, always watching his back? She'd thought she liked the air of danger surrounding him, but maybe not so much.

"I just knew." He swung a leg over his bike. "Get on."

"Okay, say there was. Who and why?"

"Don't know and don't know. Couldn't catch up with him. You gonna get on?"

Testy are we? He was definitely on edge, and he was making her nervous. She slid onto the back, but instead of wrapping her arms around his waist, locking her hands at the front of his stomach, and leaning against his back, she grasped his hips. Obviously, that didn't work for him because he took her hands and pulled them around his waist.

The ride home was uneventful, and when he pulled up next to her door, she jumped off. "I had a nice day . . . well, until the last part." She kicked at the sidewalk with her new motorcycle boots. Turned out she'd wasted her money since she'd never be on the back of his bike again. "The thing is, Alex, I don't think we should see each other anymore. There's just too much excitement in your life for me. I'm sorry."

His only response was a nod as he stared straight ahead. The lump in her throat hurt, and she willed herself not to cry as she turned away. She went into the bookstore, to the front display window, and watched him ride away, feeling like she had just let go of something special.

On the ride home, she'd almost leaned against him and told him to take her to his place, but the smart part of her mind had kept her mouth shut. She had no problem with him owning a biker bar, but what she couldn't get past was his involvement with Ramon.

What if it had been a cop, a vice detective following them? Alex had sworn that he didn't use or deal drugs, and she'd believed him until today. Now she didn't know what to think. Better to end it now than to get caught up in her cousin's world.

"I wish I could trust you," she whispered as the taillights of Alex's bike disappeared when he turned the corner.

After dropping off Madison, Alex headed straight for Ramon's. Temper still boiling, he followed the housekeeper to the back deck. The target of his rage floated in the pool, a beer bottle in one hand and a cigar in the other. Two well-endowed blondes wearing bikinis no bigger than postage stamps sat on the edge of the pool, kicking their feet in the water.

"What have we here?" one said at seeing him. Her cherry-red lips lifted in a sultry smile.

The second woman pulled her sunglasses down her nose, checking him out over the rim. "Nice. Veeery nice. I'm Misty." She arched her back, lifting her breasts.

"I'm Carlotta," the other one said. "Why don't you come sit with us?" She patted the space between them.

Not in the mood for their shenanigans, he ignored them. "Ramon, a private word."

"Dude, I'm not moving. What's up?"

"I need to talk to you." When he didn't respond, Alex considered shooting the bastard. Since that would be messy, he managed to refrain. "Now, Ramon!"

"This better be good." He paddled over to the shallow end.

Oh, it was going to be good all right. Alex walked around the corner of the house, stopping when he was out of sight of the Barbie twins. When Ramon finally appeared, he rammed his forearm under Ramon's neck, pushing him back against the wall.

"The hell's wrong with you?" Ramon gasped.

"Why are you having someone follow me?" He pushed his arm harder.

"Ca-can't talk."

Alex eased the pressure on Ramon's neck. "Start talking."

"I don't know nothing about someone following you."

"No? So one of your men took it on himself to tail me?" When Ramon's eyes flickered away, Alex pushed against him again. "You put Madison's life in danger. I could easily kill you for that."

Ramon put his hands on Alex's arm and pushed. "All right! You weren't supposed to see him."

"You sonofabitch." He let go, stepping back. "You obviously still don't trust me, so let's just call our business relationship quits right now."

"It has nothing to do with that, you dumb shit. I'm just keeping an eye on my cousin."

Bingo. Alex had suspected that was the reason for the tail. The man was obsessed with her, and even though he'd backed off when Alex had threatened him with the loss of Aces & Eights for laundering money, he clearly wasn't happy. Ramon put his hands on his hips, and it was nearly impossible to take seriously a glaring man wearing nothing but a Speedo and a thick gold chain with a large cross on the end. Alex rolled his eyes.

"As head of the family, I take responsibility for her," Ramon said. "You can't blame me for that."

Yeah, he absolutely could. "I think your father might dispute your claim as head of the family, then there's Madison. I doubt she'd like knowing you're spying on her." The dude didn't like that. No surprise there. Alex's impression of Ramon was that he was lazy but saw himself as heir to a drug cartel empire, entitled to take whatever caught his imagination, which at the moment was his cousin.

"If not for me, my father would still be a pissant wannabe."

Alex almost snorted. The man talked big when his father wasn't around. "Here's the deal. The next time I catch you or one of your people following me or Madison, our business is done." He crowded Ramon's space. "And stay out of Madison's life."

"She's just another woman, bitches all of them," Ramon said, sneering. "You should keep that in mind." He waved a hand, as if shooing Alex away. "Be back tonight. We got someplace to be by eleven."

Alex wasn't at all reassured that Ramon was taking him seriously about leaving Madison alone, but except for killing the bastard on the spot, there wasn't much he could do about it now.

"Fine. Later." He strode away before he really did lose his cool. Outside Ramon's house, he texted Nate, telling him that they needed to talk and he was on the way over. Although he fully intended to go straight to his brother's, he ended up parked below Madison's window. The curtain was closed and there was no light shining around the edges. Had she gone to bed already? She'd made it clear she was done with him, and he should go. She was better off without him in her life.

He'd just check on her, make sure she was okay, then he'd leave her be. After tapping his special code, he waited. Impatient after a few minutes, he tapped again. Nothing. Either she wasn't in there, or she was refusing to see him. He backed away.

"Smart girl," he said, determined to ignore the ache that felt like someone was stomping on his chest.

♥ ♥ ♥

At hearing Alex's boots clang against the metal stairs of the fire escape as he descended, Madison lifted the edge of the curtain. She'd almost opened her window, but even though her heart had turned cartwheels at hearing his signal, she'd somehow managed to keep her feet planted in place. As he'd stood on the other side of her window, so damn close, she'd stayed frozen. *He's not good for you. He's not good for you. He's not good for you.* had been her mantra during those long moments, and she'd clung to the words, willing them to keep her strong.

He glanced up as he swung a long, muscular leg over the bike seat. She leaned her head back, but even though she knew he couldn't see her, he seemed to sense her watching him. By a slight dip of his chin, he acknowledged her. He started the bike, turned in a tight circle, and rode away, the rumble of his Harley fading along with the bike's taillights.

The ache in her chest confused her. Her time with him was temporary, a chance to go a little wild and have some fun. So it shouldn't feel like her heart had been ripped out.

She squeezed her eyes shut against the burning tears. "Good-bye, Alex."

She had been in her room, but her message had come through loud and clear. Get lost. Alex didn't blame her. He banged his finger on the button for the tenth floor. After he'd lied to her—and oh yeah, she'd known it—she didn't trust him.

It had been a great day right up until the time Ramon's man had made an appearance. As soon as he'd said it was a road rage deal, he knew he'd lost her. That had sure screwed up his plans for tonight, but he told himself for the hundredth time since riding away from her place that it was for the best. He needed a clear head, and she needed to be as far away from him as possible. It didn't sit well, though, that she'd be anywhere near her cousin. Somehow, he'd find a way to keep an eye on her.

"Thought you had a date tonight," Nate said when Alex entered and went straight to the fridge.

Alex grabbed a beer. "Obviously not." His brothers shared a look, both knowing him well enough to pick up on his anger. "Ramon had us followed." He plopped down on the sofa, set his beer on a coaster, and tugged off his boots. "Said he was just keeping an eye on his cousin."

"You talked to him?" Court asked.

"You bet your ass I did." He released his Velcro ankle holster and set it and his gun on the coffee table. "You should try giving hell to a man wearing nothing but a Speedo." He shuddered. Nate and Court laughed. "Not funny."

After telling them what had happened, he gave them the license plate number of the Escalade. "Run it," he told Court. "It might be registered to Ramon, but maybe not."

Nate went into his bedroom, returning with his laptop and handing it to Court. Alex grabbed his beer, taking a healthy swallow. Although he and Nate were computer literate, Court was the tech nerd and could pull up the information they needed twice as fast.

"Hector Ramirez," Court said, his eyes darting across the screen. "Male, age twenty-eight, five feet nine, one hundred seventy-two pounds. Dude's got a record. Two drug busts and one grand theft." He shook his head. "Stole his mother's car when he was nineteen, and she reported him."

"Nice friends you got there, little brother," Nate said.

"Screw you." He finished his beer and set the bottle back on the table. "I have to meet up with Ramon tonight, and it's the last thing I want to do, but duty calls. I'm gonna go shower, grab something to eat, then head out."

Nate gave him a two-finger salute. "I know you'd like to shoot the bastard, but try to refrain."

"I'll try, but no promises." The dude better not test his patience, though.

CHAPTER THIRTEEN

Two weeks had passed, and Madison hadn't heard a word from Alex. It was what she wanted and for the best. Who was she kidding? For the best, sure, but it wasn't what she wanted. She missed him, and it made her grouchy. Mostly because there was no reason to miss a man she'd only intended to have fun with.

At least her mother was cheerful. Angelina bounced around the bookstore like a puppy on speed. Light had returned to her mother's eyes, and that was the only bright spot in Madison's life these days. That and the bookstore. She loved every nook and cranny, every single minute she spent here.

The coffee and tea side of the business was doing even better than expected, and Angelina had perfected her latte foam art to the point people were disappointed when she wasn't behind the counter. Angelina was proving invaluable in so many ways. She'd even found a woman who made awesome baked goods, which beat the cookies and pastries she and Lauren had been picking up each morning at the grocery store. They were so delicious that they had doubled their daily order to keep from selling out before the day was over.

Madison couldn't wait to put their other plans into motion, especially starting the book club that would meet once a month in the bookstore. She was working with a local author for their first reading and signing, and eventually they would create a children's section. Her head was full of ideas—such as having a ladies-only adult coloring book night with wine and cheese—and she had to rein herself in so that she wasn't running around creating chaos by starting too many things at once.

If not for men, life would be perfect. One thing she needed to do was tell Lauren about Ramon. There was no predicting what her cousin would get up to next, and her friend needed to be aware of what was going on.

"Got a minute?" she asked, tracking Lauren down in the stockroom.

"Sure. What's up?" She stood with a stack of books in her arms. After setting them on the worktable, she stretched her back.

"Back hurting?" At Lauren's nod, she walked behind her friend and put her thumbs on Lauren's spine, massaging her.

"Ah, that feels good."

"As soon as we can afford it, we need to get a stockroom person. They can do shipping and receiving as well as restocking the shelves."

"Sounds good."

"I wanted to talk to you about my cousin." It was embarrassing to admit her own cousin was sexually harassing her, but what if he showed up sometime when Lauren was here by herself and Ramon turned his attention on her?

"Have I ever met him?"

"No." Madison gave Lauren one last rub before sitting on the edge of the desk. She sighed, hating that she even had this kind of problem. "I've made a point of not letting you anywhere around him. He's a slimeball." She told Lauren the things he'd done to her.

"Are you kidding me? That a family member would do something like that is disgusting. What're we going to do about it?"

"Nothing." At Lauren's outraged expression, she held up her hand. "Calm down Crusader of Wronged Best Friends. I'm telling you because a few weeks ago, I saw Ramon sitting in his car across the street. I don't know if he's done that before, and I don't know if he was watching for me to come out or what. We just need to be aware, okay?"

"Since I don't know what he looks like, I wouldn't know him if I saw him."

Madison scrolled through the photos on her phone, finding one of her mother standing on the beach with Jose and Ramon. "Here. That's him and his father."

"Wow. He's hot."

"Lauren—"

"Oh, believe me, I have no interest in slimeballs no matter how good-looking. Why can't we make his life miserable or something?"

"Because I think he's dangerous." She didn't have proof that Ramon was involved in the drug business, so she kept her suspicions to herself. "He drives a black Hummer. If you ever see him or the Hummer parked outside, tell me, okay?"

"You got it. Now, speaking of hot guys, what happened with Alex? I thought you two were really into each other."

"It didn't work out, is all." She didn't want to talk about Alex.

"Well, when you are ready to talk about it, you know I'm here for you."

Madison hugged her best friend. "I know." She left Lauren to finish the restocking. Returning to the store, she stilled at seeing her uncle and cousin talking to Angelina. It was as if by speaking of Ramon, she'd conjured him up. Why the hell were they here?

She took a deep breath as she strode over to them while sending up a little prayer that Lauren wouldn't come out of the stockroom. "Uncle Jose, Ramon, this is a surprise." And not a pleasant one.

Ramon sidestepped, brushing his arm against hers. "We came to invite the two loveliest ladies in South Florida to dinner."

She inched away from his touch. "I already—" At the pleading in her mother's eyes, she clammed up.

Uncle Jose frowned. "The invitation isn't optional, Madison."

"I guess it's a good thing I didn't already have plans then."

Her uncle made a tsking noise. "Such a smart mouth isn't attractive on a young lady."

If she hadn't accepted that loan from him, she would tell him where he could stick his *invitation*. While she was growing up, he hadn't paid any attention to her. He'd once roughly pushed her away when she'd tried to show him a doll she'd gotten for Christmas. "I don't have time for silly little girls," he'd said. From that time on, she'd avoided him as much as possible.

"We would love to have dinner," Angelina said, putting her hand on Madison's arm, a plea to please be nice. "We're closing in ten minutes if you don't mind waiting."

Panic swelled inside Madison. She wanted them out of the bookstore before Ramon saw Lauren. If she knew her cousin, he would decide he wanted Lauren, too. "No, let's go now. Give me a minute to let my partner know I'm leaving, and I'll meet you all out front."

"I'll just go get my purse." Angelina hurried off.

Madison took a step away, but her uncle grabbed her shoulder, stopping her. His touch wasn't gentle. "I've been waiting for an invitation to see how you invested the loan I gave you, Madison. One never came, so I decided not to wait any longer."

A reprimand. "I wanted to be up and running first, Uncle, so you could see for yourself that the bookstore will be successful. I know you had your doubts."

When he'd offered to loan her the money to put up her share of the bookstore, she'd been surprised. He'd been so nice about it that she'd even thought he was starting to like her. Now she had to believe it had been an act, a way to assert his authority over her.

He dropped his hand from her shoulder. "You and I will sit down very soon to review your books and your business plan. We'll be in the car. Don't keep me waiting."

Blood raced through her veins, roaring in her ears. She curled her toes, trying to anchor herself to the floor to keep from attacking him as he walked away, her cousin by his side. The very day the bookstore turned a profit, she was going to the bank to get a loan to pay him back.

Ramon glanced back, a smirk on his face.

Fuck you. Fuck you both. Hands fisted at her sides, she blinked away the tears burning her eyes as she went to tell Lauren she was taking off early.

Dinner had been torture. There had been too many questions from her uncle and cousin for comfort about High Tea and Black Cats Books. She'd tried to be as vague as possible, but her uncle wasn't going to be satisfied with superficial answers for long.

"I'm going to make a run to the ladies' room," Angelina said, after their dinner plates had been removed.

Not wanting to be left alone with her uncle and cousin, Madison pushed her chair back, intending to go with her.

Her uncle wrapped his fingers around her wrist. "Stay."

Dread tossed around the food she'd eaten, and she put her hand on her stomach to try to stop the sickening roll.

"Your bookstore is going to be hugely successful, Madison. Do you know why?" Uncle Jose picked up his wine glass, giving it a critical eye. "I'm going to have to talk to Hector about serving inferior wine."

Madison wasn't sure she was even still breathing. She had no idea who Hector was. The owner? The wine steward? Whoever he was, she didn't care. It was her uncle's ominous question that had her heading for a full-blown panic. She didn't want to know the why of anything that came from him.

"I can see I have your attention, Madison. Good. I'm going to invest additional funds into your business."

And make her even more beholden to him? No thanks. "Thank you for the offer, Uncle, but it's not necessary. We're doing good, better than expected actually."

"Nevertheless, you will allow it."

Suspicion crept into her mind. Her uncle didn't do anything without a reason. There was something going on here that she didn't understand. "Why would you insist after I've told you I don't need another loan?"

Irritation flashed in his cold brown eyes. "It isn't a loan, Madison. In fact, I will keep a separate book for the funds, which you won't question."

"I don't understand."

Her uncle and cousin exchanged glances, a message passing between them, then Ramon put his hand on her shoulder, squeezing so hard that it hurt. "You don't need to understand, cousin."

Oh God. Oh, almighty God. Were they talking about some kind of criminal activity? Risk her and Lauren's dream if . . . not if, *when* they were caught? They could even go to prison. Did her uncle care so little for her that he was willing to see her hauled away in handcuffs?

She jumped out of her chair, running to the restroom. When she passed her mother, she kept going without a word. She barely made it into the stall before she lost her dinner.

"I don't feel so well," she said when she finally returned to the table. "I'm going to cut out, go home, and crawl into bed." She couldn't bear spending another minute with her cousin and uncle.

Her mother put her palm against Madison's head. "You do feel a little warm, sweetheart."

"Probably something I ate didn't agree with me, is all." Or it could be the two evil men at the table who had her wanting to pull the covers over her head, hiding from the monsters invading her life.

How had she agreed to allow Ramon to take her home? Okay, she knew the answer to that one. Because after her uncle had as much as said that he planned to laundry—was that the right term?—money through the bookstore, she'd lost the will to fight anything they threw her way.

She'd never in her life understood what it meant to be defeated. Now she did. But she was Michael Parker's daughter, dammit. Her father would die before he allowed his beliefs to be taken away. Somehow, she'd find a way to be true to what she believed in, too.

Jose and Ramon had refused to let her call for a taxi to take her home. Angelina had sided with them since Madison was supposedly sick. Her mother had said it was the only way she'd know Madison would arrive safely, and wasn't that a joke? So here she was sitting in Ramon's car, alone with him.

"How about making me a latte?" Ramon said when she reached for the door handle.

Her and Ramon alone together anywhere near her apartment where there also happened to be a bed? So not happening. "Not tonight. I'm sick, remember? And by the way, neither you nor your uncle are putting any of your dirty money through my store. Do you hear me, Ramon? It's never going to happen."

"I'm really tired of you acting like a bitch, cousin." He slammed his mouth over hers.

Her stomach lurched, and she shoved him away. "Get off me." She scrambled out of his car. "You're a pig, Ramon," she yelled as she ran, digging for her keys. After fumbling to get them into the lock, she yanked open the door.

"Madison, stop."

She tried to pull the door shut, but it bounced back when it hit his foot. "Go home, Ramon." She tugged on the handle.

"We need to talk, you and I." With little effort, he pulled the door open. "I don't think you understand the way things are going to work."

"We have nothing to talk about." She backed against the wall, crossing her arms over her chest. She'd been so stupid in allowing herself to be intimidated into letting him take her home. There was nothing in the foyer to use for a weapon, but after tonight, she was going to keep a baseball bat in the corner.

"Oh, but we do, cousin. I make the rules. The first one concerns your mother." He leaned against the doorjamb. "You're taking advantage of her. She deserves better than a life of working as a clerk, or whatever it is you call her."

"Uncle Jose put you up to this, didn't he?" The subject had come up at dinner, and her uncle had made it clear that he didn't like his sister working like *a dog*, as he'd referred to it. Angelina had laughed, telling him that she enjoyed the time she spent at the bookstore. Madison wasn't fooled when the subject had been dropped. Uncle Jose didn't like Angelina's newfound independence.

"Tell her you don't need her anymore."

"No. She likes it here. Uncle Jose can just deal with it. Good night."

Instead of leaving, he advanced on her. "You need to learn some respect, cousin. Have you forgotten I own half of this place?"

She saw red. "Like hell you do! It was a loan from Uncle Jose, not you, and I'm paying it back with interest. Nowhere does it say you own any part of my shop."

"Things will go a lot easier when you accept that I call the shots. You have a nice little business here that will prove useful in moving some money around. We don't want Angelina involved in that, so tell her you don't need her. As soon as that's done, you and I will start working together." He smirked. "Very closely together."

"Go to hell." Never would she allow her dream to be tainted by him or anyone else. She'd give it away to Lauren first.

He grabbed her arm, squeezing it so hard it brought tears to her eyes. "One phone call and I can have your business license pulled. Maybe you should try and convince me not to do that."

Would he dare? Even if he would, and she wouldn't put it past him, she would die before she'd let him touch her like that. When he leaned his face toward her, she turned her head to the side. "Get out now!"

He laughed. "I don't think so. You've been teasing me since you were fifteen and grew a nice little pair of titties. I think it's time to pay the price."

Full-blown panic exploded, almost bringing her to her knees. She tried to break free of Ramon's hold, but he was stronger and bigger than her. He spun her and then pressed against her back, smashing her chest into the wall.

"Go ahead and fight me, *chica*. Makes me hot." He nuzzled her neck.

Use the back of your head to go for his nose. Alex's instructions flashed through her mind. She leaned her forehead against the wall.

"Tell me you don't want it, cousin, and I'll call you a liar."

"Go straight to hell, *cousin*." As soon as he lifted his head, she reared back with as much force as she could muster. God, that hurt, but hearing the crunch of bone was worth the pain.

"Fucking bitch."

He let go of her, and she scrambled up the steps. As she ran, she looked back to see her cousin holding his nose, blood pouring through his fingers. Inside her apartment, she slammed the door, turning the lock. She dropped her purse on the floor before racing to the kitchen, grabbling the largest knife out of a drawer. Dragging a chair back with her, she shoved the back of it under the doorknob.

She stood back, heart hammering as she stared at the door. As she listened for footsteps on the stairs, she spied her purse on the floor. She snatched it up, taking her phone out. There was only one person she wanted, and she called him.

♥ ♥ ♥

Alex scowled at his laptop screen, frustrated that he'd come up blank again. No matter what keywords he tried, his mother's trail had gone cold the moment she'd walked down that dusty road, never to be seen again. Not that he had much to go on other than her married name, and with that he'd found his parents' marriage certificate with her maiden name on it. Neither of those names showed up anywhere since the day she'd left. Wherever she'd disappeared to, she'd done a damn good job of losing herself.

Giving up for the time being, he turned to searching for information on Madison's father. Since there weren't any witnesses to the hit-and-run, there wasn't much to go on. He scrolled down to the interview a detective had conducted with the newspaper's editor. According to his editor, that night Parker had worked late on a story that he'd sworn would be front-page news. Unlike other stories that he'd shared with his editor before publication, he'd been secretive about this one. That jived with what Madison had said.

"Interesting," Alex murmured as he read that the editor had claimed Parker didn't seem as excited as he would have expected a reporter who was about to break a big story to be.

What would make an investigative reporter both secretive and perhaps not particularly happy about the story he was writing? Only one thing came to mind, and he called Nate. After telling his brother what he'd learned so far, he asked Nate for his take.

"Sounds like the story was personal."

"Yeah, my thinking, too. What if he was on to the Alonzos? That would definitely be personal, and because of worrying about his wife's reaction, he might not have been all that happy about the story. It would have been a good reason to be so tight-lipped. Think we could get Rothmire to okay Taylor or Rand doing a follow-up interview with that editor?"

"I'll call Rothmire in the morning. You feeling any better?"

"Yeah, a bowl of chicken soup from the deli and a couple of cold capsules helped." He was fighting a head cold, and Nate had kicked him out of Aces & Eights when Alex had sneezed on his big brother one too many times.

After hanging up, he leaned forward and punched up his pillows. He took a drink of the hot tea with lemon, honey, and whiskey he'd made. The soothing liquid eased down his sore throat. Leaning back again, he pulled up some of Parker's previous work. The man had been good, and his stories were hard-hitting, many of them exposing crooked public officials.

He was halfway through a story on a councilman who'd taken bribes to push through building permits for a developer with a history of cutting corners, when his phone buzzed. Thinking it was Nate calling back, he scrolled his thumb across the screen without looking at it.

"What?" he said.

"Alex?"

At hearing Madison's voice, he shoved his laptop aside. "Yeah. Hi, Grasshopper." For the past two weeks, he'd checked his voice mail constantly, hoping for a message from her. Every time his phone had buzzed, his heart had raced, thinking it might be her. But she'd not called, texted, or left a message, and he'd forced himself to stay away since it was what she wanted. Next to watching his mother walk down that dirt road without a backward glance, it was the hardest thing he'd ever done. For two weeks, there had been an ache in his chest from missing her.

"I need you," she said, her voice quivering.

"Where are you?" He shot out of bed, his phone to his ear.

"Home. Come in through the front."

"Madison . . ." The call disconnected. It took only minutes to change from sweatpants to jeans and a T-shirt. He slipped on his shoulder holster and a lightweight jacket. After taking a couple of cold pills and drinking a hot toddy, he decided he'd best take his car even though he could get to her faster on his bike. Keys in hand, he headed to the elevator. As he waited for the door to open, he called Nate and gave him an update so his brothers would know where he was.

Ten minutes later—and thankful he hadn't been stopped for speeding—he pulled up in front of the entry to Madison's apartment. Why was the door wide open? Any other time, he would have waited for backup, or at least called Nate or Court, but Madison was in there. He eased up to the entry and, seeing blood on the floor, he palmed his gun. Careful not to walk in the blood, he quietly made his way up the stairs. At the top, he tried to turn the doorknob, but it was locked.

Although he wanted to slam his shoulder against the door, he had no way of knowing who would be on the other side to greet him. She'd said to come to the front, but what if someone had forced her to say that? A sneak attack suited him better, and he backtracked down the stairs, careful not to make any noise.

Fear for her kicked up his adrenalin, but he stepped outside and took a few deep breaths, calling on his training to get him to the place he needed to be. Until she was safe in his arms, all she could be to him was a job, one he had to do by the book. Although if he were going by the book, he'd wait for that backup he should have asked for, but fuck that.

When he reached her bedroom window, he tried lifting it, only to find it locked, which was as it should be. Her bedroom was dark, and from her panicked phone call and the blood in the foyer, he seriously doubted she was snuggled up in bed, asleep. Taking a chance, he took off his jacket and wrapped it around his fist, breaking through a corner of the window. He unlocked it, then slipped his jacket back on.

No one greeted him when he eased into Madison's room, and because it was dark, he made his way to her bedroom door using his memory of the layout. Thankfully, she was a neat person—something he'd noticed on his numerous visits—and he didn't stumble over anything tossed onto the floor.

"Jesus," he muttered when her cat let out a hiss. Alex looked down to see Hemingway crouched next to him in the doorway, the black devil's hair razor sharp on the ridge of his back. He reached down and placed a hand on the cat's head. "What's happening here, buddy?" he whispered. The cat hissed again.

He'd never been anywhere in her apartment besides her bedroom, and he wished now he'd asked her for a tour. Across from him was an open door that he guessed was another bedroom, her roommate's maybe? A dimly lit lamp sat on a table next to the bed, and he slipped into the room, making a thorough check. Once satisfied it was empty, he eased down the hallway.

Coming to the end, he paused, lifted his gun, and edged into the living room, keeping his back to the wall. Huddled in a corner with a large knife clutched in her hands, Madison caught his movement, and the moment she recognized him, she dropped the knife and lunged for him.

He held out his arms, keeping his gun pointed away from her. "Talk to me," he said, wrapping his arms around her as he watched for signs of anyone else in her apartment. "What happened?"

"Ramon," she answered, a shudder traveling through her that he could physically feel.

He pushed Madison behind him, his gaze pausing on the chair notched under the doorknob. "Where is he?"

"I don't know. He was downstairs. Did he leave?"

"I think so." He pulled her into his embrace. "It's okay. I've got you." And she wasn't leaving his sight. He led her to the living room sofa. "Tell me everything."

As he listened to what Ramon had tried to do, he considered the man lucky that he wasn't nearby. Alex tamped down his rage, not wanting to scare her. She'd had enough trauma for one night without seeing him go ballistic.

She looked up at him, her green eyes shining with warmth. "I got away because you taught me how to fight back."

"You did good, Mad. I'm proud of you." Thankfully, she'd called him instead of the police. He assumed she hadn't called 9-1-1 because Ramon was family. Unless she had been willing to file assault charges against him, there wasn't much the cops could do, and he doubted she would if for no other reason than not wanting to upset her mother.

He wrapped his hand around hers. "Go pack a bag."

"Why?"

"Because you can't stay here alone. You're coming home with me."

She pulled her hand away. "I can't. There's blood in the foyer I have to clean up, and I have to be here when Lauren comes home. She can't be here by herself if Ramon decides to come back."

He turned his face away and coughed. The relief the drink and cold pills had given him were wearing off. "You're not staying here . . ." His throat dried up, and he coughed again. "Be right back." In the kitchen, he opened cabinets until he found a glass, filling it with water.

"Are you okay?" she asked when he returned.

"Just a little cold." He sneezed. "Sorry."

"No, don't be. I didn't know you were sick when I called you." She put her palm on his forehead. "You're warm."

"You have any idea when Lauren will be back?"

She shrugged. "No. She's in Coconut Grove having dinner with one of her sorority sisters. Tomorrow's a work day, so she probably won't be super late."

"Go pack a bag. We'll call her on the way to my place, work something out." Surprised when she didn't argue, he went searching for a mop and bucket. The sooner he got home, the sooner he could die in his own bed.

CHAPTER FOURTEEN

"That was Lauren. She wants you to call off the dog. Her words not mine." Madison dropped her phone onto the bed as she sat on the edge of the mattress. "She said your brother's an arrogant asshat. Again, her words."

Alex's laugh turned into a coughing fit. "Well I know it." He put his arm over his eyes.

"Which brother is it?" Alex had made a phone call after they'd talked to Lauren, arranging for one of his brothers to go to her and Lauren's place.

"Court. The middle one."

She reached over and put her fingers on his cheek. "You're still warm. Can I get you anything?"

"Yeah. A new head."

"Sorry. Can't help you with that." Claiming he was hot, he'd changed into a pair of cargo shorts, and nothing else. Since he had his eyes covered, she seized the opportunity to admire his chest. As dark and thick as his hair was, she'd expected him to have more chest hair, but he had only a dusting of fine black hair above his nipples, then a dark arrow down the middle of his stomach. Her fingers itched to follow that trail to the hidden treasure. She blinked when the material of his shorts moved and watched, fascinated, as the shorts tented.

"You keep looking at me like that, Madison, and cold or no cold, you're going to find yourself naked and under me."

Cheeks heating, she glanced up to see him watching her from under his arm. "Ahem . . ."

He chuckled. "Yeah, ahem. You have no idea how badly I want to kiss you, but no germs for you, Grasshopper. Why don't you go to bed before I forget I'm sick."

She picked up her phone as she stood. "Are you going to call your brother? Lauren was serious."

"No. Ramon probably won't come back, but better safe than sorry. He'll crash on your sofa."

"Call and tell him he can have my bed for the night." She leaned over and kissed his cheek. "Sweet dreams."

He grabbed her hand, turned it over, and kissed her wrist. "If they're of you, they'll definitely be sweet. Now, go wash your hands and get all my germs off."

She paused at the door. "Thank you."

"For?"

"For coming when I called, especially after how I treated you."

His eyes locked on hers. "You knew I would."

Yeah, she hadn't doubted it for one minute. She smiled. "Good night, Alex."

"Night, Mad." He pulled his pillow over his head. "I'll feel better tomorrow, and then I'll let you play with my chest."

"Promises. Promises." She closed the door, making a detour to the kitchen for a glass of water before she took herself to bed. Should she have told Alex everything? All she'd said was that Ramon had attacked her. She'd kept to herself his demand that she allow him and his uncle use of the bookstore to funnel money through.

Although she wanted to tell him, she still didn't know exactly what his relationship was with Ramon. Sleep was elusive. She tossed and turned, her heart arguing with her mind. Her heart said she could trust Alex. Her mind questioned her sanity for believing that.

The smell of coffee drifted through the open door of Alex's guest room, the aroma dragging her from sleep. She'd finally drifted off sometime around dawn after deciding that she'd listen to her heart until Alex proved her wrong. Stupid maybe, but he'd sworn he didn't do drugs or sell them. She chose to believe him. Even so, she wasn't sure enough to tell him about the money laundering. Which, if she was honest with herself, put her right back to stupid.

She rolled onto her side, sighing in dreamy pleasure as she pulled the comforter up to her chin. The guest bed was better than hers at home— the mattress perfect, the sheets cool and silky, and the down comforter one she could snuggle in forever. Five more minutes and she'd get up.

"Rise and shine, sleepyhead."

Madison groaned. "Go away." The covers were pulled off, and she opened her eyes to see Alex standing over her, a smirk on his face.

"Not a morning person, are we?"

"Hate mornings, but especially hate cheerful morning people." She stretched her arms over her head.

"Then I guess we better break up, Grasshopper. Too bad about that since it means you won't get to play with my chest after all."

Break up? Did that mean he considered them back together? "Alex?"

"Mmm?"

"Thank you."

"For what? Being happy when you called me? I wasn't pleased about the reason you did, but what's important is that you're here where I can keep you safe."

She wanted to ask if they were back together, but she chickened out. What if he said no, he was only playing the hero by coming to her rescue. Besides, he wore only a pair of worn jeans that hung low on his hips. It was hard to think straight with his chest right there in front of her face. All she wanted to do was follow that trail of hair with her tongue, not stopping until she claimed the prize.

"How do you like your coffee?"

She jerked her gaze up to his face, only to see amusement in his eyes. The man knew exactly where her mind had been. "Poured down my throat. I'll be there in a minute."

"Don't go back to sleep."

"Yeah, yeah." He turned away, and she frowned at the scars on his back.

After a quick shower, she dressed, then went looking for coffee. At the entrance to the kitchen, she stilled. Alex stood at the stove with his back to her, still shirtless. A confusing mix of lust and rage coursed through her. He was magnificent! The broad shoulders, trim waist, lean hips, and mussed black hair long enough to cover the back of his neck were straight out of a woman's wet dreams. She wanted to crawl all over his body, touching, tasting, exploring.

It was seeing the scars on his back again, though, that made her want to wrap her arms around him and promise she'd never let anyone hurt him again. They were old ones, white and puckered. Feet bare, she padded toward him. She thought she could sneak up behind him, but he tilted his head as if listening.

"Nice try, Grasshopper."

His amused chuckle made her smile. She stopped inches from him, lifted a hand, and gently touched one of the scars on his right shoulder. "Who did this to you, Alex?"

"My father. How do you want your coffee?"

"Cream and two sugars." She put her hands on his waist to hold him in place, pressed her mouth against a jagged scar on the middle of his back, kissed it, then moved to the next one and the next one and the next one. What father did this to his child? It was beyond her comprehension. Her father had been nothing but loving, his hands gentle even when she had misbehaved.

As she placed kisses across his back, tears streamed down her cheeks. Tears for Alex having a father who'd tortured a boy he should have protected, and tears for the father she missed with every aching beat of her heart every damn day.

Alex stilled, unable to breathe. He felt her tears, hot against his skin, and although all the places she'd pressed her lips had long gone numb from the scar tissue, her kisses were a balm to his soul. No other woman had put her mouth on his back. Some had pretended not to notice, some had been visibly turned off by the sight of his back, and one had even asked him to put his shirt back on.

He'd long ago decided he wouldn't hide the results of his father's cruelty. It was what it was. It had happened, but he'd put it behind him. Or so he'd thought until Madison stood in his kitchen, her mouth seeking out each place a belt buckle had ripped his skin open as her hot, burning tears slithered down his back. A shudder rippled through him, and he sucked air back into his lungs.

"Madison," he whispered. Unable to take any more of the tears she shed for him, he faced her. "Don't cry, Mad." He wrapped his arms around her, pulling her against him, burying his mouth in her hair.

"I can't help it." She slid her hands up his chest, then farther up, until she clasped her fingers together behind his neck. "All children should have a father like mine, and no child should ever"—she put her feet on top of his, and he had the thought that she was trying to climb inside him—"ever, ever know the kind of pain from a parent who puts scars on his back."

He couldn't argue with that. He held her close, wishing she really could climb inside his skin and live there. Somehow she'd stolen his heart on a morning when all he'd meant to offer her was a cup of coffee and a plate of scrambled eggs. Who saw that coming?

If he didn't get her to her bookstore in the next few minutes, he'd never take her back. As he held the woman he knew he could love forever given half a chance, he glanced at the clock on the microwave. "Can you take the day off?"

She sighed, her breath tickling his chest. "I wish. But no."

"Then let's have some breakfast before I abduct you and carry you to my cave like a barbarian. Another minute and I'll drag you there by your beautiful hair." He kissed that beautiful hair. "I'm that close, Madison, so you need to back away."

Her lips curved against his skin. "And I'd love that, but I think we need to go rescue Lauren from the mad, bad dog."

"Hopefully, they haven't killed each other yet." He'd never known Court not to find a way to get along with any woman, and he was skeptical that his brother and Madison's roommate were squaring off like feral dogs.

Lauren glared at Court from the kitchen—which she'd refused to leave even after Alex had walked in with Madison tucked next to him—and if she could shoot fire from those eyes, Alex would have feared for his brother.

The two of them were like a pair of rabid dogs, each snarling from their corners, just waiting for the chance to attack. Alex had never seen his brother so worked up over a woman, and, fascinated, his gaze darted between Court and Madison's roommate.

"You kept me up all night with your snoring," Lauren said, her lips curling in a sneer.

Alex found her attitude interesting considering her gaze was locked on Court's bare chest.

"I. Don't. Snore." Court turned away, yanking on his T-shirt.

As far as Alex knew, his brother didn't snore. He leaned his mouth close to Madison's ear. "I think they like each other."

She made a noise that sounded like a half snort, half laugh. "I think we arrived just in time to keep them from killing each other. You take him, and I'll try to calm her down."

As soon as she slipped out from under his arm, he wanted to grab her and tuck her back next to him, but the snarling dogs needed to be dealt with. "What's wrong with you, bro?"

Court turned furious dark eyes on Alex. "The next time you need a babysitter, lose my number. The woman's a raving lunatic."

If that was how he felt, why did his gaze settle on Lauren's ass as Madison led her from the room, the two of them disappearing down the hallway? Alex grinned. "Methinks thou doth protest too much."

"What kind of crap are you spewing now?" Court grunted. "I'm outta here. The two of them are all yours."

Alone, Alex circled the room, eyeing the shelves, wondering which things belonged to Madison. There were a lot of books, but that wasn't surprising. A framed photograph caught his attention, and he picked it up. Madison and two adults he recognized as her parents stood on the beach. He studied Michael Parker, smiling at seeing the red hair and green eyes so like Madison's. The man stood between Madison and her mother, an arm around each, and Alex could see the affection they had for each other shining in their eyes. What would it have been like to have loving parents like that?

He set the picture back on the shelf but continued to stare at it. Had Michael Parker been killed because of a story he was working on? Their bureau chief had approved their request, and Taylor was supposed to schedule an interview with Parker's editor this week. If the editor would agree, Taylor would bring back to the office whatever files and notes the newspaper had saved of Parker's. If he didn't agree, they would ask for a court order to confiscate them. Not that they'd get it.

The thread tying Parker's last story to the Alonzo family was tenuous at best, based on nothing more than a feeling Alex had.

Hopefully, the newspaper would cooperate on the chance the agency could identify their reporter's killer. How would Madison react to him nosing into her life? He guessed she'd want the person who took her father away caught and tried, even if it was her cousin, but would she ever forgive him for the big lie sitting between them? Eventually it was going to come out that he was more than a co-owner of a biker bar, and he'd give anything if he could sit down and tell her everything.

He'd tried to stay away, but the past two weeks had felt like his heart had been ripped out of his chest. She had been the first thing he thought of on waking and the last thing before sleeping, and all the hours in between.

"Is he gone?"

Alex narrowed his gaze on Madison, prowling toward her. "He is." Reaching her, he cupped her cheeks. "My cold seems to be gone, but I'm going to wait one more day to kiss you just to be safe. Fair warning, though. I'm going to kiss you so long and deep that you'll have to ask me your name when I'm done with you."

Her eyes darkened and air swished out of her lungs. "I'm not sure what my name is right now."

"When we do make love, Madison, we'll be lucky if we don't set the bed on fire." He kissed her forehead. "I have to go, but I'll be back at six to pick you up. I have to be at the bar tonight, but I'm not leaving you alone. You can ask your roommate if she wants to come."

"She'll love that, if she doesn't have a date with her boyfriend."

The last thing he wanted to do was leave her, but he had a man to see.

"You're lucky I don't kill you," Alex said the moment he found his way to Ramon's bedroom. The housekeeper had said Ramon wasn't up yet, and Alex had brushed past her, taking the stairs two at a time, then sticking his head into three rooms before he found the one he wanted.

"What's your problem, dude?" Ramon rolled over, stuffing a pillow behind his head.

"You. You're the problem. As of this minute, Madison's off-limits to you. You don't go near her again." Alex eyed Ramon's swollen nose with satisfaction. His Grasshopper had done well.

"I didn't do nothing." He pointed at his nose. "Look what the bitch did to me for no reason at all."

He really was going to kill the man. "Just heed my warning and we're good. You don't, we're done doing business." It was doubtful that Ramon would shut him out now that the bar was laundering thousands of dollars a day for the man, so Alex had felt safe in showing up and threatening bodily harm if he bothered Madison once more.

The adjoining bathroom door opened and Trina strolled out, naked as the day she was born. "Well, look who's here. Hello, Alex." She leisurely strolled to the bed, leaned back against Ramon, and let her gaze roam over Alex. "Wanna play with us?"

Alex could appreciate that she had a killer body, but he'd rather play with a spitting cobra than take a tumble in the sheets with her. "I'll pass, thank you."

"You're no fun," she pouted as Ramon reached around her and squeezed her right breast. She pulled the sheet down to Ramon's waist and slid her hand underneath, all the while keeping her eyes locked on Alex, as if that would turn him on.

"So I've heard." His message delivered, he wanted to get away from the sick fucks.

Ramon grunted, arching his hips. "Sure you don't want to play, Alex? Trina can handle us both. She's full of tricks, dude."

He just bet she was. "Positive." He waved a hand. "Carry on." His feet couldn't get him out of there fast enough.

CHAPTER FIFTEEN

"What does one wear to a biker bar?" Madison said, walking into Lauren's bedroom. "Whoa! Look at you." Her roommate grinned as she spun in a circle. Her hair was spiked more than usual, and on Lauren it actually looked cool. She wore black skinny jeans, knee-high black boots with five-inch heels, and a white off-the-shoulder gypsy shirt with a low-cut bodice. Silver earrings, her only jewelry, dangled from her ears.

"Do you think this is okay to wear?"

Madison licked a finger, then shook it in the air. "Too hot to touch, baby. You look great." It wasn't often that Lauren was uncertain, especially about her clothes, and it struck Madison as odd that she was even asking.

"Let's get you dressed."

"Good luck with that. I'm short on biker chick clothes." She followed Lauren and stood by while her friend rifled through the closet Madison had stuffed with outfits for every occasion except hanging out with bikers. Lauren was a genius with clothes, though, and thirty minutes later, Madison stood in front of a mirror, wondering what Alex would say when he saw her.

It would have never occurred to her to pair the black leather motorcycle boots with a denim miniskirt. The boots were ankle length, and thick white socks peeked over the tops. Her black, cropped, long-sleeved silk blouse was tied in the front, and the red lace of her bra was visible when she moved. Like Lauren, the only jewelry she wore was silver big-hoop earrings. They'd curled her hair so that it had a wild look to it as it fell over her shoulders and down her back.

Lauren eyed her. "Your man's going to drool all over his shirt when he sees you."

"I don't think I've ever looked so . . ."

"Hot?" Lauren laughed.

"Yeah, I guess." Lauren had convinced her to leave the top two blouse buttons undone, just enough to give an enticing view of the valley of her breasts. Was the outfit too much? She wanted to look sexy for Alex, but maybe she shouldn't have so much on display, considering where they were going.

"Stop overthinking it. You look great."

"You tell Nelson where you were going tonight?"

Lauren's eyes widened. "No way. I told him I was hanging out with you."

"I'm glad you didn't lie to him."

"Why would I? He doesn't own me." The doorbell rang, and Lauren clapped her hands. "Party time. Let's go." She grabbed Madison's hand, pulling her downstairs.

"I can't wait to see his face when he sees you." Lauren opened the door.

"Your limo has arrived, ladies," Alex said, his gaze sliding past Lauren, locking on Madison. Without saying a word, he brushed by Lauren, walking straight up to Madison. Leaning down, he put his mouth next to her ear. "Every drop of blood in my body just went south. What are you going to do about that?"

"I have a few ideas," she whispered back.

"Thank God." He took her hand, not letting go as they walked to his car, Lauren following.

Wearing black leather pants and a black Aces & Eights T-shirt with the jack of hearts card above the pocket, he looked pretty darn hot himself. After he opened the front passenger door for her and the back one for Lauren, he skirted around the hood.

"Wow, did you see his eyes? He wanted to eat you up the minute he saw you," Lauren said.

"I might have let him if you hadn't been standing two feet from us."

Alex slid into the car, halting their conversation. "One thing about tonight, ladies. Don't feed the animals."

"What does that mean?" Madison asked, although she thought she knew, but she wanted to be sure Lauren understood.

"Some of our customers don't recognize boundaries, and both you ladies are smokin' hot." His eyes slid to her as he said that, the heat in them making her stomach twitchy. "They're a rough bunch, and any encouragement you give them could end up in me and my brothers having to fight them off you. While you're in the bar area, never venture away from one of us."

"No problem," Madison said. Not wanting to cause Alex problems, much less have strange men hassling her, that was an easy promise to make.

"What if one of those animals is your brother?" Lauren muttered.

Madison leaned around the headrest. "What's the deal between you and Court? He seemed nice enough to me." Lauren's attitude was embarrassing. Alex had arranged tonight as a favor, and it would be nice if Lauren were more appreciative.

"He's a jerk."

"Lauren!" Madison glanced at Alex to see his reaction.

He grinned. "Fireworks are grand, aren't they?"

The amusement dancing in his eyes eased her concern that he was offended by Lauren's declaration. Was he right? Were there sparks flying between Lauren and Court? If so, Lauren wouldn't be happy about that since Nelson was still supposedly the love of her life. Tonight was going to be interesting.

"Sorry, Alex," Lauren said, leaning forward and patting his shoulder. "No offense. I just don't like him, okay?"

Alex glanced back at her, a smirk curving his lips. "You sure about that?"

"Without question."

Madison gazed out the window, watching a sailboat as it approached the bridge they were traveling over. If she looked at Alex, she would burst out laughing. He'd nailed it. Lauren was attracted to Alex's brother, and she wasn't happy about it.

Back on the mainland, Alex turned right. She'd never asked where Aces & Eights was located, but it should have occurred to her that there were no biker bars in South Beach. She'd been to his condo, which wasn't too far from the bookstore, so somehow she'd thought his bar was nearby. The area they were in wasn't one she would want to travel into alone.

"Never come here without me," he said, as if reading her thoughts. He took her hand and placed it on his thigh.

"That I can promise." She loved touching him, and she squeezed her fingers into his leg. "Am I going to end up plastering myself against you, begging for your protection?" Lord, she loved flirting with him.

"All night long," he answered, his voice changing into the rough sound she loved.

Lauren thumbed Alex on his head. "Hello. I'm feeling like a voyeur here, people."

Alex chuckled. "Your roommate's touchy."

"She's jealous," Madison said.

"So am not." Lauren snorted. "Okay, maybe a little. You two are just too cute. I can see you sending adorable kitten pictures to each other on Facebook."

Alex turned into the parking lot of a building with a neon sign blinking the words "Aces & Eights." He drove around to the back and pushed a button on the remote clipped to his visor. A garage door opened, and he drove inside. Three shiny black Harleys were parked beside a black SUV, maybe a Land Rover. Including the black BMW she sat in, it appeared the bar was a successful venture for the brothers, but they did like the color black, whether it was their vehicles or their clothes.

They exited the car and Alex took her hand, tangling their fingers together. "Remember, don't wander away." He glanced at Lauren as he said it, and Madison speared her friend a look behind Alex's back.

"What?" Lauren mouthed.

"Behave," she mouthed back, ignoring Lauren's eye roll, which didn't bode well. They walked down a hallway, past a kitchen where a man was washing dishes, and then through a set of swinging doors.

"Welcome to Aces and Eights, ladies," Alex said, putting himself between them.

The first thing that hit Madison was the loud Southern rock music. The second was the rough-looking crowd. She pressed closer to Alex. And Lauren wanted to come here because . . . ?

As Alex led them into the room, she kept her hand in his. He didn't have to worry about her leaving his side. Two men approached, one she recognized as his brother Court, and the second, even though she'd never seen him before, she knew was also Alex's brother. She'd not paid much attention to Court the other night because Lauren's pissiness had distracted her, but now, with the brothers together, she was struck by how much they looked alike.

"You've both met Court, and this is our big brother, Nate," Alex said when the men reached them. "This is Madison." He smiled at her. "And her friend Lauren."

Madison smiled. "Nice to meet you, Nate, and good to see you again, Court." Neither man seemed overjoyed to see them. Nate's gaze zeroed in on her with an intensity that made her want to hide behind Alex's back. Her smile wavered when he didn't return it.

"Ladies, if you would stay here with Court, I need a minute with Alex."

Alex knew what was coming, had expected it. He squeezed Madison's hand before letting go. "Be right back."

"What the hell were you thinking bringing them here," Nate demanded as soon as they were out of earshot.

"They wanted to see the place, and apparently Lauren threatened to show up by herself if she didn't get an invite. I thought it better to control the visit." Wednesdays had somehow evolved into what the hardcore bikers called the wannabes night. The customers here tonight were non–club members, and the gangs didn't like mixing with them, so they stayed away.

"And you didn't think you should tell me you were doing this?"

Alex shrugged. "Actually, I thought I probably should, but I also knew you'd refuse."

"Damn straight I would have. Take them home."

Alex put his hand on Nate's upper arm. "Nope. Deal with it." He chuckled when his brother growled at seeing Spider spill his beer on the dude next to him at the bar. The man—a new face—squared off against Spider, who had grabbed a bar towel and was trying to dry the big guy's leather vest.

Nate sighed. "Idiot's gonna get himself killed one night."

"Guess you better go save him. Again." Alex headed back to Madison, leaving Nate to deal with the fight about to happen. He arrived at the same time as Trapper John and Hawkeye, two friends who had served together in Iraq. Alex respected that they were former military, but he didn't like them, having seen how they treated women.

"What do we have here?" Trapper said, winking at Madison. "Let me buy you a drink, sweet thing."

"I get this one," Hawkeye said, pressing up to Lauren's side.

Alex stepped behind Madison and wrapped his arms around her waist. "She's my woman. Get lost." He gave Court a glare that said, "Step up to the plate, man."

Court narrowed his eyes, letting Alex know he was going to owe him big, before putting his arm around Lauren's shoulder and pulling her to him. "And this one's my old lady. She's off-limits to you, dude."

Trapper grabbed his crotch. "You girls get tired of playing with boys and want a real man, let me know." He and Hawkeye laughed as they walked away.

"Old lady?" Lauren jerked away from Court's hold. "What are you, a Neanderthal?"

"I was saving your pretty ass, sweetheart."

The two of them glared at each other, and Alex wondered if he should get Nate to come break up another fight, or if he should find them a bedroom. He'd never seen a woman twist Court's boxers like this one was doing, and he swallowed a laugh. It was about time someone stood Court's ordered world on its head.

He took Madison's hand, pulling her away. "Let them be. They'll work things out," he said when she resisted.

She craned her neck as he led her off. "They're going to kill each other."

"I'm not so sure about that." He knew that, left alone with Lauren, Court wouldn't leave her to the resident vultures circling around the sexy new woman. "As far as I know, Court hasn't killed an aggravating woman yet."

"There's always a first time," she grumbled as they walked into the poolroom.

"Do you play?"

"No, but I've always wanted to. Will you teach me?"

Alex immediately had visions of pressing against her back as he showed her how to hold the cue, and his dick stirred awake. "Yeah." He cleared his throat, the damn thing suddenly gone raspy. "Here you go," he said, chalking a pool cue before handing it to her. She took it, and he put his hand on her shoulders, turning her toward the table. They had four pool tables in the room, two currently being used, and when the dudes playing eyed Madison, he sent them a death glare.

Once satisfied they got his message, he stepped up behind her, putting his arms around her and his hands over hers on the stick. "I've been thinking of having my body wrapped around yours all night," he said with his mouth pressed against her ear. "Come home with me." If she wouldn't come to his place, he'd be at hers, either in her bed or standing sentry on the sidewalk all night, guarding her door. He'd much prefer to guard her while in bed with her.

"Okay."

He laughed, couldn't help it. "You're so easy, Grasshopper."

"Can't deny that where you're concerned." She wiggled her ass against his erection. "I'm thinking you're a little easy yourself, Grandfather."

"You watched *Kung Fu* without me?" He tried to sound affronted, but it pleased him that she'd wanted to know why he'd given her the nickname. "And I'm far from your grandfather," he said, punctuating his words by snatching the cue stick out of her hands. "We'll have pool lessons some other day."

"Will Lauren be okay?" She pulled him toward her friend.

"Court will make sure she gets home safely."

"Okay, but let me tell her I'm leaving."

After the friends said their good-byes, he tucked Madison under his arm and led her to the car. On the way to his condo, he tried to think of something to say that didn't have anything to do with sex. Specifically, sex with her. Nothing occurred to him.

"Are you sure he'll see that she gets home safely?"

"Hmm? Who?" He put in his code to lift the gate.

"Lauren. Will Court make sure she stays safe? I shouldn't have left her."

At his parking space, he turned the key, switching off the engine. "My brother might be acting like a jerk for reasons I can only guess at, but he'll make sure she gets home without harm." Surprising him, she leaned across the console, put her hand behind his neck, and pulled his mouth down to hers.

God, yes. Getting a head start in the car hadn't been on his agenda, but who needed a plan, anyway? She pushed her tongue into his mouth, sighing against his lips, and the only thing stopping him from tearing off her clothes was the sound of another car pulling into the underground garage.

"Let's go upstairs. I have a bed that's been dying to meet you." He got her out of the car, up the elevator, and into his condo, barely managing not to drag her at a run. Had he ever wanted a woman as much as he wanted Madison? Not that he could remember.

"Can I get you anything?" he asked as soon as he'd locked the door behind them. "Wine, water, beer, a bed?" Suddenly, he was nervous. Was he pushing her too soon? From the day she'd walked into Ramon's billiard room, he'd wanted her. He'd had erotic dreams of her, waking up as hard as a steel rod. He'd often found himself staring off into the distance, thinking of her, wondering what she was doing. Wondering if she ever thought of him.

He had it bad.

"I'll take the wine and bed, please." Amusement flickered in her eyes, and one side of her mouth twitched as if she was trying not to smile.

He raised a brow. "Wanna share?" That got him the smile she'd been trying to hide.

"You've been vibrating with sexual tension all night. I thought within seconds of walking in you'd have me up against the wall. Instead, you politely offer me something to drink and a bed."

"Are you disappointed?" *Please say yes.*

She shrugged. "Maybe."

"Have I told you how hot you look tonight?" He prowled toward her. "I was sure I'd end up in a fight before I got you out of there. There wasn't a man in that bar who didn't want you, but not one of them as much as me."

He stopped in front of her, and trailed a finger down the valley of her breasts. "This red lace playing peek-a-boo every time you move and this bit of skin have been tantalizing me all night. I've been fantasizing about licking you from here"—he touched her bottom lip—"to here." He slid his finger down the opening of her blouse, and couldn't stop his satisfied smile when she shivered. "That's just for a start, Madison. Before the night's over, my mouth and tongue will know every inch of you."

Her eyes were locked on his, her pupils dilated, their color reminding him of a stormy green sea. She licked her lips, drawing his attention to them. He stepped forward, crowding her, and still keeping her eyes on his, she backed up. So, she wanted to play. Another step toward her, one back from her, and then he did it again and again, until she was up against the wall.

"Where to now?" he said as he put his hands against the wall, caging her. When her gaze darted to the left, he laughed. "Oh, no you don't. You're not running away." He pushed his body hard against hers, rocking his hips. "Feel that?"

"Yes," she whispered.

"Do you want it?"

She nodded.

"Say it. Tell me you want it."

"I do. I want it."

A moan slipped out of her when he rubbed against her again, and the needy sound almost sent him over the edge. He angled his head and covered her mouth with his. The taste of her exploded in his mouth as their tongues slid over and around each other. He could get insanely drunk just from tasting her. Trailing his thumb down the column of her neck, he kept going until he came to the top button of her blouse. He slipped his hand underneath the soft material, spreading his fingers over her left breast, caressing the silky skin above her bra.

She lifted a leg, wrapping it around his thigh, and he reached down, pulling her other leg around him. He moved his mouth to her earlobe, nipping it with his teeth. "Now I've got you right where I want you, wrapped around me." When she tugged on his T-shirt, he leaned his torso back, letting her pull it over his head.

It didn't take him but seconds to have her blouse off, and he took a moment to appreciate the sexy bra. "Beautiful," he murmured. The creamy skin rising above the red lace beckoned him, and he lowered his mouth, skimming his tongue and lips along the top of the lace.

Alex chuckled against her skin when she dug the heels of her boots into his thighs. "I never thought riding boots were all that sexy, but combined with this little skirt, and those beautiful legs of yours show-ing in between . . . I've changed my mind about that. But it's time for them to come off."

"Okay." She nestled into him, burying her face against his neck.

"Hold on." With her wrapped around him, he walked them into his bedroom. "Down you go." He lowered her onto his bed. When she reached for a boot to remove it, he brushed her hands away. "Allow me."

After he'd taken off her boots and socks, she wiggled her toes. "Ah, nice."

"Yeah?" He danced his fingers over the soles of her feet.

"Ack!" Laughing, she tackled him, landing on his chest and taking him down. As they rolled around on the bed, trying to tickle each other, giggling like six-year-olds, Alex realized two things. First, he was turned on, which made this the most unusual foreplay he'd ever participated in. Second, he was ticklish. Who knew?

For a few minutes, he lulled her into thinking she was his equal as they wrestled each other, then he attacked, pinning her under him while he captured her hands in one of his, holding them above her head.

"Now what you gonna do?" he said, pinning her legs under his.

"Surrender?" Her grin said she had no problem with that.

Her fiery red hair was spread over the pillow, and the laughter in her eyes faded, replaced by desire as they stared at each other. He didn't know what it was about her that was different from the women he'd been with before, but whatever it was called to him in a way that made him want her in his life. Maybe forever.

Unless the lie—the one that sat on his chest like a boulder—of who he was held so much weight that it would crush this thing growing between them. He knew by now that she wasn't involved with her cousin, and he believed he could trust her. It was killing him, this keeping something so big, something she deserved to know, a secret.

"Madison . . ."

CHAPTER SIXTEEN

"Mmm?" Madison said when Alex hesitated. He hovered over her, holding his weight on his elbows, intensely staring at her, but she was having trouble concentrating with his bare chest in front of her face. She lifted her hand and trailed her fingers across his shoulders and down his arms, feeling his muscles flex under her palm. Lord, she liked touching him.

He closed his eyes, breaking the connection between them, and gave a shake of his head. "Nothing." His eyes blinked open, smiling. "I was just thinking that you still have too many clothes on."

"So do you," she said, not pressing him, although she wondered what it was he hadn't said. His expression had been too serious, and the way he'd said her name had been hesitant, almost as if . . .

He covered her mouth with his, and her thoughts slipped away. For a man, he had soft lips, but his kisses were a mix of gentle and demanding. It was dizzying the way he took possession of her mouth. His tongue slipped in when she parted her lips, and he explored every crevice before tangling their tongues.

Their breaths mingled until she didn't know which was his and which was hers. She slid her palms down his sides, doing her own exploring, his skin quivering under her fingers.

He pushed away, settled on his knees, and stared down at her. "Too many clothes," he grumbled, making her laugh.

She loved that about him, the way he was both playful and intensely sensual. It was novel. Not that she had a lot of experience with men and sex, but the few she'd been with had pretty much dived in, got what they wanted, and then rolled over and gone to sleep. She thought Alex might be right when he said it was possible they could set his bed on fire.

She also loved how her inhibitions faded away when she was with him, leading her to do things like put the sole of her foot on his crotch. "I'm not the only one with too many clothes on."

He grinned as he pressed his erection against the bottom of her foot. "Easily remedied, Grasshopper."

With lightning speed, he vaulted off the bed, unbuttoned and unzipped his pants, and pushed them and his briefs down at the same time. When they got tangled up with his boots, he hopped around, drawing her attention to his erection, which seemed to be waving at her with each bounce. She couldn't help it. She burst into laughter. He stilled, narrowing his eyes, which only set her off more.

"Not good for a man's ego when the first time you see him in all his glory, you laugh, you know." His lips twitched, ruining his scowl.

Totally losing it, she pulled a pillow over her face. This was turning out to be one of the strangest preludes to sex, and she adored him for it. She could easily fall hard for this man.

The mattress dipped, and his bare leg pressed against hers. Before she knew what was happening, he had her miniskirt and panties off. She peeked out from underneath the pillow, watching him as he tossed her clothing over the side of the bed. Her laughter faded away as she eyed his erection, which was pointing straight at her.

She came out of hiding, pushing the pillow aside. "Impressive. Really, really impressive." His eyes devoured her as his gaze roamed over her, her skin prickling as if he were actually touching her.

"I aim to please, ma'am." He danced his fingers along the inside of her thighs, and when he reached the top of her legs, he paused. "No matter what happens in the future, I want you to know something."

Something like regret flickered in his eyes, and she didn't know what to make of that. It made her nervous, and she had the urge to tell him to stop talking, that she didn't want to hear whatever he was going to say. He glanced away, and when he faced her again, she added sadness to the emotions swirling around him.

She reached for the hand he had resting on her leg. "What?"

"If there ever comes a day when you wish me to hell"—he turned his hand palm up, linking their fingers—"know that I never wanted to hurt you. I think we have something special, and I've never felt this way before, but I'll probably find a way to screw everything up. For that, I'll be more sorry than you'll ever know."

She didn't know what to say. What was going on in that mind of his? For a moment, she wondered if she was in over her head. Already, he was working his way into her heart, while at the same time, warning her that he'd probably hurt her. She wasn't supposed to fall for him. He was only going to be a bit of fun before marriage and children.

She had imagined marrying a banker or stockbroker, maybe a doctor or lawyer. Someone with his feet planted firmly on the ground, a man who kissed her good-bye when he left in the morning, his briefcase in hand, and who returned home in time to share a glass of wine before dinner while they discussed their day.

That had been her dream, but she suddenly felt like yawning. As she studied Alex's beautiful face, his eyes watching her with that intensity of his as he waited for her to respond, she knew the smartest thing she could do was walk away this very minute before he stole her heart completely. But if she did, she would always regret it.

She put her palm on his cheek. "Make love to me, Alex. Make me yours."

He put his hand over hers. "And I'll be yours. If you believe nothing else, Mad, believe that." He dropped her hand, rose onto his knees, and covered her body with his. Cupping her cheeks, he angled his head, lowering his mouth to hers.

There was passion in his kiss, but something else, too. It seemed as if he wanted to make sure she would never want another man after him, and she wasn't sure she ever would. The weight of his big body on hers, the prickle of the dusting of hair on his chest over her skin, and the way he possessed her mouth sent heat spiraling through her, making her blood flow hot through her veins.

She thought she might climb out of her skin when he moved down her body to a breast, latching his mouth around her nipple and swirling his hot tongue around the tip. He nipped it, the gentle clamp of his teeth sending waves of pleasure through her. At her moan, she felt his lips smile against her skin. He should be pleased with himself. No other man had taken the time to worship her body the way he was doing, and if he wanted to feel a little male satisfaction, he was entitled to.

Her right breast was next on his agenda, and he repeated the nipping and licking, sending an aching need for him to her very core. Unable to keep still, she writhed under him, and feeling his erection bump against her thigh, she squeezed her legs together, capturing him between them.

"Please," she begged.

"All in good time." He lifted his face and blew on her damp nipple, raising goose bumps and sending more shivers through her.

He took his leisurely time kissing a path down her stomach, until she was uncontrollably squirming in anticipation of him reaching his final goal. And when he did, oh God, when he did, and his magical tongue touched her there, she grabbed the top of his head, holding on for dear life. He sucked on her, lapped her with his tongue, and teased her with his teeth, and when the tidal wave hit, she thought her entire body would have lifted off the bed if he hadn't been holding her down. She screamed his name.

"You're so damn wet for me," he said, his voice raspy as he lifted onto his knees and stared down at her with raw hunger in his eyes.

"Only for you," she whispered, and it was true. Something had changed between them in his bed tonight, and if he was the only man to ever touch her again, she would die happy.

"Damn straight." He reached over to his nightstand and opened the drawer, never breaking eye contact with her.

"Wouldn't you like me to return the favor? I mean"—her cheeks heated, and she didn't doubt her face was turning bright red—"wouldn't you like me to . . ."

"To go down on me?" he finished when she stumbled over the words, and she nodded. He grinned. "You're so damn cute when you're embarrassed, Grasshopper, but to answer you, hell yes. Not yet, though. I'm on the edge as it is. Later, you can have at me."

"Okay." It wasn't something she'd particularly enjoyed doing in the past, but with Alex? Oh yeah, she was sure it would be different with him. She watched him as he tore open a condom package with his teeth, watched him roll it on, and finally got lost in his eyes, now black and burning with desire, as he lowered his magnificent body over hers.

"Are you ready for me, Mad?" Not waiting for an answer, he slid his hand down, easing his finger inside her. "Oh, yeah," he said. "You're dripping for me, baby."

After he eased inside her, she wrapped her legs around his thighs, and then he made love to her so beautifully that tears came to her eyes. He stroked her with his hands, finding all her sensual places, and as he loved her, he put his mouth next to her ear and whispered dirty words to her, telling her all the things he was going to do to her before the night was over.

Each stroke, each touch, each filthy word, each time he thrust into her, then pulled out, only to do it again, sent her to a place she'd never been before, and she responded by sinking her teeth into his shoulder.

"Hell, yes," he said. "Show me how much you want me."

Desperate need swelled inside her until she could no longer contain it, and she arched up, meeting him thrust for thrust. She moaned, and he answered with a growl from deep in his throat, and then he took her to the heavens.

When she clenched her muscles around him, he lifted to his arms, watching with a savage intensity as she fell apart. Eyes as black as midnight held hers prisoner as his own release overtook him. His breaths were hard and fast, the cords on his neck thick and ropey as he strained, his hands digging into her hips. She'd never seen anything hotter than Alex when he looked like he might shatter. He ground his hips into hers in one final stroke, shouted something incomprehensible, and then fell against her.

After they'd both caught their breath and she could talk again, she said, "That was so burning hot, I think we did set the bed on fire."

He chuckled against her neck, where his face was buried. "Then we'll just have to go down in flames because I can't move."

"What's wrong, Grandfather? Can't keep up with Grasshopper?" She loved the feel of his warm breath on her skin.

"Shut your mouth, girl." Getting some of his strength back, Alex rolled off her, somehow managing to get his legs under him to go to the bathroom and dispose of the condom. Back in bed, he tucked Madison next to him. Still reeling from making love to her, he tried to remember if he'd ever had white spots dancing in his vision when he'd climaxed. He couldn't remember that ever happening before.

"How soon can you be ready to do that again?"

He lifted his head, looking down at her. "Is that a challenge?"

"Consider the gauntlet thrown down."

Her grin and the mischief sparkling in her eyes twisted something inside him, and he wondered if it was the beginning of love. That he felt something special for her, he'd accepted, but if it was turning to love, the timing couldn't be worse. He was feeling too good to worry, though, about what may or may not happen tomorrow or the next day.

"Still waiting," she said. "Maybe I can help you answer my question."

When she reached for his dick, wrapping her soft hands around it, he rested his head back on the pillow, fully willing to put himself in her hands, so to speak. What was it about this woman that had snared him from the beginning? He'd asked himself that question a thousand times but still didn't have an answer. Arousal stirred as her hand stroked him, and he watched her face, smiling at her intense concentration and the pink tongue stuck out the side of her lips.

At the moment she began to lower her mouth, his phone buzzed with the tone set for Nate. Madison jerked her head up, her hand stilling at the sound. Damn his brother, anyway. Dude had the worst timing. He'd ignore the call, except that Nate knew Madison was here with him and wouldn't be calling unless it was urgent.

"Do you need to answer that?" she asked.

"'Fraid so. It's Nate." He grabbed his phone from the nightstand. "This better be good."

"Court just left to take Lauren home. He said to tell you that he's not staying, so if you're worried about her being by herself, then you'd better get your ass to the bookstore."

"Did you notice him acting weird around her?"

"I got the impression he doesn't like her. Why, is there something I should know?"

"Not sure."

"I've done my duty. Don't bring those two here again."

Alex chuckled when Nate hung up on him.

"What's going on?" Madison asked as soon as he hung up.

He pulled her against him. "Court's taking Lauren home."

"Is he staying?"

"Apparently not." She scrambled off the bed. "Where you going?"

"To get my phone."

His gaze followed her as she left the bedroom. "Beautiful ass, Grasshopper."

At the door, she glanced over her shoulder, a grin on her face. "All yours, Grandfather."

"I'm not old enough to be your grandfather," he yelled as she disappeared down the hall.

When she returned, her phone was to her ear, and a frown was on her face. "This is Madison. Call me." She picked her blouse up from the floor. "She's not answering. I need to go home."

"No problem. We'll just move our next play session to your bed."

She walked straight to him, put her hands around his neck, and pulled him to her, kissing him hard. "Thank you for understanding I need to go."

"You mean *we* need to go."

Thirty minutes later, he parked on the street in front of High Tea and Black Cat Books. Court stood outside the door, leaning against the wall. He walked over, and Alex rolled down the window.

"She's all yours. Stop making me responsible for her, bro." Court glanced at Madison. "Nothing personal, but your roommate pushes all my buttons." He stepped back. "You kids have fun."

Alex lifted his hand in a wave as his brother headed across the street to his car. He wondered exactly which *buttons* Lauren pushed. There had to be more to it than he was seeing. It wasn't like his brother to have such a strong reaction to a woman, especially one he'd just met.

"I think that's Nelson's car," Madison said when a black BMW parked in front of them.

Alex whistled. The car was a BMW i8, price tag over a hundred grand. "What does he do for a living?"

"He's a model. Lauren's been seeing him for a few weeks now."

The man got out, and when he reached the door, Lauren opened it, grabbed his hand, and pulled him inside. Alex glanced across the street to see his brother standing at his car, staring hard at the turquoise door of the bookstore. A few seconds later, Court got in his car, burning rubber as he sped away. Yeah, the lady was pushing his buttons all right.

Alex chuckled as he exited his BMW, an X6 model, half the price of the i8. It was fun seeing someone finally twisting Court's boxers in a knot, and he planned to take full advantage of the knowledge to ruthlessly torment his brother.

"She must have called Nelson on her way home," Madison said as they walked up the stairs.

If Lauren had called him to come over while returning home in Court's car with his brother listening, then that was plain mean. Or she'd wanted Court to know she had a boyfriend. Either way, it wasn't a cool thing to do. When he and Madison entered her apartment, Lauren and her boyfriend weren't around.

"Wish we'd known he was going to be here," Alex said. "We would still be in my bed where I'd be doing naughty things to you."

"What? You don't think my bed's naughty worthy?" She took off down the hall, laughing as he chased her.

"Gotcha!" He pulled Madison to him, nuzzling her neck. "Take me to your bed, woman. Let's see just how naughty we can get on it."

CHAPTER SEVENTEEN

Madison rolled over, reaching for Alex. She opened her eyes when she realized he wasn't there. The sheet was still warm from his body, and she assumed he'd gone to the bathroom. When he didn't return after a few minutes, she glanced at the clock to see it was four in the morning. Had he left?

She switched on the lamp as she got out of bed. His shirt and shoes were on the chair where he'd left them, but his jeans were missing. The bathroom was empty, and she slipped on her robe before going to the bedroom door and peeking out. The hallway was dark, and she didn't hear any noises. Where was he?

A search of the apartment turned up nothing, and now puzzled, she headed downstairs. Maybe he'd gone for an early run? Would he have done that barefoot, though? Doubtful. The deadbolts were still secure, so he hadn't gone out, but then she noticed the door leading into the bookstore was open. She walked in and opened her mouth to call for Alex when a hand covered her mouth, and she was pulled against a male body. With her heart pounding in fear, she tried to bite the fingers of the man holding her.

"Shhh," he whispered in her ear. "It's me."

Alex? What the hell was going on? She pressed her hand over her chest, against her hammering heart.

"Stay quiet," he whispered, dropping his hand from her mouth.

Something furry brushed against her legs, and she almost screamed before she realized it was Hemingway.

"Shit," Alex hissed.

His foot kicked against hers, and a hysterical giggle bubbled up. She slapped her hand over her mouth. Once she was sure she wasn't going to laugh, she lifted onto her toes and whispered in his ear, "It's my cat."

Because of the streetlights shining through the windows, she was able to see him nod. He put his finger to his lips, telling her again to stay quiet, and then he took her hand, leading her down a row of bookcases. They were both barefoot, and she padded silently behind him. Hemingway brushed against her leg as he trailed alongside her, and nervous laughter threatened again. If she were an author, she'd write a scene where the hero and heroine crept through the night with their faithful sleuth cat, and the only one clueless about what was happening was the heroine.

When they reached the end of the bookcases, Alex stopped and again put his finger to his lips. He leaned his head around the shelf, then a few seconds later, pulled her in front of him. They had a perfect view of the bookstore's office, and she gasped at seeing the light from a flashlight as someone rifled through the desk.

"What the—"

"Shhh," Alex said, his mouth next to her ear.

"Who?" she asked in a whisper.

"Lauren's boyfriend."

Why would Nelson be nosing around their office? She stepped forward, intending to ask him what the hell he was doing, but Alex pulled her back.

"Easy, Grasshopper. We don't want him to know we're on to him."

She supposed he had a point, but what could Nelson possibly be interested in? It wasn't like the bookstore had a ton of money coming in, so there was nothing to steal. He opened a folder, took out his phone, and snapped a few pictures. They were too far away to even get a hint of which file he found so interesting, and it was killing her not to march into the office and confront the man she no longer liked.

As if he understood, Alex gave her a squeeze. "We'll figure it out."

Hemingway hopped onto a shelf, knocking a book to the floor. Nelson froze, clicking off the flashlight. Alex picked up the cat and tossed him toward the office. Hemingway let out an affronted yowl.

"Damn cat," Nelson said, turning the flashlight back on, putting the folder back into the drawer.

Alex grabbed her hand. "Let's go."

They hightailed it back to her bedroom, and after the door was closed, Alex held up his hand to stop her from talking. In the silence, she heard a floorboard creak, then Lauren's bedroom door open and close.

When Alex pointed to the bed, she climbed in. He turned off the lamp she'd left on and crawled in beside her. "What do you know about him?"

Taking her cue from him, she kept her voice quiet. "No more than I already told you." They were nose to nose. She shivered, feeling as if a goose had run over her grave. From how many directions did she have to watch for attacks against her, Lauren, and the bookstore? She was a simple girl with a simple dream. Own a bookstore, do her best to make that work, and live happily ever after. The universe was conspiring against her.

She wanted Nelson out of her apartment. "What do you think he was taking pictures of?" Alex wrapped his arms around her, and it was the one place she felt safe. Please let her heart be right.

"I don't know," he said, "but I saw the general area where he put the file back. Tomorrow we'll see if anything stands out."

"What should I tell Lauren? I need to warn her."

"Don't say anything until we figure out what he's up to. Turn over." After she did, he said, "Try to go to sleep, Grasshopper." He wrapped his arm around her, pulling her back to his chest.

She snuggled against him. Thank God he'd been here tonight, otherwise she never would have known Nelson was snooping in the files. Although she didn't think she could sleep, it was nice being held by a big, warm body . . . specifically, Alex's body. They'd made love earlier, when they'd first gotten into her bed. He'd told her he wanted to love her slow and easy, and he'd proceeded to do just that. It had been beautiful, the way he'd worshiped every inch of her.

Although she was sure she was losing her heart to him, she still hadn't quite figured him out. He gave the impression that he was a bad boy, and he did seem to be at times, yet she was getting glimpses of a man who was honorable and cared deeply about those who meant something to him.

He buried his nose into her hair, and a few minutes later his breathing slipped into that of sleep. She tried to blank her mind, but it was impossible. There were too many questions about Nelson floating around and, frustrated, she thought about Alex instead. Or tried to. What she wanted to do was confront Nelson, and then kick him out of both the apartment and Lauren's life. That she'd misjudged him, thinking he was a great guy, she tried not to think about. It was too close to her questions about Alex. Who was he? Could she trust him?

When sunshine peeked around the edges of the curtains, she gave up trying to sleep. Alex had an arm thrown over her waist and one of his legs between hers, and she took a few minutes to enjoy the feeling of having his body wrapped around hers. She could learn to like having him in her bed every night. He had to be a good man. He just had to be. She inched her way out of his hold until she was able to slide over the edge of the mattress without waking him.

After a quick shower, she dressed and then tiptoed out of the bedroom, closing the door behind her. In the kitchen, she started a pot of coffee, which she desperately needed. As soon as it was ready, she poured a cup. Although she wasn't normally a breakfast person, she decided to make omelets, bacon, and toast for her and Alex.

Once the bacon was cooked and on the warmer, and everything she needed for the omelet was ready, she turned to go wake up Alex and let out a yelp at seeing Nelson leaning against the wall, watching her. How long had he been there?

"Sorry, didn't mean to scare you." He smiled.

That deceivingly sweet smile made it hard to think of him as the same man she'd seen sneaking around in the office only hours earlier.

"Could you spare a cup of that coffee? Maybe two, so I can take one to Lauren?"

"Ah, sure." Alex had told her not to let Nelson know they were on to him, so she tried to act normal, as if she didn't know he was a rat-bastard sneaky night spy, for what reason she couldn't guess. "Here." She thrust two cups into his hands. *Now go away.*

"Thanks."

She stared at his retreating back, narrowing her eyes as he disappeared down the hallway. And she'd thought he was nice. No matter what Alex said, she wasn't going to let her best friend go much longer thinking Nelson was a good guy. Was he working for Ramon, or did he have his own agenda?

Alex slipped back into Madison's bedroom, watching through the crack in the door as Lauren's boyfriend walked by. Where had he seen the man before? He punched Nate's number into his phone.

"See what you can find out about Nelson Lopez," he said when Nate answered. He gave his older bother the license plate number he'd memorized the night before.

"It's six fucking o'clock in the morning, bro. Either call me back at a reasonable hour or text me all that."

When Nate hung up on him, Alex texted his brother the license plate number. After Lauren's bedroom door closed behind Nelson, Alex headed for the kitchen. "Do I smell bacon?" he said, walking around the corner.

"You do." She picked up a piece, holding it out to him.

He locked eyes with her as he approached, lowering his head when he reached her, letting her feed him. The green in her eyes darkened when he sucked her thumb into his mouth.

"Alex."

That breathy way she said his name sent him over the edge. He reached over and turned off the stove before picking her up and throwing her over his shoulder in a fireman's carry.

"You're insane," she said, laughter flowing from her as he carried her down the hall.

"That's what you do to me, so don't blame me."

He almost dropped her when she grabbed his ass cheeks with her hands, letting out a low moan as she kneaded them with her fingers.

"Mad, you're playing with fire again." He dropped her on the bed.

"I know. I'm such a bad girl." She blinked far-too-innocent eyes at him. "Are you going to punish me?"

"Oh, yeah. I sure am." This girl was either going to be his doom or his lifeline. Right then, as he lowered his body over hers, he didn't care which.

"The file he was looking at was somewhere in the middle of this drawer," Alex said, flipping through the folders.

Madison sat at the desk, twirling a pen around her fingers. "I can't imagine what he was looking for."

"Here." He pulled out a folder, memorizing the bank account numbers as he handed it to her. "I'm guessing this."

"Why would he be interested in our bank statements?"

"Good question." He needed to talk to his brothers and bring them up to speed. By the time he got home, Nate and Court would have the background on Nelson Lopez.

"I'm going to head home. Do some investigating on the man."

"You mean google him? What will that tell you besides he's a model and some pictures of him pop up? I can do that right now."

He had to stop slipping, saying things that raised her curiosity about him. "No, I mean I'll ask around. Put some feelers out on the street with some dudes I know."

She didn't know he and his brothers were FBI with unlimited resources available to them. As far as she was concerned, he was a friend of Ramon's, maybe even involved in the Alonzos' drug business. Although knowing that, he had to question her intelligence for letting him anywhere near her. What did that say? That she had deep feelings for him, enough to overlook everything she thought she knew about him?

Damn, he wished he could come clean, tell her everything, but that wasn't wise. She could easily blow the operation, intentionally or unintentionally. More worrisome, if Ramon learned who he was, it could put her in danger. Her cousin would be suspicious that she was passing on information. And, his brothers would kill him if he did.

"I'll come back tonight when I can get away. It might be late, so I'll come in through your bedroom window." He walked to her, took the pen away, dropping it on the desk, and leaned down and kissed her. "See you tonight, Grasshopper." He meant to only give her a quick kiss before leaving, but just one taste of her, and he was lost. When he finally pulled away, he thought his eyes were probably as glazed over as hers.

"Keep your window locked until I signal you, okay?"

At her dazed nod, he grinned. He liked that his kisses zoned her out.

♥ ♥ ♥

"I remember where I saw him before," Alex said, tapping the computer screen as his brothers looked on. "The night I met Ramon at Rage, Nelson Lopez was there. He was with a woman, and the only reason I noticed him was because they stood not far from Ramon's table. The dude kept glancing at me."

They were in the office at Aces & Eights. Nate went to the wall and pushed the button that lowered a whiteboard. On it were pictures of Jose Alonzo, Ramon, his minions, and a timeline of events since they'd started the undercover investigation.

This was primarily Alex's show, his first lead on an operation, and he was determined to prove himself not only to the FBI, but also to his brothers. It was an understatement to say that his involvement with Madison was a complication they hadn't prepared for. Tough. The bureau and his brothers could just deal with it because he wasn't giving her up. On the plus side, because of her, they were getting intel they might not have otherwise.

As for his brothers, Nate was spending a lot of time with the prosecutor, preparing for an upcoming trial for a human-trafficking ring, the victims mostly underprivileged teenage girls, while Court was in the early stages of an investigation into a gang of luxury car thieves based in Miami and rumored to be operating worldwide.

"Why are you smiling like you just swallowed the canary?" Court said.

"Trust me, if I swallowed a damn bird, I wouldn't be smiling. But I was thinking how righteous it would be if your car thief dudes stole Lopez's i8."

Court snorted. "That would be funny."

"Children, pay attention." Nate tapped the whiteboard with his knuckles. "Here's what we know about Lopez so far."

Alex settled back in his chair, giving him a salute. "Yes, sir!" He grinned when Nate growled. The three of them were a team, and no matter how busy they might be with their own investigations, they were always there for each other. Whenever he thought of how far they had come and what they'd made of themselves, he wished the old man were still around so he could laugh in the bastard's face.

"I think we have to assume, until we learn otherwise, that Lopez is working for the Alonzos," Nate said.

Alex nodded. "Agree. So the question is, what does he want with the bookstore's bank information? If he's working for the Alonzos, then he's following orders, meaning they want those numbers."

"Only one reason," Court said. "They want to use the bookstore to launder money, with or without Madison's or Lauren's knowledge." He glanced at Alex, giving him a shrug. "I doubt Lauren knows anything about it, at least not yet. But I can't see how Madison wouldn't know."

Alex gripped the arm of his chair to keep from punching his brother. "She doesn't know." Did she?

CHAPTER EIGHTEEN

That afternoon, Madison made two lattes. "Looks like things have slowed down a little. Come sit with me for a few minutes." She handed her mother one of the coffees.

Angelina took the cup. "Lovely. I could use a break. We had a busy few hours."

"Oh, I ran into Mrs. Anderly yesterday," Madison said as she set her cup on the table before her shaking hands spilled coffee on her slacks. "She said she saw you in the park. Are you taking walks there now?"

"Who's Mrs. Anderly?"

"A customer. She usually comes by in the mornings when you're not here, but she saw you one afternoon when she stopped by to pick up a book we were holding for her."

Angelina shrugged. "Can't place her, but yes, I've started walking for thirty minutes in the mornings."

"That's great. I'm glad you're getting out more."

"Me, too. It's about time, don't you think?"

"I do." It was past time her mother started living again. "Listen, I need to talk to you about something. Uncle Jose doesn't want you working here. He told me to . . . well, to fire you."

"What?" Angelina set her cup down. "Why would he say such a thing?"

Because he doesn't want you around when the cops bust me for money laundering, maybe? "I don't know, Mom. He didn't say. It wasn't a request, though."

"Is that what you want, Madison?"

"No, absolutely not. I love you working here, and you're so good with the customers. I think you enjoy it, right?"

"Oh, I do. My brother is just old fashioned. Thinks women shouldn't have to work." Angelina patted her hand. "You leave him to me."

Which was going to really make him angry, but she didn't care. "It wasn't actually Uncle Jose who told me, but a message from him delivered by Ramon."

God, she had a splitting headache. She was a simple bookstore owner. Drugs and threats and perverted cousins were just too much to deal with. If her uncle and Ramon would disappear from the face of the earth, she'd be the happiest person in the world. She rubbed her forehead, wishing she could close her eyes and forget all her problems.

"Are you all right, Madison? Your cheeks are pale."

She forced a smile for her mother. "I have a little headache, is all." Actually, she had a major headache, which she didn't know the cure for.

"Why don't you go upstairs, take something for it, and have a little nap? It's almost time to close. Lauren and I can finish up."

"Thanks, I think I will," she said, giving her mother a hug. She should stay and help close, but she couldn't resist the offer. All day she had put on a front, pretending everything was as it should be.

Through it all, she'd somehow managed not to tell Lauren that her boyfriend was a scumbag. Oh, but she wanted to. Knowing Lauren, though, she'd go straight to Nelson, demanding an explanation.

Madison locked the door to her room, kicked off her shoes, slipped her bra out from under her blouse, and crawled into bed. She needed time to think and formulate a plan before she went off half-cocked. What would her father have done?

He'd investigate, dummy. Could she do that? Learn everything there was to know about Nelson Lopez? Was he spying for her cousin and uncle, or was he up to something unrelated to them? Whatever his reason, she needed to find out soon so she could tell Lauren. Having him in their home at night was unacceptable. No way would she be able to sleep if he was here for the night. Nor did she want to stay at Alex's, knowing Nelson was up to no good. Whatever he was doing, it had to stop.

For sure, she was going to ask Alex to stay over at night until Nelson was gone. She decided to take a nap so that she could stay awake if Nelson did spend the night. And she really did have a headache, which, hopefully, a few hours of sleep would cure. Later tonight, she'd get on her laptop and see what she could learn about him. That decided, she closed her eyes, but before she could drift off, there was a scratching at the door. Rolling her eyes, she got up and let Hemingway in.

"Come to take a nap with me?" He followed her onto the bed, and she fell asleep to his purrs.

♥ ♥ ♥

When she awoke, she glanced at the clock to see it was almost midnight. After her sleepless night, she'd needed the rest, although she hadn't meant to nap that long. Leaving Hemingway curled up on her pillow, she went into the bathroom, splashed water on her face, and brushed her hair. Her clothes were a wrinkled mess, and she changed into a tank top and a pair of boxer panties.

She'd left her laptop in the living room, which meant she was going to have to get it. She eased her bedroom door open a few inches, seeing that Lauren's door was closed. Was Nelson in there? She crept down the hall, careful not to step on the two boards that creaked. The laptop was on the coffee table, the top open. Weird. She was sure she'd left it on the side table with the lid closed.

Back in her bedroom, she locked her door and sat on the bed. The first thing she looked for was the computer's search history. Nothing unusual showed up, and because the laptop was password protected, she decided she was getting paranoid. Even if Nelson had tried to get into her computer, he would never guess her password.

She spent the next hour searching for anything she could find on him, turning up very little. What did surprise her was that he was the only son of a famous Cuban actor and a Cuban woman the actor had divorced early in his career. According to one interview with the actor, the divorce was amicable, and growing up, Nelson had spent time with both parents. He had a Facebook page, but his last post, a photo of him with his arms around two gorgeous women, had been eight months ago. It looked like some kind of fashion show, which wouldn't be unusual, considering.

The tapping at her window startled her, and she yelped. It was Alex's signal. Smiling, she unlocked the window. "Hey you. I'm so glad you're here." The arms he wrapped around her were strong, his breath warm on her cheek as he hugged her.

"Missed you, Grasshopper," he said, then kissed her.

His mouth hungrily devoured hers, and his tongue slipped through her parted lips, tangling with hers. Madison sank against him, and he lowered his hands to her hips, his fingers digging into her skin.

"Bed," he gasped between kisses.

"Yes." She laughed when he scooped her up. The man made her happy, made her feel sexy and wanted. If he ended up breaking her heart, she would find a way to deal with it. She would eat gallons of pistachio ice cream and cry buckets of tears for a few weeks, and then she'd be over him. Wasn't that how it worked?

Alex listened to the steady sound of Madison's breathing as she slept. They'd made love twice, and now she was curled up to his chest, her bottom pressed against his erection. Yeah, he wanted her again. It was crazy, the way he couldn't get enough of her. He'd never been in love before, so he wasn't sure if that was what was happening to him. And it wasn't just the sex that had him wanting to be with her. It was everything about her.

He flattened his hand over her stomach, his hold on her possessive. The investigation with Ramon was nearing its end. They had enough evidence on Jose, Ramon, and Trina to make an arrest. The only thing holding them back was knowing that Ramon was meeting a new customer on Friday, and he and his brothers wanted the man's name. Once they had his identity, arrest warrants would be issued for the Alonzos, Trina, and the distributors.

Alex couldn't wait for it to be over. He wanted Madison to know the real him, if she was still willing to let him be a part of her life. She sighed as she turned onto her stomach. He fell asleep with his palm resting on her ass.

The next morning, he awoke to see Madison sitting cross-legged at the end of the bed with her laptop open. She wore boxer shorts and a little shirt with straps, and her hair was mussed. He smiled at the way the tip of her tongue stuck out of the corner of her mouth as she concentrated on whatever she was reading. It was a little quirk he'd noticed before when she was intent on something.

"Morning, beautiful."

She glanced up at him and grinned. "Morning. I didn't mean to wake you."

"You didn't." Obviously, a little morning fun wasn't going to happen. That was too bad. "Be back in a minute." He went to her bathroom, used the john, and then found the toothbrush she'd given him the last time he had slept over. Not much he could do about his face without a shaving kit. Would she mind if he kept some toiletries here?

When he returned, her gaze roamed over his body. "It always amazes me how men walk around nude so easily."

"It always amazes me why women are so shy about their bodies." He sat behind her, putting his chin on her shoulder. "What has you looking so serious this morning?"

"Nelson Lopez. Did you know his father was Rafael Lopez?"

"Yeah, found that out yesterday."

She tilted her head. "What else do you know?"

"Not much. Still checking him out."

"Have you ever seen him around Ramon's?"

"No, why do you ask?" Their assumption was that he was spying for the Alonzos, and if she was asking that question, she might be coming to the same conclusion. He hoped she was. It would be easier if the idea came from her.

She closed the laptop. "I honestly don't know if I can trust you. I want to. My heart tells me that I can, but I don't understand why you hang out with Ramon. I think he sells drugs. My uncle, too. Is it really because you and Ramon are just friends?" She drew circles on the comforter. "Because I have to tell you that I have trouble believing that."

He scooted around to face her. "Look at me, Madison." He waited for her to lift her eyes to his. "I told you the truth when I said I don't use drugs. I don't sell drugs. I've never even smoked a joint because if my brothers had caught me doing anything like that, they would have beaten my butt raw."

"Yet, you're friends with a drug dealer?"

"Not really. The more I was around him, the less I liked him. Since I've learned how he treats you, I've pretty much avoided him." His lies to her were coming home to roost. It would be over soon, and he'd be able to tell her everything. He couldn't wait for that day to come.

"Okay, I'm going to trust you, but if you go straight to Ramon—"

"I won't. I swear it on the lives of my brothers." He hadn't been sure he'd ever see that kind of trust shining in her eyes. It made him want to promise that he'd never hurt her, but that was going to happen as soon as he made his confession. Aware that he was walking a fine line between what he had to do for the job and being as honest with her as he could for now, he stayed silent.

"I know how much you love your brothers, so that's good enough for me." She let out a sigh. "I think Nelson's spying for Ramon and my uncle."

Smart girl. "That's one possibility. Is there a reason you think that?"

"Yeah. Here's my problem. My uncle loaned me the money for my share of the bookstore. Now he's holding it over my head."

"How?" That problem was going to be solved soon, but he couldn't tell her that either.

"He wants me to launder money through the bookstore. I don't even know how that works. What really upsets me is that he doesn't seem to care about the risk to Lauren and me. We could go to prison, Alex."

"No, baby. Not ever going to happen." He pulled her to him.

"You can't know that."

Dammit. He did know it. "You said you trusted me. Do you mean it?" At her nod, he said, "Here's what we're going to do. Tell Lauren that you caught Nelson snooping, but you don't know why. That gives you a good reason to ban him from staying over. If she wants to see him away from the bookstore, that's her business." Not that she would be seeing him for long. He'd go down with the Alonzos.

"Good. I was going to talk to her today, anyway. And I already told Ramon I wasn't going to let him use the bookstore to wash his dirty money." She frowned. "Do they really wash the money?"

"I think if it's new bills they do." He had to be careful not to be too knowledgeable about all this. "Listen, you really need to stand firm with your uncle on that."

"I know. It's just that . . . he's always been intimidating, but I can't let him force me into risking everything. Ramon didn't take me seriously when I told him it wasn't going to happen."

"Then he's stupid. I sure wouldn't mess with you, Grasshopper." That earned him a smile, which went straight to his heart. He wanted to strip her of those sexy little boxers and pass the morning making love to her, but he needed to talk to her about her father. He hated to pile more on her, but since they were already having a heavy discussion, maybe now was better.

"I'm going to make us a pot of coffee," he said, pulling on his jeans. "There's something else we need to talk about." He leaned down, giving her a kiss, and when she slipped her hand around his neck, her fingers warm on his skin, he almost said to hell with talking.

She pushed him away. "Hurry back."

While he waited for the pot to brew, his phone buzzed, Court's name coming up. "Where are you?"

"Madison's." Alex peeked around the corner to make sure no one was in the hallway. "She thinks Lopez is spying for the Alonzos. She also said that her uncle wants her to launder money through the bookstore."

"Not surprised. If nothing else, we now know that if she's confiding in you, then she's not involved with them."

"I've always known it." Almost always, anyway. Maybe he wasn't sure in the beginning, but it hadn't taken him long to realize it.

"I'm glad you were right, little brother. Have you talked to her about her father?"

"About to do that."

"Good. I called to tell you Nate wants you to get her to let us into her father's study. See if we can turn anything up."

"I'll see what I can do." After hanging up, he headed back to Madison's room, eyeing Lauren's closed door. Was Lopez in there? He didn't like not knowing.

Shutting the door behind him, he held out a cup. "Here you go."

She took the cup from him. "Thank you, kind sir."

She sat on the bed, legs stretched out in front of her, and he settled next to her, stuffing a pillow behind his back. While he was gone, she'd dressed in what he thought of as her bookstore clothes—a blouse and pants—and he was sorry for that. It was probably for the best, though. Those little boxer panties messed with his concentration.

"I have about forty-five minutes before I have to go downstairs, and I want to catch Lauren before we open. What did you want to talk about?"

He leaned to the side so that their heads were touching, inhaling her lemony scent, wishing all their problems were dealt with and in the past. All he wanted to do was spend time with her when there were no lies between them, no investigation happening with her family, and no one spying on her. When this was all over, if she was still talking to him, he wanted to take her away for a few days. Just the two of them some-place romantic where they could talk about mundane things instead of drugs and all the other shit they were both dealing with.

"It's about your father."

She sucked in a breath, pulling away. "What about him?"

Already, her eyes were pooling with tears, and he'd give anything to not have to tell her. "After you told me it was a hit-and-run, I did a little investigating." He reached for her hand, enfolding it in his. "Did you ever read the police report or ask for details?"

She shook her head. "Uncle Jose and Ramon came to the house to tell us. The news was devastating, and my mom fell apart. Between my own grief and taking care of her, I never thought to ask. I just knew it was a hit-and-run when he was crossing the street."

"Who told you that?"

"Uncle Jose. Why?"

Tears rolled down her cheeks, and Alex wiped them away with his thumb. "Because he wasn't crossing the street. The accident investigator was able to pinpoint where he was on the sidewalk. He was several feet away from the pavement. There isn't proof, but the investigator concluded that the car aimed straight for him without trying to stop. There was also a traffic camera, but it was pointed down the street. All it picked up was a fast-moving dark car, could have been green, blue, or black. The license plate was missing, meaning someone removed it so no cameras would pick it up."

She gave a violent shake of her head. "No. No."

"I'm sorry, baby. Come here." She crawled onto his lap, and he held her while she cried. If he had to guess, she'd been too caught up in taking care of her mother to grieve properly. As her warm tears soaked his shoulder, he considered her uncle's reasons for hiding the truth from her. It could be as simple as protecting Madison and Angelina from knowing someone wanted Michael Parker dead. Or he didn't want them looking into it too closely, which Alex instinctively thought was the case. And how had the Alonzos known about the accident before Madison and her mother found out? The police would normally contact the next of kin, not their relatives. Another avenue to investigate.

"I drooled on you," Madison said, her voice muffled as her mouth was pressed against his shoulder.

He smiled into her hair. "Maybe you should give me a bath?"

She made a giggling, sobbing sound. "Men."

"Yeah, we make inappropriate comments at the worst times, but Mad?" He waited for her to look up at him. "About that bath?" As he'd hoped, she giggled. It was at that moment—when her beautiful green eyes were both teary and sparkling with amusement, and her fiery red hair curled around her face and down her shoulders like some kind of mythical goddess—that his chest ached with the knowledge that he loved her. Knowing that hurt, because his lies were going to tear them apart.

"How did you get the accident report?"

"It's public record. Anyone could have gotten it."

"I should have thought to do that."

"You were told it was a hit-and-run. Why would you question that? You were also grieving. I do wonder how your uncle knew about it before the police notified you." His theory was that her uncle or Ramon had somehow found out her father was writing a story about them and had ordered a hit.

"I don't know. I never thought about it." She leaned back, furrowing her brows. "Alex, I have to know what happened to him. An accident, I could . . . accept. Is that the right word? Is there a right word for losing your father?" She drew circles on his thigh. "But murder?" She looked up at him, her eyes glittering with rage. "I'm going to find the person who killed him."

"*We* are. Together. Okay?"

"Why? I mean, I'll take all the help I can get, but I don't even know exactly what you can do."

"As to the why, because I care about you, Madison. I want to help if this is important to you." He tucked a strand of hair behind her ear.

"It's maybe the most important thing I'll ever do."

"I know. As to how I can help, my brothers and I deal with a pretty rough crowd on a daily basis, men who know things most people don't. We've picked up a trick or two here and there. If you'll allow it, you'll have the Gentry brothers on your side."

"I don't know what to say except for thank you. Are you sure your brothers are okay with you volunteering them?"

"I'm sure. Do you know what your father was working on?"

"No. Like I told you, he was being very secretive. How can we find out?"

CHAPTER NINETEEN

"Nothing," Madison said after she'd searched her father's desk. "Either of you find anything?" The last thing Madison wanted was for her mother to know what they were up to, so she'd brought Alex and Court to her mother's house while Angelina was working at the bookstore.

"Nothing yet," Court said, his fingers flying over the keys of her father's computer.

"Nope." Alex lifted a painting, checking behind it. "Did you get a chance to talk to Lauren this morning?"

"I did and got a nice surprise. She broke up with Nelson. Before I could tell her about his spying, she told me that things had cooled between them, and she decided it was time to end it with him." She shrugged. "That's Lauren. She'll be in love with some other guy next week."

Court muttered something.

"Pardon?" Court shook his head, and she exchanged a glance with Alex. He shrugged, obviously no more clued in about what was going on between his brother and Lauren than she was. She wondered if Lauren's breaking up with Nelson had anything to do with Court, because the air definitely crackled whenever Court and Lauren were in the same room together. What she didn't understand was why they pretended to hate each other.

"Did you tell her about catching Lopez in your office?" Alex asked.

"No, not after finding out they'd broken up. Should I?"

"Probably best not to right now. She might decide to confront him. Better that he doesn't know we're on to him yet."

"That's what I thought." She looked around, wondering if her father had a secret hiding place. "Should we look for a loose floorboard or something?"

Alex laughed. "You read too many books."

Court gave an exasperated grunt. "I've tried all the common things he might have used as a password, like birthdates, but no go. Your dad have a pet name for you when you were little?"

"Yeah, he did. When I was really young, he called me his little snuggle bear. Why?"

"Just something else to try." His fingers moved over the keys, then he glanced up at Alex, and a message seemed to pass between them. "Can I take his computer with me? Work some more on it tonight?"

When she hesitated, Alex said, "You can trust him, Mad." He came and knelt in front of her, taking her hands in his. "Your father's computer is safe in his hands." He glanced at Court. "Excuse us a minute."

"Sure." Court set the laptop on the desk, then left.

Madison watched him go, marveling again at how much the brothers looked alike. But it was Alex who made her heart race when he focused those black eyes on her, the way he was doing now.

"With everything going on, we really haven't had a chance to talk about us," he said. He glanced around the office. "Maybe this isn't the best place to do it, or maybe it is because I think your father's spirit is here. From the moment I first saw you I wanted you in my bed. As I got to know you, I knew I wanted you in my life. What I'm saying is that I'm falling hard for you, Madison Parker."

"Alex—"

"Let me finish. Where you're concerned, I'll protect you at all costs, and that goes for my brothers, too. They know how I feel about you, and they know that they'll have to deal with me if they do anything to hurt you. Trust me, Mad. I'm on your side, and because I am, so are my brothers."

She wanted to, but she still had that feeling that there was more to him than what he showed her. Yet, she believed he did care for her, and if he was falling for her . . .

Alex squeezed her hands. "What's going on in that beautiful head of yours?"

Everything. If she was right, she was a member of a crime family, Lauren's boyfriend had spied on them, her father's death might have been a murder instead of a horrible accident, and, well, she could go on, but that was enough to start.

In spite of the questions she still had about Alex, there was one thing she knew, prayed that she knew. She leaned forward and kissed him. "I trust you," she whispered against his lips. And she did. Mostly.

"Thank you." He slipped his hand up to her shoulder, circling his fingers around the back of her neck and his thumb under her chin.

As he deepened the kiss, she cradled his cheek with her palm, his stubble a rough scrape against her skin. A sexy rumble sounded low in his throat, and heat crashed through her. She loved the taste of him, the scent of him, the feel of him.

He chuckled as he pulled away. "Another minute and we'll be rolling around on the floor."

"Alex," she said before he opened the door to let Court back in.

"Yeah?"

"I'm falling for you, too." It hadn't been easy to put that out there, making herself vulnerable to him, but the soft smile on his face and the way his eyes warmed reassured her.

He winked. "I know."

"Arrogant ass." She threw a pen at him, which he deftly caught, laughing.

Court left with her father's laptop, and she squeezed her fingernails into her palms to keep from ordering him to give it back, praying her trust in the Gentry brothers wasn't misplaced.

"Ready to go, Little Snuggle Bear?"

She laughed. "I should have known you'd grab on to that one, the way you like giving me pet names."

"That's not all I like giving you." He tucked her next to him.

"You're impossible, Biker Boy." She stuck her fingers into his back pocket as they walked out, leaving the office as they'd found it, minus the laptop in Court's possession.

Later that night, Madison stared at her window, waiting to hear Alex's signal even though he'd told her he wouldn't be coming. It was his night to close the bar, he'd told her, but his eyes had shifted away as he spoke, making her wonder if he was lying. She flipped onto her stomach, punching her fist into her pillow to make an indentation for her face. She'd said she trusted him, so she shut down her suspicions. Questioning his every move wasn't the kind of woman she wanted to be. Hemingway jumped on the bed and bumped his nose against her head.

"Hey, sweetie. You come to keep me company?" She wished Alex were here, but a warm, purring body was the next best thing.

Alex hated Ramon Alonzo, but maybe he hated Trina more. He hadn't decided yet. They had no shame, either one of them. At the moment, Trina was humping Ramon's leg, while her hand was down the man's unzipped jeans, going at it in Ramon's billiard room. Alex lined the cue stick up for his next shot, doing his best to ignore their grunting.

Once he had this last name, they would get their arrest warrants, and he couldn't wait. Supposedly, the deal was a big one. The dealer had called as they were leaving, postponing the meet for an hour, resulting in a bored Ramon and Trina, thus the porno show going on behind him.

All in a day's work, Heart Man, all in a day's work. True, but that didn't mean he had to like it. Give him badass biker gangs and Spider all day long over these two sickos.

"Yes! God, yes!"

Wishing he had earplugs to shut out Trina's screams, Alex hit the cue ball harder than he'd meant to, and sixteen billiard balls bounced around the table, not one of them falling into a side pocket. He straightened, set down the stick, and walked out of the room. At the end of the hallway, he took out his phone, stabbing Nate's number with his finger.

"I quit," he said when his brother answered. He scowled at the phone when Nate laughed. "Not funny, bro. These two morons make my skin crawl."

"Not much longer and you can have the satisfaction of slapping handcuffs on them. Rand phoned, said you hadn't left yet. I thought you were supposed to be at the meet right now."

"Postponed for an hour," he said, keeping an eye on the door to the billiard room. Rand Stevens and Taylor Collins were sitting in a car down the block from Ramon's house. Ramon had been secretive about where they were going, and Nate had decided to play it safe and have the two FBI agents tail them to the meet.

"We should be leaving soon. Meanwhile, Trina's humping Ramon's leg like a damn dog in heat and has her hand stuck down his pants. When I get home, I'm washing out my eyes with bleach."

"You just call to whine then?"

"Screw you." Ramon walked out, and Alex disconnected at the sound of more laughter from his brother.

"Who're you talking to, man?"

Stuffing his phone into his pocket, Alex headed down the hall toward Ramon. "My brother. He wanted to know what time he could expect me to drop off the money."

"The dude just called. We can head out."

"Great. Let's do this." Alex followed Ramon and Trina to Ramon's Hummer.

They pulled up in front of a warehouse surrounded by a chain-link fence. A large man with an AK-47 slung over his shoulder stepped out of the shadows, peered into the car, and opened the gate.

"Not liking being closed in like this. You ever been here before?" Alex said after they entered, the gate closing behind them. Even Trina seemed subdued, and that said something.

"Once." Ramon met his gaze in the rearview mirror. "Dude's a little weird, but he's cool."

A garage door opened, and another man with an AK-47 motioned for them to drive into the warehouse. "Not liking this at all," Alex muttered. He wished he were wired, but they'd decided that would be too risky, and the decision turned out to be a wise one.

After getting out of the car, they were ordered to turn around and put their hands on the roof of the car. With a weapon pointed at them by one of the guards, another frisked them. When the man found the gun in his boot, Alex said, "You take that away from me, dude, we're gonna have a problem." The big man stood, giving Alex a smirk. Understandable, since Alex's one handgun was no match for the AK-47 pointed at his chest.

"Long as it stays where it is, *dude*, we got no problem." He moved over to Trina, taking twice as long to frisk her, not that she seemed to mind.

Alex mentally rolled his eyes. A fruitcake had more sense than the woman. The man finished fondling her, moving on to frisk Ramon. The warehouse interior was dimly lit by one lightbulb hanging from a long wire directly overhead, making it difficult to see much past where they stood. Alex sensed they were being watched, though.

Once the guard was satisfied, he picked up the AK-47 he'd placed on the table before searching their bodies. The two gun-toting thugs stepped back behind the table, and from a door on the far wall, a man dressed as if he were on the way to a society ball walked out.

Before he could even see the man's face, Alex sensed power emitting from the dude. He was big, his long strides were assertive, his broad shoulders were posture perfect, and his chin was held high. Tinted glasses hid his eyes. He stopped just outside the circle of light that the weak bulb gave off.

The man's gaze traveled from Ramon, to Trina, and then to Alex, staying on him the longest. For the first time since he'd become an FBI agent, working undercover operations, Alex had the urge to squirm. Who the hell was this dude? The mystery man gave a slight nod to one of his men.

"He would like to view the merchandise," the bodyguard said.

The whole setup was meant to intimidate them, but Alex, feeling ornery, said, "And we'd like to see the money." That intense gaze focused back on him, but Alex refused to cower. Raising a brow, he stared right back at the man. There was something about him that reminded Alex of James Bond. It was his evening clothes, his arrogance, and his coolness. As much as Alex hated to admit it, the dude was pretty damn cool.

As if highly amused, the man lifted one side of his mouth in the slightest of smiles. He snapped his fingers. From the same door, another man walked out, carrying a silver briefcase. He brought it to the table, opening it. James Bond gave another nod, this one directed at Alex.

"Check it out, Trina," Alex said, refusing to take the bait. It was obvious by now that Bond wasn't going to talk. Alex watched as Trina fanned the packs of bills, ignoring the piercing glares coming from Ramon. If Alex had to guess, Ramon was afraid of pissing off James Bond. Too bad.

Trina closed the briefcase. "Good to go." She flashed Bond a sultry smile. "I'm Trina. It's a pleasure to meet you, Mr. . . ."

The man bowed, putting his hand over his heart. He nodded to one of his guards.

"Mr. X," the guard said.

Mr. X? There were rumors of a big-time dealer everyone called Mr. X who operated out of Atlanta. The word was that he controlled the state of Georgia, and if the stories were to be believed, he was looking to expand his operation into Florida. If this was the same man, his being here gave credibility to the rumor. No agency, state or federal, had been able to put a name to him. And if it was the same man, and they were able to take him down, their boss and several bosses above him were going to be very happy.

Damn, Alex couldn't wait to tell his brothers. He eyed Mr. X. The dude was smooth. He kept his features hidden by the tinted glasses and the shadows, no voice to identify, and no name. And if Alex wasn't mistaken, the man was wearing an expensive wig. Taylor and Rand would follow him when he left, hopefully learning who he was.

The guard who'd been doing all the talking pointed to the table. "The merchandise."

Alex opened the back door of Ramon's car. When both guards aimed their AK-47s at him, he paused. "The bags are in the backseat." One guard nodded, but both kept their weapons on him. He grabbed the two large totes, handing them to Ramon.

Why hadn't X simply had one of his men do the deal? Why risk any of them even knowing he existed? Ego? Did he enjoy toying with them? Or maybe he didn't trust his men with the amount of money and merchandise involved in this deal.

As one of the guards used a kit to test the heroin, Alex kept his gaze pinned on X, memorizing everything he could about the man—mannerisms, build, height, weight. Were his shoulders made broader by pads? Maybe.

Once the heroin was deemed acceptable, X nodded to one of the guards, who picked up the heavy totes with the heroin. X then tipped his hat before walking away, the guard at his side.

"You can go now," the remaining guard said, motioning at their car with his AK-47.

♥ ♥ ♥

Court stacked the packs of money from the briefcase on the table. "Six hundred thousand to the penny."

Alex eyed the money. "Anyone want to go on a shopping spree?" They'd closed up the bar before gathering at their favorite after-hours table, each with a beer.

Court snorted. "Sure. I could use a few new shirts."

"If you're going to go to the dark side, have a better reason than new shirts," Nate said. "Go back over everything again."

Alex set down his bottle, twirling it in a circle. "Do you want me to start with Trina humping Ramon's leg?" He narrowed his eyes at Nate. "Oh, right, I did tell you about that. You laughed. You should be more sympathetic to your poor baby brother's sensibilities."

"If you're angling for hazard pay, forget it." Nate smirked. "I could probably arrange for trauma counseling."

"She didn't," Court said, grinning.

"Oh yeah, she did. I'm gonna have nightmares for a month." He gave an exaggerated shudder. "Let's just skip to us arriving at the warehouse." After relating the events of the night, he said, "X seemed to treat the whole thing as a game. The word that comes to mind is *arrogant*. Do you think he's *the* Mr. X we've been hearing about?"

"If he is, and we manage to arrest him, even the director is going to know your name," Nate said. "Rand and Taylor will report in as soon as they see where he goes."

Alex couldn't care less if the top boss knew who he was. "As long as we keep an eye on the heroin. I don't like that much being out of our sight." He wanted this operation over and done with. Although they had no choice but to allow drug deals to happen during an operation, he hated that he played any part in letting that shit hit the streets.

Nate's phone buzzed, and Alex listened as his brother talked to Taylor. "I'll notify Rothmire," Nate said. "Hopefully our SWAT team will get there before they take off. If not, shoot the plane's tires out, but don't approach. They're heavily armed. Stay safe, and you and Rand come to my place as soon as you can. We'll regroup."

"Plane?" Alex cocked a brow.

Nate nodded. "Stand by. I need to call Rothmire."

Rand Stevens leaned his head back on the sofa, closing his eyes on a sigh. "Long night, huh?"

"Truth." And Alex was ready for it to be over. The other four agents around Nate's living room seemed to be as tired as he was, if the way they slouched in their seats was any indication. Considering it was three in the morning, no surprise they were beat.

His gaze rested on Taylor, his curiosity caught by the way her eyes turned soft whenever she looked at Nate. She was a beautiful woman, one who, as far as he knew, had no man in her life. He caught the moment Nate met her gaze, and he could almost feel the electricity crackling between them. She blushed, suddenly seeming to find the arm of her chair fascinating. If Alex wasn't mistaken, that was longing shimmering in his brother's eyes, and wasn't that interesting?

"SWAT got there about five minutes after we shot out the Lear's tires," Taylor said. "They had the plane surrounded and were trying to talk our suspects out when we left."

Rand peeked open an eye. "Rothmire's on the scene. He said he'd call when he had something to tell us."

Just then, Nate's phone buzzed. "Rothmire," Nate said, eyeing the screen. They all fell silent, waiting to hear the news. He listened for a few minutes, then his gaze fell on Alex. "I'll tell him."

"Tell me what?" Alex said when Nate disconnected.

"That a commendation letter is going in your file. Because of your investigation, we just took down Anatoly Gorelova, a man the Russians call the Ghost. The Ghost is wanted by half the countries in the world, but no one knew who he was. There's not much he's not involved in, from drugs, to arms dealing, to assassinations."

Stunned, Alex stared at Nate. "Holy shit." Suddenly energized, he sat up. He was actually glad he hadn't known who Mr. X was when the deal went down. While he'd like to think he could handle anything that came his way, dealing with one of the world's most wanted on his first lead case might have tested his ability to stay cool. But damn, this would probably be the biggest arrest of his career, and he couldn't help the smile that crossed his face.

Court reached over and slapped him on the back. "Way to go, baby brother. You'll be a legend now."

Not something he'd aspired to. He'd just been doing his job, but he'd never been more proud to be an FBI agent than he was this night. "I'm surprised he's talking already."

Nate shook his head. "He's not. He lawyered up immediately. One of his men is talking in return for a deal." He grinned. "Good job, Alex. Damn good job."

The other agents in the room echoed Nate's praise, but it was his big brother's approval that meant the most.

"The bad guys better watch out for the Ghostbuster," Court said, making everyone laugh.

When the conversation quieted, Nate glanced at Taylor. "One last thing we need to talk about before we can hit the sack. Update us on your interview with Michael Parker's editor."

She straightened in her seat. "The editor's name is Jack Candor. He doesn't know what Parker was working on, only that Parker told him the story would merit a front-page headline. Parker did make one comment that caused Candor to wonder if the story was hitting close to home. Parker said, and this is a direct quote from Candor, 'I just hope when the story breaks that I don't end up in divorce court.'"

From what Alex knew of Madison's mother, there was only one thing that could refer to. "He was investigating the Alonzos. Madison mentioned that she's worried about how close her mother is to her twin brother. If Jose or Ramon had anything to do with the hit-and-run, that's going to crush her . . . Angelina, I mean. I think Madison wouldn't at all mind seeing handcuffs on those two." That was his hope, anyway.

Court stood. "I need my bed. There's some stuff I want to do a search on, but tomorrow when it doesn't feel like I have a pound of sand in my eyes." At the door, he gave a wave over his shoulder. "Night, Ghostbuster."

"Night." And what a night it had been. Alex was still reeling from the revelation that he'd accidently helped to take down one of the world's most wanted.

Rand was the next to leave, and Alex followed him out. If it wasn't so late, he'd go straight to Madison's, but he doubted she'd appreciate him tapping on her window at this hour. Too bad, because he was now feeling like the Energizer Bunny, ready to go again and again.

As he walked out Nate's door, he glanced back to see his brother put a hand on Taylor's arm as she slipped her purse over her shoulder. Alex smiled to himself. He'd not seen that one coming. What was up with his brothers and the women they pretended not to care about?

CHAPTER TWENTY

Madison dropped her clothes in the hamper before stepping into the shower. She and Lauren had spent a few hours after closing reorganizing the stockroom, and she was dirty and sweaty. Alex had texted, saying he was on the way over. She poured shampoo into the palm of her hand and lathered her hair.

A soft knock sounded on the bathroom door right before it opened, and Alex poked his head around the doorframe. "Don't scream, Mad. I'm coming in."

She watched through the glass as he quickly stripped, then stepped into the shower with a wicked grin on his face. Her gaze roamed over his muscular body, finally understanding why women in romance novels licked their lips at the sight of their man naked.

"I missed you last night," she said.

He put his hands on her waist and turned her. "Bet I missed you more, thus the reason I'm here in your shower with you."

She moaned when he massaged her head. "That feels good. How'd you get in? Not that I'm complaining."

"Lauren let me in. Put your head under the water so I can rinse the shampoo out."

A man had never washed her hair before. Actually, she'd never bathed with a man before. It was sexy, and apparently he thought so, too, because he pressed against her back, letting her know he was aroused.

"Did I mention that I missed you?" He poured body soap onto his hands.

"I think I remember you saying something like that." With his slick hands gliding over her body, she wasn't sure what she remembered. His fingers brushed across her breasts, raising goose bumps on her skin where he touched her. She leaned her head back on his shoulder again, closing her eyes as his hands roamed over her body, sending a burning need through her. He flattened his palm on her belly, pulling her tight to him.

"I love how warm and soft you feel, Mad." He angled his head, finding her mouth with his.

With one hand, he toyed with her breasts, teasing her nipples to hard pebbles, while the hand he had on her stomach inched lower. When his fingers slid into her sex, she moaned, getting an answering growl from him. Their tongues tangled as he stroked her with clever fingers.

"Alex," she whispered, as desire so sharp that it bordered on exquisite pain spiraled through her.

"Come for me, baby."

As if her body was his to command, her core muscles squeezed around his fingers, and pleasure raced through her. Her knees buckled, refusing to do their job of holding her up, but Alex was there to catch her. His mouth trailed down to her neck, and she felt him smile against her skin. He was damn pleased with himself, but she couldn't fault him for it. Still struggling to get air back into her lungs, she was pushed against the tile, his large body covering hers.

"I'll die right here in your shower if I'm not in you this minute," he said, then sucked on her earlobe.

"Yes, please." Else she might die right along beside him.

"Don't move." He opened the shower door, bent down, and picked up a condom from the floor.

"Pretty sure of yourself," she teased.

Black eyes smoldering with heat pierced hers. "Hoping."

"Put that on and come here."

A wicked grin curved his lips. "Yes, ma'am."

She watched as he unrolled the condom, and when he was sheathed, he stood still for a moment as his gaze roamed over her.

"You have no idea how beautiful you are, Madison." He lifted a finger and trailed it down the valley of her breasts. "All that beautiful red hair, wet and curling down your back, the drops of water snaking down your body, making your skin glisten . . ." He thumped a fist over his heart. "You slay me right here."

Was it possible for a person to melt? "I think you're beautiful, too." And, God, he was. She wanted to lick up every pearl of water dripping down his perfectly sculpted body. His mouth softened into a smile that made her heart flutter.

He pressed against her, staring down at her. "Let me love you, beautiful girl."

She nodded.

"Thank you," he whispered. He wrapped his hands around her upper arms, made a slow slide of his palms down to her hands, and laced their fingers together. The next second, he had her arms lifted over her head, held there by his hard grip.

She sucked in a breath when he took himself in hand and probed her entrance, then made a slow slide up and down her sex. "Want," she said. "Please, Alex."

He rested his forehead against hers, letting out a breath that blew warm on her cheeks. "I can't decide whether to make love to you hard or slow and easy. You decide."

"Both."

He laughed. "I might be good, but I'm not that good. Let's go for hard now, then slow and easy the rest of the night. That work for you?"

She nodded.

"Have I made you speechless, Grasshopper?" Without giving her a chance to answer, he plunged into her.

Madison gasped. The way he filled her, the way he wrapped his big body around hers, making her feel like there was nowhere else she belonged but with him, was like nothing she'd ever felt before. "Not speechless. Touch me. Touch me everywhere."

"Christ, Mad, I can do that."

And he did. While he kept her arms captive above her head with the strength of one hand, his other hand explored and caressed her breasts, her stomach, her thighs, and finally, came to rest on her bottom, where he dug his fingers into her skin. Because her hands were held against the tile, and because he'd brought her to a crazed state like he was so talented at doing, she lifted a leg and wrapped it around his thigh, trying to climb him.

"Madison. Damn," he gasped with his mouth pressed against her ear. He let go of her hands and pulled both of her legs around him so that the only thing holding her up was his body and the wall behind her.

"Now, baby. Now." His mouth crashed down on hers, his tongue tangling with hers when she parted her lips on a gasp as he thrust into her in a frenzy, their bodies slapping together.

Pinned between Alex and the wall, she could do little more than hold on to him. He lowered his mouth to a nipple, sucking it, then nipping it with his teeth. The water rained down on them, making their overheated bodies slick, and she scraped her teeth across his neck. She curled her fingers into his hair and pulled. "Alex."

"Hell, yes," he said, his voice raw and rumbling.

Pleasure blazed a burning fire through her, every nerve ending in her body sensitive to his touch, to the water sluicing down her skin, and she screamed his name as he thrust deep into her. Her heart slammed against her chest, robbing her of breath and vision. His body, a coiled mass of muscles, stilled, and he buried his face against her neck as a great shudder rolled through him. She closed her eyes, loving how he filled her.

"Breathe," she whispered.

He laughed. "I don't think I can." He lifted his head, looked searchingly at her for a moment, and then kissed her.

"I love you, Alex," she whispered against his lips. The words had slipped out, leaving her mind as soon as she thought them, surprising her.

Alex froze as the words he wasn't ready to hear echoed around them. How could she love him? She didn't know him. The man she thought she loved wasn't real. He wanted her to love him with a need that ran so deep he wasn't sure where it ended. But he wanted to hear her say those words when she knew the real him.

The happiness that had been shining in her eyes waned as the seconds ticked by and he didn't respond. He had to say something, but his mind had gone blank.

"I didn't say that so you'd say it back." She smiled but it didn't reach her eyes. "Actually, I didn't mean to say it at all, so don't stress over it, okay?"

He brushed her damp hair away from her face. "Okay, I won't." And he'd just piled another lie on top of the others because he was definitely stressing over it. "It's late, beautiful girl. Let's get some sleep."

If she only knew what was in his heart, she wouldn't be looking at him with those wounded eyes. He dried her off, then himself, the silence between them killing him. Once in bed, she turned her back to him, and he pulled her against his chest, holding her as he called himself every name in the book.

I love you, too, Grasshopper. But it would be wrong to tell her when the words would come from a man she didn't truly know. Soon he would arrest her uncle and cousin, and she would learn that he'd been lying to her from day one. She would see it as a betrayal, and it would be.

The only right thing to do was to let her go. What was the saying? If you love someone, let them go and hope they come back? That wasn't right. Hell, he couldn't remember, but he had to do it for her.

If she would let him, after everything was over, he would try to explain the reasons for his lies, and if he were a very lucky man, she would agree to start over. Whatever her decision, it would be her choice. If he lost her, he would only have himself to blame.

Alex stayed awake long into the night, holding his girl, memorizing her scent, how she felt in his arms, and how her silky hair tickled his chin. Although he wanted to sneak out like a coward so he wouldn't have to see her tears when he told her he wouldn't be back, he stayed. Would she cry? If she did, he might confess everything.

At dawn, he crept out of bed and quietly dressed. He sat in a chair for the next two hours, watching her sleep. She was on her stomach, her small hands disappearing under the pillow, and one beautiful leg outside of the covers.

Just go back to bed and hold her like you want to. She'll learn who you are soon enough. Alex crushed the voice, although he wanted to be selfish and do just that. It was because he loved her that he refused to listen.

She pulled a hand out from under her pillow and, even in sleep, reached for him on his side of the bed. *His side.* Would he ever sleep beside her again? He rubbed his chest. Damn ache.

"Alex?"

Her voice was soft with sleep, and sexy as hell. "I'm here." He gripped the arms of the chair to keep from going to her.

She sat up, her hair falling messily over her shoulder, also sexy. "You're dressed. Did I oversleep?"

He'd never hated himself more than he did at this moment. "Madison—"

"If you're dressed, I guess you need to leave early? You have time for breakfast? I'll go start the coffee."

"Madison, no coffee. I need you to listen for a minute."

"Okay." Those green eyes that he loved turned wary, and she sat back against her pillow, pulling the sheet up, covering her beautiful breasts.

Any other time, he would have smiled, even teased her about her modesty. She was everything he dreamed of finding someday—beautiful, kind, funny, intelligent. He cleared his throat, swallowing the lump that had lodged there.

"Ahem . . . I've been thinking." He scrubbed a hand over the stubble on his chin. Christ, he hated this, for both of them. For a brief second, he almost gave in to the voice that said he didn't have to do this. He could take what he wanted and gamble that she would understand when she learned the truth.

Love had ambushed him when he least expected it, and as he sat there while the woman he would die for chewed on her bottom lip, waiting for him to speak, he accepted that he had to do the right thing. This being-in-love shit sucked. It hurt.

Blinking against the burning in his eyes, he leaned his elbows on his knees and stared down at the floor. "Yeah, well, I think things are moving too fast between us, and we should step back. You know, take a break for a while." Her face paled, and he gritted his teeth to keep from telling her everything.

"I thought . . ." She shook her head. "I guess it doesn't matter what I thought."

"I'm more sorry than you can possibly know."

"Don't. I don't want to hear it. Just go, Alex." She turned her face away.

He stood, wanting to take back everything he'd said, but he reminded himself he was doing this for her. If they had a chance for a future together, it had to be when she fell in love with the real Alex Gentry. Not that he believed he'd get another chance.

At the door, he paused, turned to look at her, and hated himself for hurting her.

"Just so you know, I take it back," Madison said when Alex hesitated at the door. She forced her eyes to meet his. "I don't love you." She didn't care if that made him flinch. "In fact, as far as I'm concerned, you can go to hell."

"That's entirely possible. I'm sorry."

It took every ounce of willpower, but she managed not to shed a tear in front of him. Not one damn tear. As soon as the door closed behind him, her lips trembled uncontrollably and the water pooling in her eyes overflowed. How had she been so wrong about him?

She buried her face into her pillow, realizing too late he'd left his scent there. The dam broke as she remembered the beautiful night before, when she thought he might be falling in love with her. There'd been such warmth and tenderness in his eyes as he'd stared down at her, but it'd all been a lie. She shouldn't have told him she loved him. No, she was glad she had. Apparently, he hadn't wanted to hear her damn love declaration, so now she knew she meant nothing to him. Better to learn that sooner rather than later.

The horrible ache in her heart made her wish she'd never met him. Her life had been just fine before Alex walked into it, and now she was crying her eyes out because of a lying jerk. She jumped out of bed, stripping the sheets from the mattress and dumping them next to the door before getting in the shower and scrubbing herself raw to wash his smell from her body.

"Good-bye, Alex," she whispered as the water and soap carried his scent down the drain. Fresh tears came when she could no longer smell him on her skin, and she let them flow. She would do her crying, and then she would forget about him. She swore it.

Once dressed for the day, her tears buried along with her aching heart in a deep hole, she headed to the kitchen for a much-needed cup of coffee, which she just might inject directly into her veins. And if there were a pill for wiping a man from her memory, she'd add that to the mix.

She wasn't kidding herself. There would be more tears, more questions about how she'd fallen so quickly for a man she should have run from the minute she saw him. He was a friend of her cousin's after all, and that should have been a gigantic red flag. Well, it had been, but she'd chosen to ignore it, so more fool her.

"I'm done with you, Alex," she muttered, bringing that first sip of coffee to her lips. Yes, there would be more tears over him in the late hours of the night, but she was determined to be done with him.

"Who're you talking to?"

Madison choked on the coffee going down her throat. "Dammit, Lauren. You scared me."

"Why? I do live here. And I do walk into this kitchen every morning."

Madison blinked, trying to hide her tears from her roommate. "Alex doesn't love me." The words slipped out along with her sobs. "He's not . . . not coming back."

"Oh, sweetie."

Madison sank into the arms Lauren wrapped around her. "I was so stupid to fall in love with him."

"The Gentry brothers have a way of making you do that."

Well, one in particular sure had that talent. She lifted her head from Lauren's shoulder. "That's an odd thing for you to say. Care to explain?"

Lauren's gaze shifted away. "Not really."

There was pain in her friend's eyes. Her own heartbreak put aside for the moment, she said, "Yes, really. What's the deal with you and Court?"

"I know him, all right?"

"I don't understand what that means."

Lauren poured coffee into a cup and then turned to leave.

"Lauren?"

At the door, her best friend paused. "I met him a few years ago," she said, not looking back as she left.

"How do I not know that?" Madison said, but Lauren disappeared down the hall without answering.

Hemingway rolled over, his body following the slash of sun on the floor that came in from the kitchen window.

Madison eyed the black cat. "Hemingway, you're the only male I'll ever say I love you to again. Go ahead. Say you're honored."

Hemingway snored on, apparently not impressed.

CHAPTER TWENTY-ONE

"Madison thinks I've abandoned her," Alex said, wearing a path across Nate's floor. Every day—morning, noon, and night—since he'd walked out, he'd had to stop himself from calling her, telling her that he was the world's biggest idiot.

"But you haven't. She'll know that soon enough." Nate set his phone on the coffee table. "That was Rothmire. He's preparing the search warrants on the Alonzos. We should have them by tomorrow afternoon."

So she'd know the truth then. She still wasn't going to forgive him. He had to do something. Get out and go somewhere. Anywhere. Ride his bike to hell and back. That would work. As long as there was air he could breathe because there sure as hell wasn't any in Nate's damn condo.

"Where you going?" Nate asked.

"Don't know. Just have to get out of here."

Court looked up from his laptop. "Want me to come with you? We can get some lunch or something."

"Some other time." As much as he loved his brothers, he needed to be miserable alone. In the underground garage, he grabbed his helmet out of the storage bin.

After a long ride up the beach highway, trying to clear his head, he gave up. All he could see was the way Madison's lips had quivered when he'd walked out on her. Had she cried after he left? Had she convinced herself that she hated him during the following days?

He turned the bike back toward home, but when he reached his building, he rode past, ending up at Ramon's. The high from catching one of the most wanted men in the world had worn off, paling beside the thought of losing Madison.

The housekeeper let him in, telling him Ramon was in the pool out back. Alex headed that way. He wanted to see the bastard one last time while the dude thought he was on top of the world. Watch him brag about the big deal he'd set up while knowing that the man was going down. The operation shouldn't have turned personal, but it had. He didn't really care.

"Mr. Gentry, a moment of your time, please."

Alex paused at hearing Jose Alonzo's voice. He stepped inside the man's office. "Mr. Alonzo." The man had never given him more than a brief nod before, so this was an interesting turn of events.

"Have a seat." Alonzo gestured to a chair in front of his desk. He leaned back, steepled his fingers under his chin, and stared at Alex.

If he was supposed to be intimidated, it wasn't working. Alex stared back, waiting to hear why he'd been summoned.

"Ramon tells me that you are proving to be useful, and for that you have my appreciation."

"The association is beneficial to my brothers and me," Alex said.

"Of course, and you have the perfect setup to accommodate our needs. Perhaps at a later date we will discuss how to expand into other areas."

Alonzo's gaze flicked to a photo on a nearby shelf, one of Ramon, Angelina, Madison, and him, taken on the beach, probably the one only steps away. "I love my family, Mr. Gentry, and only want what is best for them." He turned cold eyes back to Alex. "You are not what is best for my niece. There is no insult intended, but you must agree that she deserves better than a part owner of a biker bar, a man who associates with the scum of society."

Present company excluded, of course. Alex counted to twenty the way Nate had taught him to do when as a boy he couldn't see past his rage. He badly wanted to ask if the old man thought it was okay for Ramon to assault his cousin, but he bit back the words. By this time tomorrow, the Alonzos would be in handcuffs. He would take his satisfaction from that.

"Madison's an adult, an intelligent woman. I believe she is capable of deciding who is worthy of her attentions. I will, however, consider your feelings on the matter, sir."

So Madison hadn't told anyone they'd broken up? If she'd told her mother, then surely Jose would have been informed. The rage still burned low in his belly, though. If the man was so concerned about his niece, then he should be worried about protecting her from his own son, not Alex.

"I trust you will make the right decision on the matter, Mr. Gentry." He stood. "I believe you were on your way to see Ramon. Don't let me keep you."

Dismissed, Alex gave a curt nod before walking out. Instead of heading for the pool, he turned for the front door. He'd had enough of the Alonzos for one day. Back on his bike, he drove straight to the gym, found a punching bag, and did his best to kill it.

Hours later, Alex sat at the bar in Aces & Eights, spoiling for a fight. "You'd think the room was filled with a bunch of nuns the way they're all getting along tonight," he grumbled.

Nate tightened the band on his ponytail as he scanned the room. "The night's not over. If you want a fight that bad, go start one."

Tempting. He shrugged. "I think I'll just bug out instead. You and Court can manage a few more hours without me."

"Are you in love with Madison, baby brother?"

"For what good it'll do me, yeah. She's going to hate me, already hates me." He missed her. There was a hole in his heart that made it hard to breathe when he thought of her, which was every minute of every day.

Nate leaned against the bar, crossing his arms over his chest. "This will be over tomorrow, then you can start winning your girl back."

If it was possible to win her back. "Someone sitting on Lopez?"

"Yeah, Rothmire's got a couple of detectives watching him. They'll pick him up in the morning at the same time we take the Alonzos down."

"I want to know why he was snooping in the bookstore's files."

"We'll get that answered soon enough." Nate narrowed his eyes, his gaze on the door. "That fight you've been itching for just walked in the door."

Alex glanced over to see who'd come in. He smiled at seeing Dirty Dan. "He still banned?"

"Yep."

Cracking his knuckles, he stood. "Just what the doctor ordered."

A little before dawn, Madison used her mother's key to let herself in to her uncle's house. She hurried to the alarm and entered the code that she hoped hadn't changed since the last time she'd used it. Familiar with the layout, she headed for Ramon's office with only the moonlight coming in through the windows lighting her way. If she couldn't find what she was looking for there, she'd have to search her uncle's office.

After Alex had left, she'd had trouble sleeping. She'd even put the sheets with his scent back on the bed, hoping that would help. It hadn't. Between the deep ache in her heart from missing him and the questions about her father, she was a hot mess. Since Alex wasn't around any longer to help her investigate her father's death, she'd just have to go it alone.

One comment Alex had made had preyed on her mind during those sleepless nights. How had her uncle and cousin known about the accident so fast? The police wouldn't have contacted them first. And why hadn't her father wanted to discuss the story he was working on? The only reason she could think of was that he'd somehow found out about their criminal activities and planned to expose them.

There was no more honorable man than her father had been. That the Alonzos were family wouldn't have stopped him from writing the story, and it would explain why he hadn't talked about it. She was her father's daughter, and she owed it to him to find the truth. If her suspicions were right, she would see that his story was told.

She'd decided the best time to search would be early in the morning when she was sure her cousin and uncle would be asleep. She crept into Ramon's office, closed the door, and turned on a lamp. Where to start? She moved to his desk, easing down onto the chair. The middle drawer was a mess of pens, pencils, paperclips, and sticky notepads, and she resisted the urge to organize everything. In the next drawer, she found a box half full of cigars, a stapler, a roll of stamps, and several pairs of eyeglasses.

"Didn't know you wore reading glasses, cuz," she murmured, holding one up and peering through the lenses.

The bottom drawer, big enough to hold files, was locked, but she'd seen a key in the mess of pens and pencils. It fit, and she pulled the drawer open. All the folders had tabs, and she flipped through them.

"What's this?" she said, seeing a tab with her father's name on it. The only thing in the folder was an envelope with her dad's initials on the front. It wasn't sealed, and she frowned when she looked inside. Why would Ramon have a thumb drive that she recognized as one of the green logoed ones she'd given her father for Christmas? Was this the proof she needed?

Unease slithered through her as she turned on Ramon's computer, slipping the thumb drive in. Her eyes scanned the document, which she recognized as a draft of one of her father's investigative reports. After reading Michael Parker's investigation into Jose and Ramon Alonzo's illegal activities, Madison sat back in the chair, her heart pounding. It wasn't proof that her own family members had either killed or ordered her father killed. That the thumb drive—one her father would never have let out of his sight—was in Ramon's possession was as damning as it got, though.

How could they do such a horrible thing? Tears streamed down her cheeks as she thought of her beloved father. If it turned out to be true, it would devastate her mother. Hell, it was devastating her. She remembered a conversation she'd overhead between her parents a few days before he died.

"Is there anything I could ever do to make you stop loving me, Angie?"

Her mother had laughed. "Of course not, silly man. You are my heart."

Had her father been thinking of the story he'd written when he'd asked that question? Madison angrily swiped at her tears. She had to get out of here before she did something stupid, like demand answers from her cousin. The thumb drive seemed hot and heavy in her hand, as if it might burn right through her skin.

She had two choices. Go straight to the police or go to her father's editor. Convince him to run the story with her father's byline. Would that be sufficient for the police to open an investigation into her father's death? She needed time to calm down and think.

"What the hell, Madison?"

She jerked her gaze up to see Ramon standing in the doorway, his hair on end, wearing nothing but a pair of boxers. *Shit. Shit. Shit.* She palmed the thumb drive, and tried to delete the document still up on the screen, but Ramon was on her too fast.

His eyes darted to the monitor, then to her. "Little girls shouldn't be nosing into things that are none of their business, cousin." His grip on her wrist tightened, and he pulled her toward the door.

"I'm not going anywhere with you." She tried to pull her arm away, but he dug his fingers into her skin, causing her to whimper.

"I didn't offer you a choice."

"You're hurting me." There was no warmth in her cousin's eyes, no affection for her on the face of a man who had lost his soul. He scared the living hell out of her. She still held the thumb drive—her evidence—tight in her palm, and, not wanting to drop it, she kept her hand fisted. But she wasn't going without a fight, so she lowered her face and clamped her teeth down on the flesh of Ramon's upper arm, while aiming for his shin with the heel of her shoe the way Alex had taught her.

"Bitch," he snarled. "You're going to pay for that."

When he let go of her wrist, she took advantage of her freedom to run for the door. She'd made it halfway down the hallway when Ramon grabbed her hair, yanking her to a stop. Tears stung her eyes, both from the pain radiating down her skull, where he twisted her hair hard around his hand, and from the defeat sinking into her heart. He walked past her, dragging her along behind him. She shoved the thumb drive into the pocket of her shorts and then grabbed on to his arm, trying to ease the pull on her hair.

"Stop it, Ramon! You're acting crazy."

Ignoring her, he kept dragging her, forcing her to bend over and stumble sideways. If she'd had any doubt that he'd had a hand in her father's death, the cruel hands of her cousin vanquished it.

"FBI! Open up."

Ramon froze. "Fuck." He turned back the way they came, not letting go of her hair. "Did you call them, Madison?"

The door burst open before she could answer, and she heard the pounding of feet and the yell of men's voices as Ramon dragged her back into the office, kicking the door closed behind them.

He pushed her against the wall, lowering his face to within inches of hers, his eyes blazing with fury. "Did you?"

"No. I swear it."

Cursing, he jerked her around, snaked his arm around her throat, and backed up to the bookcase. From a humidor, he pulled out a gun, putting it to her head. With his arm squeezing her throat, and the barrel of the gun digging into her skull, Madison feared this was the day she would die.

CHAPTER
TWENTY-TWO

Because he knew the layout of the Alonzos' house, Alex was the first in. Movement in the hallway caught his attention, and his heart stuttered painful beats. He would know that flash of red hair anywhere.

"Ramon's got Madison," he growled.

"You sure?" Nate said from beside him.

"Yes. Jose's bedroom is up there, second door on the left." He lifted his chin toward the stairs. "Court, you take some men and get him. Nate, just you and me are going after Ramon. We go busting in there, guns blazing, God knows what he'll do." As Court and a handful of men made their way up the stairs, Alex told Rand and Taylor to split the remaining agents between them and start searching the house.

"I don't know if the housekeeper's a live-in or not. Her name's Mrs. Gutierrez if you run across her." He forced himself to do his job as lead on this operation instead of racing down the hallway and killing Ramon for touching Madison.

When he reached the door to Ramon's office, he glanced at his older brother. "If he hurts her, I'm going to kill him."

Nate put a hand on his shoulder. "Understood, baby brother."

"Let's do this," Alex said. He flattened himself against the wall on one side of the door, while Nate did the same on the other. Because he worried about Madison's reaction to hearing his voice, Alex used his mimicking skills to make his voice sound like Rand's.

"Ramon Alonzo, it's the FBI. We have a warrant for your arrest. Come out with your hands on your head." When there was no response, he chanced turning the knob, pushing the door open. Peering around the doorjamb, his blood turned to ice at seeing Madison held against Ramon with a gun at her head.

"He's got a gun on Madison," he whispered. What the hell was she doing at Ramon's at this time of the morning? "Give it up, Ramon. You're not getting out of here."

"Back away from the door, and I'll come out."

Nate shook his head, and Alex gave a nod that he understood they couldn't let Ramon control the situation. A commotion sounded from the living room, and he heard Jose Alonzo demanding a lawyer.

"Papa!" Ramon yelled.

The team pushed Jose out the front door, and it got quiet again. Rand and Taylor came down the hall, stopping a few feet away. Nate backed up to them, quietly bringing them up to speed. When Nate returned to his position, he nodded, and Alex slipped around the doorway, Nate at his back, both their weapons pointed at Ramon.

"Drop your gun," Alex ordered, still using Rand's voice. Madison furrowed her brow, giving him a hard look. Although he wore a black ski mask, he saw the recognition hit as she stared into his eyes. He gave a slight shake of his head when she opened her mouth. Ramon would probably go crazy if he realized the man he'd thought was his friend was actually FBI.

She pressed her lips together, and the betrayal in her eyes was a punch to his gut. But he'd expected it, thought he was prepared for it. There was so much fury in her expression that he wasn't even sure she remembered there was a gun to her head. Whether she would ever forgive him didn't matter at the moment. Getting her to safety was all he could allow himself to think about.

Alex took another step into the room. "You're not getting out of this. Lower your gun to the floor, nice and easy." He kept his gaze on Ramon. "Do it now."

"Hell no." Ramon held Madison in front of him, his finger on the trigger of the gun. "Unless you want to see her dead, you'll get out of my house."

"You pull that trigger, man, it'll be the last thing you ever do."

Ramon turned the gun on Alex, and the minute he did, Madison kicked his shin just the way he'd taught her, and then fell to the floor.

That's it, Grasshopper, Alex thought right before Ramon pulled the trigger, the sonofabitch shooting him above the edge of his Kevlar vest. A weapon fired next to his ear, and a second later, blood colored Ramon's chest red.

"Good shot, bro," Alex muttered before crumbling to the floor.

"Alex!"

That was Madison's voice, and she sounded worried. Did that mean she forgave him? When he felt her hands touch his face, he tried to reach for her, but he couldn't see her. Had someone turned out the lights?

"Alex," Madison pleaded, tears streaming down her face as she crawled to him. She pulled off his ski mask, searching his face for any sign of life. She'd known those eyes almost from the minute he'd walked into the room, dressed in black with the FBI letters on his vest. All she could think while standing there with a gun stuck to her head was that Alex had used her to get close to Ramon.

Never had she felt so betrayed. As she watched him try to talk Ramon into surrendering, she'd looked for any warmth for her in his eyes, and all she'd seen was cold determination to get his job done. And as she'd waited to learn how it would feel to have a bullet blast through her brain, her heart—already broken in half—had shattered into a thousand pieces.

And now, he was dying. "Don't die, Alex. Please don't die." She took his hand and brought it to her face.

"Hold this over the wound."

A piece of cloth torn from someone's shirt was thrust at her. She grabbed the material and pressed it to Alex's chest where blood gushed out. There were other people in the room now, she could hear them talking, their voices terse. A man dropped to his knees on the other side of Alex, and he tore off his face mask.

He put his hands over hers, pressing her palms harder against Alex's shirt. She peered up into the tear-filled eyes of his older brother, Nate. "Please don't let him die."

"Never," Nate said, sounding as if he meant it with everything he was.

Another man joined them, and she recognized Alex's brother Court.

"Dammit, Alex," he said, his voice cracking. "You fucking die, I'll kill you myself."

The pain radiating from him turned what was left of her heart to ashes. Alex wasn't going to make it. Did she even belong here with them at such a tragic time? Should she leave him to his brothers? Even if she should, she couldn't make herself step away from his side. The two brothers shared a look, and despair flooded their eyes. She understood. Her heart was breaking, too.

"I've got him," a man said, pushing his hands under hers. Startled, she fell onto her butt and was pushed out of the way by a trio of EMTs. Alex's brothers surrounded the EMTs, who were doing CPR. Unable to watch, she ran out the door, hitting the hard body of a man she'd never seen before.

"Whoa. Easy, Madison." He circled his arm around her waist, pulling her with him toward the front door. "I'm Rand." He handed her a wet washcloth he'd gotten from who knew where, and she stared at her hands as she tried to scrub Alex's blood away.

A woman fell into step at her other side. She recognized her as Alex's date from the night he'd met her and Ramon at the Flamingo Bar. What was she doing here? Madison glanced at the gorgeous woman, who had tears rolling down her cheeks.

"Do you love him?" she asked, thinking she should just shut up, but she had to know.

The woman leaned her head down, resting her chin on Madison's hair. "As a brother agent, yes, I do. As a lover, we've never gone there and never would have. He's yours, Madison. Don't think otherwise."

Did everyone know about her and Alex? "Doesn't matter anymore, does it?" she said, wishing she could stop crying. She had seen him take his last breath, had seen his body go slack, had even seen one paramedic glance at the other two, giving a shake of his head.

As soon as she walked outside with a wall of those who loved Alex surrounding her, she broke away and ran to the end of the house, losing everything left in her stomach. Too much blood had poured out of his chest for him to survive.

She hated him for using her to get close to her cousin, and she loved him with every fiber of her being. The front door of her uncle's house flew open, and two EMTs rushed by with a gurney while the third one straddled Alex, pushing on his chest.

"He's dead," she whispered as her knees gave out. Someone picked her up and carried her away, but she was too lost in her heartbreak to know who, much less care.

"I'm not leaving," Madison said, refusing to be daunted by the room full of what she assumed were Alex's fellow FBI agents, some sprawled over chairs in the hospital waiting room, others holding up the walls.

"Only family can see him," the woman she remembered as Taylor said, kindness in her eyes.

"Then I'll just sit over here." Madison moved to a far corner, away from the curious stares of some of the most intimidating people she'd ever seen. Nate had been the one to call and tell her that Alex was hanging on to life by a thread, and he would always have her gratitude for thinking of her during what had to be one of the hardest times in his life. She clasped her hands together, bowed her head, and prayed for God to save Alex's life.

"Madison."

A gentle hand cupped her knee, and she opened her eyes to see Court kneeling in front of her. "Is he . . . is he . . ." She couldn't finish the question, certain that Alex was gone.

"He's still the same. Will you come with me to see him?"

"I thought only family could go in." Why was she questioning the offer when she needed to see him more than she'd needed anything in her life? Court smiled, and it was so much like Alex's that tears pooled in her eyes.

"I'll flash my badge if a nurse tries to stop you."

"Or you could just smile at her. That should do it." Oh God, had she just said that? It was only because there was so much about him that reminded her of Alex, plus all the brothers had lethal smiles.

He chuckled. "I think you're giving me more credit than I deserve. Come on." Taking her hand, he pulled her up. "Come talk to him, Madison. Bring him back to us."

Why would he think she could do such a thing? Alex didn't care for her. She'd only been a means to an end, a link to Ramon. After an ambulance had whisked Alex away, Taylor had taken her home so she could wash off the blood and change her clothes. In spite of her resolve not to like the woman, she had. Although she'd dreaded it, she'd broken the news to her mother that Jose had been arrested and Ramon killed, staying with Angelina to console her until Nate had called.

The biggest surprise had been Angelina. She'd shed endless tears for her twin brother's arrest and the death of his son, but she'd placed all the blame on the two of them for the way things had gone down. As for Jose, all Madison knew was that he was in federal custody, right where he belonged.

She hadn't the heart, though, to tell her mother that it appeared Uncle Jose had a hand in her husband's murder. Maybe she would someday; she hadn't decided. Ramon was dead, and if Uncle Jose got sent away for life, what would be the point in telling Angelina? It would only add to her grief.

Court kept her hand in his as they walked to Alex's room, and it seemed a brotherly type of gesture. What would it be like to have been with Alex and have Nate and Court as her brothers? It wasn't going to happen, and she still didn't understand why he thought her presence would help.

"Alex ended things between us," she said, wanting to make sure he knew. "I doubt he'll want me here."

He just gave her a mysterious smile, as if he knew things she didn't. They walked into the room, and she gasped. The man on the bed was deathly pale, and she wondered if it was only the machines hooked up to his body that kept him alive.

Nate sat in a chair pulled up to the bed, his head bowed as if in prayer. Court let go of her hand, and tears fell freely down her face as she approached. Nate lifted his head, and she saw the fear and pain in his eyes, thinking it must mirror her own.

"Come sit, Madison." He stood, motioning her to the chair he'd been sitting in.

Her throat closed, making it impossible to swallow. How could the man on that bed be her vibrant, beautiful Alex? She sat in the chair

Nate had vacated, taking Alex's hand. It was cold and lifeless, and a sob escaped her lips.

"We almost lost him three times, twice in the ambulance and once in the emergency room." Nate put his hand on her shoulder, giving her a gentle squeeze before moving away.

There was so much pain in his voice, and she didn't know if she could bear it. They seemed to think she was important to Alex, that she could perform some kind of miracle, and the weight of their faith was a burden she wasn't sure she could endure. She exhaled a shuddering breath as tears flowed like a river down her face.

Court handed her a handkerchief, then moved to the foot of the bed next to his brother. The two of them stood with their shoulders touching as if drawing strength from each other, or maybe they were simply leaning on each other for support. She didn't know, only that there was incredible love between the Gentry brothers. That they were FBI agents was still something she was trying to process.

"He was only with me to find out if I knew anything about my cousin's activities." She didn't know why she needed them to understand she'd meant nothing to Alex, but they seemed to think all she had to do was talk to him and he'd wake up.

"Is that what he told you?" Nate said.

"Not in so many words, but . . ." She sighed. What good would it do to let them know how much he'd hurt her?

"Talk to him, Madison. He'll hear you."

She didn't know what to say to Alex. That she'd fallen in love with him? That no man had ever hurt her the way he had? Even though he had wounded her down to her soul, she didn't want to see him like this.

"Alex, your brothers seem to think that you'll hear me. I don't know why they believe that, but please open your eyes." Nothing. She shook her head. "I don't think—"

"Just keep talking," Court said. "He'll hear you." He moved back to the far wall, leaned against it, tucked his chin against his chest, and closed his eyes. Nate moved over next to him, gave her an encouraging nod, then closed his eyes, too.

She talked to Alex for hours. She told him about her father, about her favorite books, and funny stories about Hemingway. She told him she loved him even though he probably didn't want to hear it. When her voice grew hoarse, one of the brothers handed her a glass of water.

As she talked to Alex, she kept her hands wrapped around his. Her back hurt, and she was getting a headache, but she kept talking, not even noticing that the sun was coming up until a bright beam shining through the window fell across Alex's face. She sucked in a breath, fearing it was a sign that God was taking him away.

"Please, Alex, stay with us. Your brothers need you." She gave a hysterical laugh. "Hell, the world needs you in it." *I need you.* She squeezed his hand, and she almost fell out of the chair when he squeezed it back. "Alex?"

"Grasshopper?" He opened his eyes, looked at her, and smiled. And just as fast, closed them, his hand going slack again.

Nate and Court were next to her in an instant. Nate put his hand on her shoulder. "What did he say?"

"Grasshopper." She tried squeezing his hand again, getting no response.

"Why would he say that?" Court said.

"That was what he called me, you know, from *Kung Fu.*"

Nate chuckled. "He loves that show. I'm going to find a doctor."

A few minutes later, he returned, a doctor and nurse in tow. Madison stepped out of the way, watching as Alex was examined.

"His heartbeat's stronger, and he's responding to light," the doctor said, shining a penlight into his eyes. "That combined with him waking up and speaking are very good signs."

"Thank God," Nate and Court said in unison, giving each other a hug.

No longer needed, Madison said her own prayer of thanks before slipping out of the room. "Good-bye, Alex," she whispered as she walked out.

CHAPTER TWENTY-THREE

"Did you see her? Did she ask about me?" Alex paced his living room like a caged animal, which he was. His brothers, damn them both, had practically sat on him to keep him in his bed or on the couch ever since he'd come home from the hospital. They had tied up the loose ends of his case, rounding up Trina and all the others. Granted, the first few days he'd not wanted to do more than sleep, but he was recovered and had things to do. Namely he needed to figure out how to win back Madison.

Court rolled his eyes. "Can I get in the door before you grill me? Yes, I saw her."

"And?"

"She said she was happy to hear you were home and doing well." He dropped two books onto the table. "Happy reading."

That was it? "Nothing else?" Damn, he hated how pathetic he sounded. Did he even have a chance with her again? It didn't sound like she was even thinking of him.

"Nope. Her roommate was there, so maybe she didn't want to say much in front of Lauren. I don't think she likes me."

"Madison?"

"No, dumbass. Lauren. Next time you want someone to check on your girlfriend, send Nate."

"What's the deal between you and her, anyway? You're like two hissing cats, ready to tear the fur off each other."

"Beats me." Court went to the fridge and grabbed a beer. "Want one?"

"No thanks." He sat on the sofa. What he needed was a plan. When he'd sent Court to get some books, just so he could talk to Madison, get the lay of the land, he should have told his brother to find a book on how to seduce a woman.

Court plopped down in a chair. "Lopez is out on bail."

"That's good." Should he send Madison flowers? Maybe write her a letter, explaining everything? That seemed too ordinary. He needed to think of something special.

"No, it isn't. He's sticking to his story that he was just curious about how well the bookstore was doing since he was thinking of hitting Lauren up for a loan. With Ramon dead, we haven't been able to prove otherwise. The damn charges against him will end up being dropped. Lauren will probably welcome him back with open arms."

"It's her life." What if he bought Madison something expensive and wrote a letter, sending them to her together? Nah. She wouldn't care about a costly bracelet or necklace. There had to be a way to get her to listen to him.

"Maybe I should talk to her."

"I would if I thought it would work. I just can't help thinking I need to do something special."

"I meant Lauren." Court pushed himself up. "You're not even listening to me. Do you need help changing your bandage?"

"No, I'll do it when I take a shower."

"I'm off then." He leaned down, put his hands on Alex's knees, and stared him in the eyes. "Do not leave here. *Capisce?*"

Alex stuck out his tongue.

"I mean it, baby brother. One of us will stop by later, and your ass had better be here."

"The two of you are worse than having a nursemaid."

"We almost lost you." He squeezed Alex's knee. "We're still traumatized. Deal with it."

If it had been one of them almost dying, he'd be traumatized, too, but he might need resuscitating again just from pure boredom. After Court left, Alex roamed the confines of his condo, looking for something to do. He'd cleaned everything twice already. His clothes were washed, dried, and put away. The bills were paid. He'd even bleached the grout on the bathroom floor.

He'd give his brothers one more night of peace, and then it would be time to put his plan to win Madison back into motion. Deciding to shower and call it an early night so tomorrow would get here faster, he went into the bathroom. As he stood in front of the mirror, he gritted his teeth when he tore off the bandage covering the wound that bastard Ramon had put in his chest. He stared at it, trying to remember anything from the time he'd been shot and when he'd woken in the hospital, asking for Madison.

He'd opened his eyes to the sound of her voice, but she hadn't been there. He'd been too afraid of the answer to ask his brothers if she'd even visited once.

Coming that close to death, he should have experienced some kind of epiphany, or at the very least, a conversation with an angel who would have told him the meaning of life. But other than the bullet hole in his chest, nothing felt different. There had been no tunnel with a brilliant white light at the end.

Nothing had changed. He still wanted to be an FBI agent, putting bad guys away. He still loved his brothers, the same as he always had.

And he still loved Madison. The only thing almost dying had done for him was make him more determined than ever to use this second chance to win her back. Although he was still under "house arrest," he could make his first move.

He studied the photos a jeweler friend had sent, decided on the one he liked, and then texted his friend, telling her to have the item delivered tomorrow.

She immediately responded.

Any note with it?

He considered, then texted back.

No

After taking a shower, he put on a new bandage, pleased with how well the tissue was healing around the wound. Tomorrow the stitches would be removed, which he was looking forward to because the damn things itched. For dinner, he reheated the leftover pizza Nate had brought over. Finished eating, he turned on a ball game and fell asleep on the sofa while waiting for one of his "jailers" to stop by and do a bed check.

"Is Madison Parker here?" a messenger asked.

"She's Madison," Lauren said, pointing at her.

He thrust a padded envelope into Madison's hands. "This is for you."

"What is it?" Only her name and the bookstore's address were on the front.

Lauren grabbed it and shook it next to her ear. "Well, it's not a bomb. You might try opening it. That'd be one way to find out."

"Smarty pants. Give me it." She opened the flap and peeked inside. "Nope, not a bomb." It was a white velvet jewelry box, and when she opened it, she stared at it for a moment, wondering who would send her a bracelet. Then she saw the grasshopper charm on the delicate silver chain and sucked in a breath.

"What? You know who it's from?" Lauren fingered the charm. "It's so cute."

"Alex." Tears stung her eyes. She had missed him every day, had felt the ache in her heart from the moment she woke up each morning, and had fallen asleep each night thinking of him.

"Oh, sweetie." Lauren took the bracelet from her and put it on her wrist. "Let's take a break." She pulled Madison to the coffee bar. "Angelina, would you mind covering the front for a few minutes? Madison and I are going to treat ourselves to a latte."

Madison smiled at her mother, hiding the ache in her heart. Angelina gave her a hug before going to cover the front. Although still sad with the turn of events involving her brother, she had bounced back faster than Madison had expected. Maybe she'd been wrong to think Angelina had been too fragile to deal with Ramon's creepy behavior.

Latte in hand, she followed Lauren to their office. They had a sofa in the office, and as soon as they were seated, Lauren said, "Start talking. What happened between you and Alex? I thought there was something really special going on there."

So had she. Was the bracelet an apology for using her to get information on her cousin? She lifted the grasshopper charm with her finger. It was an exquisite piece. The eyes of the grasshopper were small emeralds, and the charm had obviously been handmade.

"I thought so, too. Maybe things were just moving too fast for him."

She thought about the moment with Nate, when he'd pulled her aside while they were keeping vigil at Alex's bedside. "I'm sorry you got caught in the middle, Madison," he'd said.

"It wasn't your cousin who threatened to kill you, so nothing to be sorry for." She'd almost given him the thumb drive then, but she'd been so mixed up. Ramon was dead, and apparently they had all the evidence they needed to send her uncle to prison for a long time, if not forever. It would break her mother's heart all over again to learn that Jose and Ramon might have been the ones responsible for her father's death. So the thumb drive had stayed in her pocket and was now hidden in a box in her closet.

"When he gets well"—Nate had looked over at Alex, lying deathly still in the hospital bed, his eyes locking back on hers with a fierce determination—"because he will, the two of you need to have a long talk. Until then, I'm going to ask you to keep who we are to yourself. The rest of it, the arrest of your uncle and the death of your cousin, will be front-page news, but we've managed to keep your name out of it. As far as anyone knows, you were never there."

"Thank you for that," she'd whispered, grateful that reporters hadn't shown up at her or her mother's door.

"Give him a chance to explain, Madison."

Not knowing if she ever wanted to talk to Alex again, she had said, "I'll promise to keep the secret of who you guys are if you'll promise not to tell him I was here."

The man who looked so much like Alex, except for the long hair pulled back in a ponytail, had pressed his lips together, his eyes glittering with displeasure. She didn't care, didn't want to hear Alex try to explain why he'd thought it was okay to use her. There was nothing he could say to justify making her fall in love with him when it had only been a job to him.

"You never said what happened."

Lauren's voice brought her back to the present, and she met her friend's gaze. "Honestly, I don't really know. He made love to me, and I thought . . ." Embarrassment burned her cheeks. "Stupid me, I thought I saw love in his eyes, and the words just blurted out of my mouth . . . that I loved him. Guess he didn't like that. The next morning he said things were moving too fast for him. End of story."

"Oh, Maddie, I'm so sorry."

"Speaking of men, when are you going to tell me how you met Court?"

Her friend shook her head. "That story's buried too deep to dig up."

"If you ever decide you need to talk about it, you know I'm here for you."

"I know. What do you say we swear off the creatures?"

Madison laughed. "For how long?" She couldn't see Lauren lasting more than a week.

"For today." Lauren's lips quivered with mirth as she shrugged. "You know me. One day's about my limit."

They dissolved into belly-aching laughter, and Madison was able to forget about a black-eyed bad boy for a few minutes.

The next day Madison received a telegram. Was it even possible to still send such a thing? She eyed the piece of paper, delivered to the bookstore from iTelegram. Obviously, it was. She opened it.

> Did you know grasshoppers' ears are located in their bellies? I miss you something terrible, Mad.

She didn't know whether to laugh or cry. No, she didn't know that grasshoppers' ears were in their bellies, and she missed him something terrible, too. But she still couldn't bring herself to forgive him. The man she'd thought she'd fallen in love with didn't even exist.

"What's that?" Lauren said, walking up and snatching the telegram out of her hand. "Wow," she said after reading it. "He's funny and sexy all at the same time. You don't want him, I'll take him."

"Hands off, girlfriend." Madison took the telegram back. "I don't know what to do."

"Maybe listen to what he has to say?"

She probably should, but she couldn't imagine anything he could say to make her trust him again. "I don't know." Why was he sending her these things? She was trying to forget him, but he was making that damn hard to do.

The next day, a bouquet of wildflowers was delivered. Attached to one of the stems was a beautifully painted ceramic grasshopper. He was killing her. For a week, little gifts arrived. Nothing too expensive—except for the bracelet, which she wore every day—but clever little things like a *Kung Fu* CD; *Are You a Grasshopper?*, an illustrated children's book about a day in the life of a grasshopper; and a small oil painting of a grasshopper in a garden of daisies.

He was wearing her down, but she didn't respond. She didn't know what to say.

CHAPTER TWENTY-FOUR

Alex didn't know what to do next. Madison hadn't responded to anything he'd tried, not even a thank-you text. Not that he blamed her after what he'd put her through.

"Why don't you just go over there and talk to her?" Nate said as he held up the remote, clicking between ball games.

"Because I'm afraid she'll slam the door in my face."

"You're such a dumbass, baby brother. That girl's in love with you."

"Not. She didn't even come by the hospital to check on me. I don't think she cares if I live or die." He sounded like a pouty kid.

Nate scrubbed at his face. "About that."

"What?" He didn't like that guilty look in his brother's eyes.

"She was at the hospital. Sat by your bedside, holding your hand, and talked to you until her voice was hoarse."

"The hell, Nate? You didn't think that was something you should tell me? Why wasn't she there when I came to?"

"She asked us not to tell you, and after what she'd gone through, she had the right to ask almost anything of us."

If that was what she'd wanted, he had to respect that, but it changed everything.

"Where you going?"

He glanced over his shoulder as he headed for the door. "To climb a fire escape."

He'd tapped his signal twice now on her window, and she either wasn't in her room or she was out. Was she on a date? That didn't bear considering. A third possibility was that she was ignoring him. So be it. He'd come back the next night, and the next one, and the next one until she opened her damn window.

Although he could walk into her bookshop during the daylight hours and see her, he didn't want to. This was how they'd started—with her opening her window to him, inviting him in. That was how he wanted it to be again.

He was halfway down the stairs when he heard the creak of her window opening, and he stilled.

"Alex."

That soft, sleepy voice saying his name flowed through him, bringing a sigh to his lips. He walked back up to the landing. "Hello, Mad." Her hair was a messy riot of curls around her face and down her back. He wanted to smile, wanted to tell her how sexy she looked, sitting there in her window, wearing a white tank top and red boxer underwear, her long legs sleek and pale in the moonlight. Her eyes were wary, though, so he didn't tell her any of that.

"Why are you here?"

Because he was miserable without her, but he didn't tell her that either. She put her hand on her knee, and the silver bracelet slid a few inches down her arm, catching his attention. His racing heart eased a little. If she hated him, she wouldn't be wearing it.

"You're beautiful, Madison," he said, the speech he'd prepared forgotten.

Her gaze shifted away, looking back into her dark room, as if she were considering a retreat. He was screwing this up. Desperation drove him, words he hadn't meant to say yet pouring out of his mouth.

"Dammit, I'm in love with you. The things I said—"

"Were for my own good?"

He let out a relieved breath. She understood. "Yes."

"Men are so stupid."

He couldn't argue with that. She gave a snort that sounded uncomfortably sarcastic, slid out of the window seat, and slammed the window down. Okay, so she hadn't understood. He stared at the pane of glass separating them, and thought about forcing his way in and making her listen, but then he'd only prove to her just how stupid men really were.

"This isn't over, Madison," he said before heading down the stairs.

The next night, he was back, and she didn't take as long to open the window, which he took as a good sign. That, and she was still wearing the bracelet. The sexy little shorts and top were gone, replaced with sweatpants and a loose T-shirt, which was too bad. But she was still gorgeous, even when she was trying not to be.

This time, he was ready with what he wanted to say. "Give me five minutes, Madison. Then you can tell me to go to hell if you want, and I swear I'll leave you alone."

"Why not? I have nothing better to do tonight."

Ouch. He leaned back, bracing his hands on the railing, and curled his fingers around the metal. He'd thought he had exactly what he wanted to say mapped out, but he was about to bare his soul, and what if she stomped on it?

"Four minutes, Alex."

"Right, better get to it." He took a deep breath. "The last night we made love, it rocked my world . . . what I felt for you. And then you told me you loved me." How could he make her understand how much that had meant to him?

"That sucker punched me, Mad. I watched you sleep for hours, and all I could think was, she doesn't know me. How can she love me if she doesn't know me? That's what I thought."

He pushed away from the railing, moving to the edge of the window, and leaned his shoulder against the frame. "I'm an FBI agent, and you didn't know that. I got it in my head that we needed to start over, that if we had any chance of a future together, it could only happen if you knew the real me."

"Why didn't you tell me? Didn't you think that was something I should have known about you?"

He saw the hurt in her eyes, and if he didn't think she would slap his face, he'd scoop her up off that window ledge and carry her to bed where he'd show her how sorry he was.

"I couldn't tell you. I wanted to, but I had a job to do. What if you had let something slip to Ramon, even if you didn't mean to? That would have put you in danger, and I wasn't about to let that happen."

"So I was a means to an end? Get close to me so you could find out what I knew about Ramon?"

He dropped to his knees, putting himself at eye level with her. "No. Please don't think that. Did I ever ask you about him?"

"No. I thought that at first, when you showed up at Ramon's wearing an FBI vest. But when I tried to remember if you asked me even one question about him, there was nothing. I had to ask, though."

"So where do we go from here, Mad?" It was probably too much to hope that she'd invite him to climb into her bed. Green eyes searched his, and he kept his gaze on hers, waiting to hear her answer.

"You said I don't know you. I think we should start over, get to really know each other this time."

Not what he'd wanted, which was mainly to pick up where they'd left off, but she was calling the shots. "Start over how?"

She put her fingers on the bracelet and twirled it around her wrist. "Figure it out."

His brain was starting to hurt. "You said it yourself. I'm just a stupid man. Help me out here."

That earned him a half-second smile. "The bracelet's beautiful. I love it. All the gifts were lovely, but no more. Good night, Alex." She closed the window in his face. Again.

What just happened?

"That was your boyfriend on the phone," Lauren said.

"Alex?" A streak of something hot coursed through her—something that felt a lot like jealousy. Why would he call Lauren?

"The one and only."

"And?"

Her friend grinned. "Promised I wouldn't tell you. If you need me, I'll be in the back. We just got five boxes of books delivered."

"Get back here!" Madison glared at Lauren's retreating back. "And stop laughing," she yelled.

What was Alex up to? When he'd explained why he had acted the way he did, she understood his reasoning. In some ways he was still the man she'd fallen in love with, but in a big way that really counted, he wasn't. An FBI agent? She was still trying to wrap her head around that one.

When he had showed up at her window, her world had righted itself again. He'd even said he loved her, and she'd almost thrown herself into his arms right then, but she needed him to prove that she was worth fighting for, thus her challenge to him to figure out how to win her back. He was up to something, and she loved nothing more than a good surprise.

"What was all the yelling about?" Angelina said, walking up next to her.

"Just Lauren being her aggravating self. You're in early today." She gave her mother a hug, inhaling the familiar scent of gardenias.

"I was restless and decided I'd rather be here than at home with all my thoughts."

She didn't like the dark circles under her mother's eyes. Maybe she wasn't handling things as well as Madison had thought. "Let's have dinner tonight, and then go visit daddy." Even though Angelina visited his grave every Sunday, Madison thought a special trip might be in order. Her mother always returned lighter of spirit after talking to her husband.

"I'd love that."

"Then it's a date." A customer walked up to the counter, and she smiled. "Can I help you find something?"

Three days passed, and Madison hadn't seen or heard from Alex since he'd last tapped on her window. Maybe he hadn't meant a word he'd said. It was Saturday night, and Lauren was getting ready to go out with someone she'd met after she'd run into the back of his car at a red light. And wasn't that so Lauren? Crash into a car and end up with a date with a hot guy.

The only plans Madison had were to drown her misery in the bottom of an ice cream container while she streamed more episodes of *Kung Fu*. Damn Alex for getting her hooked on Grandfather and Grasshopper. She put on her most comfortable staying-in clothes— baggy harem pants and a Miami Dolphins football shirt.

Determined she wouldn't think of him all night, she poured a glass of wine to go with her pint of salted caramel and chocolate fudge swirl. "The dinner of champs," she said, carrying the two items into her bedroom.

She was halfway through her glass of wine and waiting for the ice cream to get soft when her bedroom door flew open. Hemingway used her arm to get traction, taking off as if shot from a cannon. Startled, Madison choked on her wine, which dripped down her chin as Lauren barged in, followed by Alex. Madison swiped her hand over her mouth.

Of course Alex would show up on a night when she had on her rattiest clothes, and she narrowed her eyes at Lauren's smirk.

"What's going on?" Her gaze landed on Alex, and her heart did a happy dance, not that she was going to let on how thrilled she was to see him.

Alex leaned his shoulder against the doorway and stuck his hands in his front pockets. "You're being kidnapped."

"Huh?" She frowned at the wicked grin he gave her. And why was Lauren rummaging in her closet?

"Here, put this on." Lauren dropped a sundress on the bed before disappearing into the closet again, coming back out with a pair of sandals.

"I'll ask again. What's going on?"

"Your boyfriend's kidnapping you. Get dressed."

Maybe she should have been more specific when she'd challenged him to figure out what she wanted. "So we're going out to dinner?"

"Among other things." Alex lifted his chin toward the dress on the bed. "Either put the dress on, Madison, or I'll carry you out in what you're wearing. Your choice."

And he would. What was he up to? Although a little giddy from the excitement bubbling up, she didn't let it show. "I'll get dressed after you tell me where we're going."

He tsked. "Don't say you weren't warned."

There was that wicked grin again, birthing butterflies in her stomach. He started for her, and she scooted off the side of the bed away from him. "Fine, I'll get dressed, but you need to go wait in the living room."

"Why? I've seen you naked."

"Alex!"

"Madison?"

Lauren laughed, and Madison shot her a glare. "Whose friend are you, anyway?"

"Yours, and you should trust me. You're going to like being kidnapped." She waved a hand at Alex. "Go away. I'll make sure she gets dressed."

"What's going on?" she asked after he left.

"My lips are sealed, but if you don't want to be kidnapped by the hottest guy you've ever dated, I'll take your place."

"In your dreams." She was dressed and ready to go in fifteen minutes. When she walked into the living room, she eyed the suitcase sitting by the door.

Alex stood. "Ready for your adventure?"

"That's my suitcase."

He glanced at it. "Yes, it is." Taking her hand, he said, "Thanks for your help, Lauren."

"Are you kidding? This was the most fun I've had all week. See you Monday."

"Monday?" Madison said. She really was being kidnaped.

CHAPTER
TWENTY-FIVE

"This is the bridge to the Keys," Madison said.

Alex glanced at the woman who'd given him the silent treatment for the last hour. "There's no getting anything over on you, Grasshopper."

"I don't agree. You've pretty much managed it from day one." She turned her gaze back to the window even though it was nighttime and impossible to see the passing scenery.

Ouch. After racking his brain, trying to think of how to start over with her, he'd decided on a romantic weekend away. At first he was going to ask her to go somewhere with him, but what if she refused? Since he didn't have a clue what her answer would be, he'd decided to just abduct her, not giving her the chance to say no.

If she'd adamantly refused, he wouldn't have followed through. But he'd seen the excitement in her eyes, and he'd breathed a sigh of relief. He'd have a whole day to romance her with no one bothering them, and he hoped they'd spend most of that time in bed. At the moment that wasn't looking promising, though.

He estimated he had another hour of driving to set things right between them. If he failed, he might as well turn the car around and go home.

"I have some things I need to say to you, Madison. Will you listen?"

"I'm here, aren't I? That must mean something, although I don't think I should have let you talk me into this."

He hoped to hell it meant something. Traffic grew heavier as they crossed the first of forty-two bridges that would ultimately take them to Key West, and he let his foot off the gas pedal as he collected his thoughts. He had to get this right.

"When you told me you loved me—"

"I took it back."

"Yeah, you did. You sent me to the devil." He'd been proud of her for telling him off. Hadn't at all liked it, but he'd deserved it. "The thing is, Mad, that man didn't deserve your love."

"No, he didn't."

She sounded so sad, and he glanced at her. Maybe it was a mistake to try to have this conversation while he had to pay attention to the road, but he wanted things settled between them before they arrived at their destination.

"Why did you come with me tonight?"

The look she gave him implied he was stupid. "Because you kidnapped me?"

"Not really. I think you know I wouldn't have forced you. Let's be honest with each other, okay? I'll go first." After crossing another bridge, he saw a pullover on the gulf side and turned the car in. Once stopped, he released his seat belt and shifted to face her. He wasn't good at talking about his feelings. Hell, what man was? But if he didn't, he'd lose her.

"I'd hoped to say this in a more romantic setting, but this will have to do." He locked eyes with her. "I've never told another woman I loved her. You're the first." He scrubbed at his face. "I'm a man and when we're in love, we really do get stupid."

"That's a fact."

He chuckled. "You don't have to be so agreeable, Grasshopper. Anyway, if nothing else, I want you to know that I regret lying to you. I don't know how else I could have handled being in love with you and doing my job . . . Well, I just don't know, okay? I can't undo any of it, but I'd do it all over again if it meant keeping you safe. If you can't accept that, now's the time to tell me."

What was it about this one woman over all the others he'd dated that had his heart pounding so hard he could literally hear its beats as he waited for her to speak?

"You should have told me." She turned her gaze back to the window. "But I suppose if they had no qualms about killing my father . . ."

"That they wouldn't hesitate to come after you?" he said when she didn't finish. At her nod, he said, "What makes you think they did?" They still hadn't found proof that the Alonzos had murdered Michael Parker.

"If I tell you, are you going to use the information against my uncle? Because it would kill my mother to know her brother had anything to do with it."

He had to touch her, and he reached over the console, putting his hand on hers. "We have enough to put Jose away without it."

"I'm not sure why I trust you after everything, but I do." She turned her hand over, lacing her fingers through his. "I found a thumb drive in Ramon's office that belonged to my father. It had all his notes from his investigation and the first draft of the story he was writing. How would Ramon have that if he didn't have anything to do with killing my dad?"

At the tears rolling down her cheeks, he squeezed her hand, wishing there weren't a console between them so he could wrap his arms around her. "Are you going to tell your mom?" He hoped not.

"No. I put the thumb drive in a safety deposit box. I plan to forget it exists."

"I think that's wise. I'm so sorry, baby. That had to be an awful thing to learn."

"God, it was. Right now, I don't even want to think about it. On the plus side, I guess I won't have to pay back the loan from my uncle."

"It's over. Neither one of those poor excuses for a man will be able to hurt you again," he said. "What about us, Madison? I meant it when I said I love you. Where do we go from here?" She rubbed her thumb over the top of his hand, and he wanted to close his eyes and do nothing but feel her touching him.

"I have no idea. You're the one who kidnapped me."

"That's not what I meant, and you know it." Pushing aside the disappointment that she'd avoided answering, he started the car. Although quiet settled around them as he drove, it wasn't uncomfortable, and she still held on to his hand.

He used the time to think about everything from her side, and in her place he'd want to get to know the real her, not the person he had thought she was. So he would give her that. The question he asked himself, would he still love her after everything? The answer was a resounding yes, and he counted on her feeling the same.

"Are we going all the way to Key West?"

"Nope, we're going here," he said as they drove off the causeway onto Little Torch Key. He'd done an Internet search for romantic getaways, and this one had caught his eye.

"Oh my God, are we going to Little Palm Island Resort?"

Surprised, he glanced at her. "You've been there?" He didn't much like the idea of her being here with another man.

"No, but my dad brought my mom here for their anniversary one year, and she couldn't stop talking about it." She bounced in her seat like a kid about to get an ice cream cone, making him smile.

"You're being kidnapped, woman. You're supposed to be bargaining for your freedom."

"I have no money, Mr. Kidnapper."

He waggled his brows, giving her a lecherous smirk. "I'm sure you have something to offer that will *satisfy* me."

"Dirty old man." She ruined her reprimand by giggling.

"You ain't seen nothing yet, baby." Her mood had definitely improved. Had she forgiven him?

He got them checked in, and when he led her by the hand into the thatched-roof suite and heard her gasp, he thought this might have been his best idea ever. The suites were detached and private, with a veranda that sat right on the Gulf of Mexico. Through the glass walls and doors, he could see the moonlight glistening on the water like a ribbon of diamonds.

A king-sized bed with butterfly netting took up the left side of the room, and on the right was a sitting area. On the coffee table were a complimentary bottle of champagne in ice and a platter of fresh fruit and assorted cheeses.

"This is amazing, Alex." She lifted onto her toes and pressed her lips to his.

Coming here had definitely been a genius move on his part. "Am I forgiven?"

"I'm very close. The thing is, I never stopped loving you, even when I didn't like you. I thought about everything you said, and I get why you couldn't tell me who you were. Just don't do something like that again, okay?"

"Never." He dropped their bags at his feet, circled his arms around her waist, and lost himself in the taste of her. He had his girl back. Christ, he'd missed her. Her stomach growled, and he leaned back, peering down at her.

"Hungry?"

"Starving." She eyed the feast laid out for them.

Right. Change of plans. Eat first, sex later. "Then let's eat."

She shook her head, the red hair that had captivated him from the moment he'd seen her catching his attention as it curled around her face. "Have I ever told you I love your hair?" He wrapped a strand around his hand. "You want a few minutes before we eat?"

"Yes."

He gave her ass a light spank. "Go on and do whatever you need to. I'll be waiting for you."

She grabbed her bag, and at the bathroom door, she glanced over her shoulder. "I'm so happy to be here with you, Alex. Just want you to know that."

Before he could answer, she shut the door behind her, and he stared at the space where she'd been. "No happier than me," he said to no one.

He heard water running in the shower and decided to get comfortable. Since he'd showered before kidnapping her, he pulled out a pair of white silk lounge pants he'd gone and bought right after deciding to abduct her, putting them on and nothing else.

By the time she found him out on the veranda, he had set up a table with the champagne and food and was leaning against the railing. His heart figuratively—and almost literally—stopped. Right then and there at seeing her wearing nearly sheer green silk pajamas that were a perfect match to her green eyes.

"Wow," he said, stupidly.

She ducked her head, but a smile curved her lips. "I didn't buy this."

"Lauren did." He stalked toward her. "I asked her to find something that would make you feel sexy but not slutty."

"You have a problem with slutty?" Her eyes lifted to his, daring him to deny it.

"Not a thing." He slipped his thumb under the collar, sliding his hand down until he could touch her breasts. "Not a damn thing."

If she knew he would crawl on his hands and knees over hot coals to get to her, she would own him. He thought about whether that would bother him. It didn't. She owned him, and he was good with that.

Keeping his fingers curled around the edge of the sexy green top, he tugged her out onto the veranda, and down in front of him on a lounge chair. After pouring champagne, he clinked his glass against hers. "To the most beautiful lady on the planet."

She lifted her head and smiled, and he had the thought that the first thing he wanted to see every morning when he opened his eyes was that smile. They sipped champagne and fed each other morsels of food as they watched the moonlight dance over the water. With only a few questions, she had him telling her how their mother had left them in the hands of an abusive father.

"I sensed you were close to your brothers. Now I understand why." She lifted her glass, and he refilled it.

"I'm not sure I would have survived my father's cruelty without them."

"When I hear stories like yours, it makes me thankful for the parents I was blessed with. Have you ever tried to find your mother?"

"A little, but she seems to have disappeared the day she walked down that road. Nate doesn't like it when I talk about looking for her."

She peered up at him, her eyebrows scrunched together. "Why not?"

"I don't know. He refuses to talk about it." He took her empty glass away. "And I don't want to talk about it right now. Can we go to bed, please?"

"To sleep?" She grinned, mischief filling her eyes.

"Silly girl." He stood, bringing her up with him.

"Jeez, you're strong."

"It pays to be strong when you're in the kidnapping business."

At the edge of the bed, he stilled and stared down at the woman he held in his arms. She cupped his cheek with her palm, sending warmth straight to his heart.

"Make love to me, Alex."

"God yes." He turned, falling onto the bed with her on top of him. "I can't get enough of you," he whispered, pulling her mouth down to his, greedy for her taste. "Champagne and berries," he said. "That's what you taste like."

From her mouth, he kissed his way down to her neck, and as he licked his tongue over her skin, and nipped at her with his teeth, he unbuttoned the silk top. He slipped his hand under the material, brushing his thumb over her nipple, feeling it harden at his touch. Her soft moan shot an electrical current of need straight to his groin. Leaving her top on, he hooked his fingers under the waistband of her pants, tugging them down.

She lifted, and kicked them off. "Now you."

"In a minute." He flipped them, putting her under him. "Do you feel the magic?"

"Yes," she whispered.

"I want you. Desperately." He spread the two sides of her top apart, soaking in the beauty of her body. "I want my mouth on every inch of you, Mad." He started with her mouth, kissing her deeply. He kissed each of her eyes, her cheeks, her neck and shoulders, and proceeded to make good on his promise of having his mouth on every part of her. When she screamed his name, he almost lost it.

He grabbed the condom he'd put on the table while she was showering, rolling it on. "This might not last long," he muttered after he slid into her warm heat.

"You didn't see anyone else after you broke up with me?"

"No, and I didn't break up with you. I just made you think I did."

She let out a sigh that sounded pleased, then put her hands on his upper arms. "Love me."

"I do. God, I do." He pushed into her, deep and hard, filling her. As he took them to a world he'd only ever visited with her, she dug her fingers into his arms, matching his rhythm. The sound of their breaths and the slapping together of their bodies filled the air around them. When he felt her muscles clench around him, and knew she was close, he lifted onto his elbows, wanting to watch her face when she came for him.

"AlexAlexAlexAlex," she chanted as shudders racked her body.

"Sweet Jesus," he gasped as he followed her into oblivion. He managed to stay on his elbows and not crush her, even though his arms shook from the force of his climax. Brushing her damp hair away from her face, he stared at his beautiful girl.

"What?"

He chuckled. "What what?"

"Why are you staring at me like that?"

"Because you're beautiful. Because I love you." He rolled over, taking her with him. "Say it back, Mad."

"Say what?" Madison lifted onto her elbow and blinked innocently at Alex. "Did you just growl?" She loved teasing him. To hear him say he loved her sent her heart soaring into the stratosphere. But he'd played his little game with her, and he deserved to sweat some.

"Say it."

She looked into his eyes, and seeing the love he had for her, she let the last of her resentment go. Even though she didn't like that he hadn't been honest with her, she understood his reasons. The days without him had been torture, and she couldn't bear the thought of not being with him.

"I love you, Special Agent Alex Gentry. I love who you are and what you stand for. My heart belongs to you. No conditions. No if, ands, or buts. I love you."

"That's my girl." His mouth came down on hers, and he kissed her with such tenderness that tears burned her eyes. He made love to her again, worshipping her body with every soft touch of his hands, showing her with his lips, tongue, and mouth over every inch of her skin how much he wanted her. By the time he finished with her, she felt cherished and thoroughly loved, and as she fell asleep with her back tucked against his chest, listening to the gentle splash of water hitting the veranda's foundation, she sighed with contentment.

Early the next morning he woke her up with lazy morning sex, and when she snuggled up against him afterward, she smiled against his chest. "You're insatiable."

He hugged her. "I never was before you, so it's your fault."

"Oh, blame me, will you?" she teased, although it thrilled her to hear him say that.

"Definitely." He slapped her butt. "Put your bathing suit on, and let's go play."

After a delicious breakfast delivered to their veranda, they spent the day exploring the small island and playing in the water. All too soon, the sun was setting, and they headed back to their suite. She couldn't wait to take a shower and wash her salt-encrusted skin.

"Thank you for kidnapping me," she said as they walked into the room, hand in hand. "Feel free to do it again anytime."

He tilted his head and smiled down at her. "Maybe next time you should kidnap me."

"I might just do that. Want to join me in the shower?" There was a large soaking tub in the bathroom, but the shower was outdoors, surrounded by a bamboo fence and lush foliage.

He snorted. "Silly question, Mad."

They kept their bathing suits on long enough to rinse them off, and then Alex removed hers. "About my insatiable problem . . . I feel it coming on again."

"Oh dear. Anything I can do to help?"

"Uh-huh." He pushed his board shorts down, kicking them away.

Sweet Lord, he was magnificent. She would never get enough of looking at him, and that wicked smile of his made her toes curl. As she swept her gaze over him, she paused on the scar where Ramon had shot him.

"I was so scared," she said, tears stinging her eyes as she gently touched her finger to the healing wound. "I thought . . ." She shook her head, not able to say it.

"Hush, baby. I'm here." He wrapped his arms around her, rocking them under the warm spray of the water. "Why didn't you want me to know you stayed at my bedside?"

"Who told you?" She pressed the side of her face against his chest, listening to his heart beat strong and steady.

"Nate, but only because he said I was being a dumbass. Tell me why you didn't want me to know."

"Because you'd broken up with me. I didn't think you would want me there."

He leaned away, his eyes locked on hers. "I heard you talking to me, but when I woke up and you weren't there, I thought I was dreaming. I didn't see a white light or anything like that, but your voice kept me from leaving."

At that, she burst into tears. What if she hadn't gone to the hospital, or what if she hadn't agreed to sit in that room and talk to him for hours? Would he have died? She couldn't bear to think of a world without Alex in it.

"Don't cry, Mad. I'm here and not going anywhere." He cupped her chin, tipping her face up, and kissed away her tears. "Have I told you how much I love your hair?"

It hadn't been until she'd reached adulthood that she'd come to terms with having red hair. As a young girl, she'd been teased unmercifully. Alex was only the second man to say that, the first being her father.

"It reminds me of the flames of a fire. Lean your head back so I can rinse the shampoo out. There you go." He poured conditioner into his palm. "The first time I saw you, I wanted to wrap my fist around this beautiful hair of yours, pull your head back, and kiss you so hard you wouldn't know what day it was. You own me, Madison. Heart, body, and soul."

"Can I just melt at your feet?"

"No. If you're a puddle I can't do this." He trailed soapy hands down her belly until he reached her sex, and then he cupped her mound as his warm breath tickled her ear. "Or this." He slid a finger inside her, and she put her hands on his lean hips for support as he played with her. His thumb found all the right places, while his finger slid in and out of her until she called out his name, falling against him as exquisite pleasure exploded throughout her body.

"I think I lost all the feeling in my legs."

"You're so beautiful when you come," he murmured. Reaching over, he turned off the shower and then lifted her into his arms. "I didn't bring a condom in with us or I'd have your legs wrapped around me right now while I buried myself to my balls inside you."

He carried her to bed, and an hour later, she lay across his body, as limp as a noodle. "I don't think I'll ever be able to move again."

"Are you complaining?" He combed his fingers through her hair.

"Never. Just stating a fact."

"I'm sorry, but you're going to have to move. We have dinner reservations."

She groaned. "Can't we just have something delivered?"

"Nope." He rolled them over and smiled down at her. "I love you. Now go get dressed. I've got something special planned for us."

And did he ever, she thought later as she sat at the beautifully set private table on the sand. Lit torches surrounded them, the warm tropical breeze making the flames dance.

"Happy?" Alex asked, putting his hand over hers.

She turned her hand over, lacing their fingers. "Yes. Can we live here forever?"

"I'll have to rob a bank, but if that's what you want, sure."

A waiter appeared, setting a plate in front of each of them. "Prime beef chateaubriand, Caribbean lobster, and grilled asparagus with a hint of lemon," he said. He refilled their wine glasses before bowing and walking away.

"Oh my God, this is amazing," she said after taking a bite of the chateaubriand. She smiled at Alex. "You, this magical night, and this food. I think I've died and gone to heaven."

He set down his knife and fork. "You take my breath away, Madison. Sitting there with your gorgeous hair blowing in the breeze and the moonlight on your face . . . How did I get so lucky?" He put his hand over hers again. "I want to wake up with you every morning and fall asleep with you in my arms each night. Move in with me."

That was a question she hadn't expected.

CHAPTER TWENTY-SIX

She needed to think about it? What the hell was there to think about? He loved her. She loved him. Moving in together was the logical next step, right? It wasn't like he'd proposed marriage. Although he'd considered it, Alex didn't think either one of them was ready for that.

A week had passed since he'd asked her to move in with him, and even though they'd spent every night together since returning from the Keys, she was still thinking. How long did it take to make a decision, anyway? Between his job as a federal agent and the long hours he put in at Aces & Eights, he wanted to make sure that Madison could deal with who and what he was before she found herself trapped in a marriage that made her miserable.

This morning she'd left his place to go home and change before she met her mother for breakfast. Today was Michael Parker's birthday, and Madison and her mother were going to church and then to the cemetery. He was to meet them in a few hours for a late lunch, the first occasion he would spend time with Angelina so she could get to know him better.

He held up the remote, channel surfing. Not much on of interest on a Sunday morning, and he finally left it on an ESPN sports show while he dressed. After a few minutes of indecision, he settled on a pair of gray pants and a dark purple silk shirt. It was his first time to be in the position of having to impress a girl's mother, and it was irritating that he was nervous.

The few occasions he'd seen Angelina in the bookstore, she had been politely pleasant toward him, but privately, she'd expressed her concern to Madison that he was the part owner of a biker bar. He'd talked it over with Madison, and they had decided it was time to tell Angelina that he was FBI. That could go either way. It would either improve her opinion of him, or not, considering it was the FBI who'd arrested her twin and killed her nephew.

It was a bit disconcerting how much he wanted Madison's mother to approve of him, although he thought he'd rather go one-on-one with Menace, the meanest son-of-a-bitch member of the Demons. Shaved, bathed, and dressed, he slapped a little of his favorite cologne on his face, put his gun in his boot, and headed for the door. He was a little early, but he wanted to stop and purchase some flowers for mother and daughter.

Since the flower shop was closed on Sunday, he headed for the grocery store. For Madison, he chose a bouquet that looked like wildflowers. He had no idea what they were, but they suited her. For Angelina, he took longer to decide, finally going with a dozen yellow roses.

He was headed to his car when his cell phone buzzed, Nate's name coming up.

"Yeah?"

"Where are you?"

"On the way to Angelina Parker's house." Nate and Court both knew it was Impress the Mother Day.

"Jose Alonzo escaped from jail."

"How the hell did that happen?" He unlocked his door and tossed the flowers onto the passenger seat.

"He pretended to be having a heart attack, and when the night guard went into the cell —alone, I might add—Alonzo kicked him in the balls and managed to get his gun away. He forced the guard to hand over his uniform and then tied him up with strips he'd made from his pillow."

"So he walked right out?"

"Yep. Wearing the guard's clothes and packing his gun. They're a similar height and weight, and he averted his face from the cameras. It was an hour before anyone discovered the switch. I just got the call a minute ago."

"He'll go for his sister."

"That's what I'm thinking. Where are the ladies right now?"

Alex glanced at his watch. "They should be at Angelina's. I'm five minutes away." He started the engine. "SWAT on the way?" He knew Nate would have called in the FBI's team, not the police department's.

"The call just went out, so they should be there in thirty minutes or so. Court and I are leaving now."

"See you there."

"Dammit, Alex, don't go in until we get there."

Alex disconnected. He could only go so fast on the narrow residential streets, but he pulled up in front of Angelina's house in just under three minutes. The blinds were closed, which he didn't like. Maybe Angelina preferred her house dark, but most people liked sunshine brightening their rooms.

There was no place in his clothes he could put his gun that wouldn't be obvious, so he left it in his boot. Fortunately, he'd worn a long-sleeved shirt. He opened the middle console and took out the knife in an arm holster. Unbuttoning his sleeve, he strapped the knife onto his lower arm, and then rebuttoned the cuff. It would be fifteen minutes before his brothers could get here. He wasn't leaving Madison and her mother alone in that house with Alonzo. The man would be desperate, and who knew what he'd do?

Alex grabbed the flowers as he exited the car. Alonzo didn't know he was FBI and would have no reason to think Alex was there for any purpose other than to see his girlfriend. He rang the doorbell and waited a full minute before ringing it again. Maybe they weren't home yet. He pushed the button one last time. When all stayed quiet, he stepped back, catching the sight of a window blind dropping back into place.

Shit. They were in there. He rang the bell again, and finally the door cracked open. Angelina peered out. "I'm sorry, Alex, Madison's sick and can't see you today."

He held up the flowers. "Then it's a good thing I brought these to cheer her up." While he talked, he edged his foot in the opening so she couldn't close the door on him. "I'll just give her these and then be on my way." He pushed passed her, made an eye scan of the foyer, and, not seeing anyone else, turned to Angelina. "Where's my girl?"

"In bed, asleep. You need to leave, Alex."

There was desperation in her eyes, and he wondered if it was for herself and Madison, or for her brother. Hopefully, the former. "I'll just put these in water for you. Your kitchen this way?" He headed for the first door he saw.

It led into a family room, which opened up to the kitchen, where Madison sat at a breakfast table, her hands clasped together so tightly as they rested on the table that her knuckles were white.

"Hey, babe. Your mom said you're sick." He walked straight to her. "I brought you flowers." He put his mouth to the side of her head as if to kiss her. "Where is he?" he whispered before stepping back. Her eyes shifted to what he guessed was the pantry. "How about I put these flowers in water for you?"

"I'll do that," Angelina said, coming toward him. He wished she had sense enough to run out of the house when given the opportunity, leaving him with only Madison to save.

The door to the pantry was at Madison's left side, and Alex made an educated guess that her uncle had a gun pointed right at her head. Delaying until his brothers and SWAT showed up wasn't going to be possible with Angelina trying to get him out of the house. Alonzo would get suspicious if Alex stuck around, so he needed to act.

"You should go, Alex," Madison said. "I don't want you catching what I have."

"I don't want to get sick either, so as soon as we get these flowers in water, I'll take off."

With her eyes, Madison pleaded with Alex to leave. If he got shot again, she would never forgive herself. How her uncle had escaped, she didn't know, but he was dressed in a police uniform and had a gun, which he'd said would be pointed at her until they got rid of whoever was at the door.

Of course, it had been Alex, and of course, he'd barreled his way in, apparently already knowing that Jose was here. Her uncle was watching everything through the slats of the pantry door. She didn't doubt he would shoot her or Alex if he felt threatened.

She'd had such a wonderful morning with her mother. They had gone to their favorite restaurant for crepes and coffee, and from there they'd gone to morning mass. Madison knew she didn't attend church as much as she should, but when she did go, the ritual of the service always comforted her. After church, they'd gone to the cemetery, spending time at her father's gravesite.

She loved listening to her mother talk to him, especially today when Angelina had told him that although she loved him and missed him, she was starting to live again. Madison knew her dad would approve.

Before they'd left the gravesite, she'd told her dad about Alex. Her mother still had doubts about him, considering what little she knew—mainly that he was a co-owner of a biker bar. What would her mother think when she learned the truth about him? The afternoon ahead, and how Alex and her mother would get on, had been on her mind when she and Angelina had come home, walking arm in arm, happier than they'd been in a long time as they talked about the lunch menu they had planned.

"Hello, ladies," Jose had said, waving a freaking gun at them when they'd walked into the house. He'd gone to Angelina, pulling her into his arms and kissing her cheek as the gun stayed trained on Madison. Why hadn't she stayed in bed with Alex this morning?

Her first thought had been to fish her phone out of her purse so she could text Alex, but her uncle had taken their purses away before she could sneak her phone out. What he'd hoped to happen, she didn't know. Alex had arrived right after them. Her FBI-trained lover was ignoring the message she was sending with her eyes, begging him to leave. He glanced at her and winked. Winked! As if this were all a game.

He walked behind her, kicking her chair out from under her, sending her to the floor, and before she could suck in another breath as she watched from under the table, he twisted his body in some martial arts kind of way she'd only seen in the movies, his feet splintering the pantry door. If she'd blinked, she would have missed the speed with which he'd produced a knife from God knew where, sticking the point into the back of her uncle's neck.

"You move one inch, you'll end up a paraplegic," Alex said to her uncle, and she didn't doubt he meant it.

She only hoped Jose got how serious Alex was. And holy sweet Mother Mary, her man was jaw-dropping badass. The sound of booted footsteps filled the air, and she peered at the pairs of legs running into the kitchen.

"Dammit, Alex, I told you to wait for us."

Madison recognized that voice. His brothers were here. Court pulled her up, and the first person she looked for was her mother. Nate had his arms around Angelina, holding her safely against him. The next person she looked for was Alex. He had Jose facedown on the floor, his knee pressing into her uncle's neck. She stumbled to her mother, and they hugged each other as Nate pushed them out of the room.

"Are you okay?" she asked, pulling Angelina into the downstairs bathroom and locking the door.

"My brother was dead to me the minute he pointed a gun to your head." Tears streamed down her face. "Oh, Madison, I was so afraid for you."

They hugged again, and Madison inhaled her mother's familiar gardenia scent, grateful the situation hadn't turned tragic.

"If you won't live with me, then marry me," Alex said, glaring down at her, his hands fisted on his hips.

"Now isn't that the most romantic proposal ever?" They were both on edge after the events of the afternoon. She turned her own glare on his brothers at hearing their dual snorts from where they were propping up the wall. An FBI SWAT team had arrived and carried her uncle away. After the house was cleared out, the Gentry brothers had sworn her mother to secrecy and then had confessed all. Angelina had taken the news of who they were in stride and even seemed charmed by the three men.

Sitting next to her, Angelina squeezed her hand. "Your father was just as insistent I marry him. It worked out wonderfully."

Had she walked onto the set of a romantic comedy? "Get out. All of you."

"Not you," she yelled, standing and grabbing Alex by the back of his shirt.

He gave her a wicked grin that turned her knees to jelly. "That fiery temper of yours is a real turn-on, Mad."

"Don't be an ass. If you want a yes to your question, do it right."

The man she loved with every fiber of her being backed her up, put his hands on the wall behind her, and kissed her hard. About the time she was ready to climb up his body, he leaned away, locking eyes with her.

"You have to marry me."

"Do I?" He'd pretty much kissed her senseless, and it was hard to think.

"Yes. I've decided I won't shame your mother by living in sin with you. Make an honest man of me, Madison."

"So you only want to marry me to make my mother happy?" She let out an exaggerated sigh. "And here I thought when I married it would be for love."

"Silly girl." He pressed against her, letting her feel his arousal. "Even in your sainted mother's house, where I should be behaving, just being near you does this to me. Marry me for love, baby."

"For love then." She wrapped her arms around his neck. "And to make an honest man out of you. Don't forget that part."

"So that's a yes?"

She nodded. "It's a yes."

"I love you, Madison Parker, soon to be Gentry." And with that, he kissed her long and hard, until she really did forget her name.

EPILOGUE

Kinsey Landon stood at the edge of her mother's open gravesite as hot tears streamed down her cheeks. "I love you, Mom," she whispered, dropping a bouquet of lilies—Wanda Landon's favorite flower—into the gaping hole. They landed on the middle of the casket with a soft thud. Two cemetery workers stood off to the side, waiting for her to leave so they could pour dirt on top of her mom, the only family Kinsey had ever known.

The few people who had attended the ceremony had long since left. Kinsey touched her fingers to her lips and then blew a kiss for the last time. Blowing kisses to each other when one of them was leaving the house had been their ritual for as long as she could remember.

Unable to bear watching a pile of dirt being dumped on top of her mother, Kinsey walked away. The day was sunny, not a single cloud marring the brilliant blue of the sky. She wished it were raining, that the heavens were weeping for the loss of a beautiful woman. Taking a pair of sunglasses from her purse, she put them on, and then looked up at the sky. Maybe it was a beautiful day because God was happy to have a new angel. The thought pleased her, and she smiled as the tears still flowed.

Not wanting to go home to an empty house, she tried to think of someplace she could hang out for a while, but she hadn't been in Jacksonville much the past three years. All her local friends were still at college, so she had no one to call. With a heavy sigh, Kinsey turned her car for home.

Her friend, Cheryl Ryding, had promised to email Kinsey class notes, which would give her something to do. She'd taken the week off after getting excused absences from her professors, but she wished she could return right then and immerse herself in school. Before she could leave, though, she had to go through her mother's things, decide what to keep and what to donate, meet with a realtor, and put the house up for sale. She'd thought about keeping it, but it was too empty without her mom there, and it always would be.

After returning home, she kicked off her shoes, then went to her room and changed into comfortable sweatpants and an oversized T-shirt that she had never returned to her last boyfriend. There wasn't an email from Cheryl yet, so she made a cup of green mint tea, and as she stood in the middle of the kitchen, she debated curling up on the couch and trying to take a nap versus facing the chore she'd been putting off. It had been easy to ignore the need to go through her mother's belongings when she had first arrived, what with having to make arrangements for the funeral.

The call from their next-door neighbor that her mother had suffered a heart attack had come as a shock. Wanda Landon ate healthy; walked several miles a day; gardened; spent an hour a day, every day but Saturday and Sunday, at yoga class; and didn't smoke or drink more than her one glass of wine a day.

Kinsey choked down a sob. She'd cried enough for one day. Steeling herself, she headed for her mother's small office. Setting her teacup on a coaster, she sat at the desk and wondered where to start.

"I so don't want to do this." Speaking out loud made her realize how quiet it was, and she turned on the small TV, tuning it to a music channel. An hour later, she had shredded old bills and other unimportant papers. In front of her was a small stack of documents—including her mom's will—that she needed to keep. The will wasn't a surprise. Her mother had made sure that Kinsey was given a copy before she'd left for her freshman year at the University of Miami. A brief scan confirmed it was the same one she had, leaving everything to her except for the garden trolls, which her mom's neighbor coveted. As far as Kinsey was concerned they were creepy. Lucy was welcome to them.

In the last drawer, she found a Bible. By the wear and tear, it was old and one Kinsey had never seen. Curious, she flipped through the pages. She was about to put it in the *keep* pile when she caught a glimpse of writing. Opening it to the middle, she saw that it was a page for marriages. Kinsey frowned as she read the names.

Wanda Little had married Gordon Gentry thirty-three years ago? Who the hell was Gordon Gentry? And neither Little nor Gentry was her mother's last name. Kinsey turned the page to see it was a record of births. She stared at the names, trying to comprehend what she was seeing. "Nate Gentry, Court Gentry, Alex Gentry, Kinsey Gentry," she read aloud.

"What's going on here, Mom?" Considering that her world seemed about to be turned on end, she decided it wasn't too early to pour a drink. The only alcohol her mother kept in the house was wine, and although Kinsey wished there were something stronger, wine would have to do. As she stood and went to close the Bible, an envelope fell onto the desk. She picked it up and saw her name in her mother's handwriting.

Instead of pouring a glass, she brought the whole damn bottle back into the office with her. The first glass, she poured to the rim, drank half of it, then opened the envelope and began to read.

My darling Kinsey,

If you are reading this, then I am no longer with you. Please don't cry too much, sweetheart. I've been blessed to have you in my life, and having you has kept me sane.

You see, I had three sons who were taken from me, and my heart has cried each day from missing them. Without you in my life, I don't know how I would have gone on.

Kinsey dropped the letter, unable to read any further.

ACKNOWLEDGMENTS

Here I am again, writing acknowledgements for a book. Where has the time gone? My ninth published book kicks off a new series, Aces & Eights. I hope you love the Gentry brothers as much as you loved my K2 team.

Since I started on this journey, I've made some amazing friends, many I've never met in person, but that doesn't lessen my love for each and every one of you. I hope you know just how special you are to me. So, my heartfelt thank-you for reading my books, for telling your friends about them, and for being impatient for the next book to come out. I love that you are, and I'm writing as fast as I can.

To everyone who has taken the time to write a review for one of my books, thank you, thank you, thank you! That means the world to me.

My family rocks! They love me and I love them. It's the way families should be, and I'm truly blessed to have them in my life. Of course, they're blessed to have me, so it all evens out.

To my critique partners Jenny Holiday and Miranda Liasson, thank you for helping me make my stories better. I'd be lost without you. It is such an honor to be critique partners with two such amazingly talented authors. I love you both!

In 2013, the first K2 Team book, *Crazy for Her*, was a finalist in a Romance Writers of America's Golden Heart® contest. One of the judges was an editor from Montlake Romance, and she requested the full manuscript. Not long after, I received an offer from Montlake Romance. I signed a contract with them, and it was the smartest thing I've ever done. So, thank you Montlake Romance for taking a chance on a relatively unknown author. I've loved every minute of being a Montlake Romance author. Maria, Jessica, Melody, and everyone else, love you all.

If you've read the acknowledgements in my previous books, then you know that I always save my agent for last. Courtney Miller-Callihan of Handspun Literary is my agent extraordinaire, and I'm so lucky to have her on my side. Love you, Courtney. xoxoxo

ABOUT THE AUTHOR

A bestselling, award-winning author, Sandra Owens lives in the beautiful Blue Ridge Mountains of North Carolina. Her family and friends often question her sanity, but have ceased being surprised by what she might be up to next. She's jumped out of a plane, flown in an aerobatic plane while the pilot performed death-defying stunts, flown Air Combat (two fighter planes dogfighting, pretending to shoot at each other with laser guns), and ridden a Harley motorcycle for years. She regrets nothing.

Sandra is a 2013 Golden Heart® finalist for the contemporary romance *Crazy for Her*. In addition to her contemporary romantic suspense novels, she writes Regency stories.

You can connect with Sandra on Facebook at Sandra Owens Author and Twitter @SandyOwens1. Her website is www.sandra-owens.com. For the latest news from Sandra, sign up to her newsletter at http://eepurl.com/50OaD.